BEER! BEER! BEER!
by
AVRAM DAVIDSON

COPYRIGHT

DEDICATION

For our family - Jill Davis, Sawyer Davis, Cody Davis & Ethan Davidson.

OR ALL THE SEAS WITH OYSTERS PUBLISHING

Welcome to Or All the Seas with Oysters Publishing, where you are about to embark upon a voyage into The Avram Davidson Universe. Within this Universe, you will find the works of Hugo, Edgar, and World Fantasy Award-winning and genre-transcending Avram Davidson, who is considered one of the finest authors of the 20th century, and the works of Grania Davis, Avram's onetime life partner and frequent writing collaborator, a dedicated preservationist of Avram's works, and a talented and acclaimed author in her own right. Or All the Seas with Oysters Publishing is dedicated to bringing both the out-of-print and the never-before published writings of both Avram and Grania back to life in print, audio, and e-book formats, and we look forward to making this treasured legacy accessible once again to readers, ranging from longtime fans and scholars to those just beginning this journey.

Avram's Universe is calling—we invite you to step inside.
avramdavidson.com/join-the-fan-club/

INTRODUCTION

In a strange way, I will always cherish 2020 because it allowed me to rediscover Avram's writing. When the pandemic forced me, for the first time in years, to stay home from the office and slow down my life, I came across something that had been hiding in the attic all along—a treasury of my godfather's works, both published and never-before-seen by the public eye. I'd become the beneficiary of his literary estate some time before, but I'd never realized the immense artistic value of what I'd held. When I looked through the collection, I was astounded by the sheer number of manuscripts. There were short stories, novels, and yellowed, hand-typed pages marked up with pen and pencil. There were beautifully illustrated science fiction and mystery magazines from the mid-20th century, and there were pieces with introductions by such luminaries as Ray Bradbury, Ursula K. Le Guin, and Neil Gaiman. I had no idea my godfather had been so well-known and so well-received, and I realized I'd stumbled upon something priceless that I owed Avram's fans a chance to see.

Beer! Beer! Beer! is one of the discovered novels, and I'd like to present it to you as a personal favorite. I can't believe it was never published. The book is 99% Avram's work as first written, incorporating his hand-written notes from the original manuscript. Little quirks in phrasing, a bit of roughness to a passage here and there—what you're getting here is Avram's writing, with minimal editing. In any case, he was never a fan of editors, so in respect to his legacy, we changed *Beer! Beer! Beer!* as little as possible.

In this book, in Avram's typical fashion, he plays with the setting such that it's a bit more special than reality. *Beer! Beer!*

Beer! exists at the intersection of magical realism (just a hint) and historical fiction, with the streets of Yokums representing the Yonkers of his youth in the 1920s and 1930s much in the way that the British Hidalgo of *Limekiller!* parallels Belize. While reading Avram's true story *Beer Like Water*, I learned that much of *Beer! Beer! Beer!* was very real; of course, there's a little extra sparkle in the novel, alongside something a little darker hiding around the corner. And if you pay attention, you'll notice little nods to you, his readers, along the way—could Yokums somehow be connected in Avram's universe to the goings-on in the fantastical empire of Scythia-Pannonia-Transbalkania?

Growing up with Avram in my life was magical in itself. He was married to my mother, Grania Davis, for a time, and our home was a magnet for some of the greatest literary talents of the era. It was pretty astounding when I later realized that my favorite childhood author, Hugo- and Nebula-award winning Robert Silverberg, had been down the hall partying with my mom and Avram, and that Philip K. Dick and Harlan Ellison had been swinging by to say hi. Avram was beyond kind to me. He was my loving, doting godfather, and we were close enough that he Bar Mitzvahed me. I adored him, and when he passed in 1993, I went for a run and sobbed. This book publication is not only because of the obligation I feel to Avram's readers, both old and new—it is a tribute to my beloved family member.

My mother was as devoted to preserving Avram's posthumous legacy as I, then a college student, was devoted to copying his old stories for her under Kinkos' fluorescent lights. As I worked on scanning documents for seemingly endless hours, I had no idea how extraordinary these stacks of paper would turn out to be, becoming such works as *The Avram Davidson Treasury*, edited with the help of Robert Silverberg; *The Investigations of Avram Davidson*, with Richard Lupoff; and *The Other Nineteenth Century*, assisted by Henry Wessells. Grania was also instrumental in publishing her collaborative work with Avram, *The Boss in the Wall*, which dabbled in the horror genre.

I can't end this without thanking everyone in my life who have helped bring *Beer! Beer! Beer!* to fruition. Greg Feeley spent tireless hours editing and preparing the manuscript for publication (I apologize for not agreeing to several of the edits), and I am indebted to him for his efforts to preserve Avram's work. Henry Wessells, Michael Swanwick, Darrell Schweitzer, Eileen Gunn, and Jacob Wiseman have been indispensable along the way. And of course, there is my brother and Avram's son, Ethan Davidson.

With that, I bring you *Beer! Beer! Beer!*. I hope you like it as much as I do. – Seth Davis, 2021

PREFACE

Oh, it's beer, beer, beer
That makes you want to cheer,
In the stores, in the stores,
Oh, it's beer, beer, beer
That makes you want to cheer,
In the Quartermaster's Stores.

—from an old Army song

CHAPTER ONE

One day in the early Fall of a year in the early 1930s, Elmer Dugan, a boy in his early teens, his very early teens, was wandering slowly around "The Village," as the downtown part of Yokums, New Jersey, was called. The streets were for the most part narrow, and paved with stone blocks, called cobblestones by the ignorant; and the houses were all of red brick, gone dim through decades of dust and dirt and smoke. On this street, this afternoon's walk took him along a block where the buildings were all tenement houses—*mostly* all —with business premises on the ground floors. Elmer had a wide mouth and a thin nose and sharp eyes; he wore a woolen jacket and linen knickers and long stockings. Not long *black* stockings, those, with short pants (*long* short pants), formed an important part of the unofficial uniform of parochial school boys: and Elmer and his family were not Catholic. His shoes, which he frequently bent to tie, were partly laced through holes and partly —the upper part—around metal hooks. By rights he should have been wearing a cap as well, at this time of the year, a regular cloth cap with a brim, but his mother, who had ambitions—she saw him as district manager of an insurance company or something like that—wouldn't let him wear a cap. She said that only Polacks and Slovacks wore caps. "People will think you work in The Sugar House," she said. Boys of his age were, some of them, already beginning to wear long pants, but, although Opa had even brought over a pair which had not been called for at the tailor shop and (he said) never would be—"Worsted, good as gold"—still Elmer's mother flatly refused to allow it.

"I don't want him looking like no midget," she'd said.

"*Nakked besser*?" asked Opa.

"I said NOOO!"

So Opa shrugged and sighed and folded them under his arm and left.

Also, Elmer wore a clean white shirt every day. Until not long ago they had been starched, too: but not now. They were still ironed, though. His mother ironed them every night with a wet cloth to keep them from singeing. And Oh Boy how she muttered when she did so. And gave his father such looks.

When he was there, that is.

Every day, a clean white ironed shirt.

And a necktie.

But *every* day.

Even Saturday.

His shoes needed shining, though.

The shoes he had on had worn through before they had worn out. They always used to buy shoes from Vanderpole in City Hall Square. The ones he had on, though, they bought from the Economy Shoe Store, right near here on Valleydale Avenue. When he showed his mother the hole she held the shoes up and yelled, "LOOK AT THESE *SHOES*!" And his father said, "Oh leave me alone for Christ's sake."

And she yelled, "Whaddaya *mean*, 'Leave you alone'? *I* said, Look at these *SHOES*!"

So the old man got up and walked out while the old lady was yelling, "OM the one who should be walking out! Some one a these days Om gunna go so far away, you'll never FIND me!"

They took the shoes to the shoemaker, who shrugged and just put another half-sole over the one with the hole in it. The leather around the hole dried up real soon and became hard and curled and hurt his foot. She didn't look inside when he wanted to show it to her; she said that if he would shine them every day they'd feel better. "That keeps the leather soft," she said. But when Elmer tipped the polish bottle, nothing came out.

It was too late in the year for anybody to go barefoot and

anyway he was never allowed to go barefoot in the city. That summer they hadn't gone to the country. As he was always on the go except when in school, his foot hurt a lot of the time and he stopped often and when he stopped he would look around, there was always a lot to see, except where there were gas stations and new buildings and these he avoided as they were hateful and dull. Right now he was in the last block on Valleydale Avenue near Main Street and there were no gas stations and no new buildings. He turned off the blue-grey flagstone sidewalk and went tentatively into the live poultry market.

The live poultry market stank of something awful but was interesting just the same. There were always cages of squawking chickens, sometimes ducks, sometimes rabbits who didn't squawk. Turkeys always before Thanksgiving; *some*times before Christmas, geese. Otherwise that was an extra-special day, when there was a goose. Once upon a time he used to come in with Oma and she would feel the chickens to pick out a nice one and then Chris the Market Man used to give him a penny for candy and when he came back the chicken already had its head chopped off and was scalded and being plucked. Nobody ever *said* he couldn't stay to watch it getting its head chopped off and he often thought of waiting but the temptation to spend the money was too strong. And sometimes the Market Man would give him a penny anyway even when he was by himself.

Over in the kosher side of the live poultry market the old rabbi looked at him incuriously as he walked by, and returned to smoking his long pipe and reading his newspaper with the funny letters that looked like music. And Chris the Market Man was talking to some lady. Oma always used to say, in her slow, choppy way, as though each word was being hacked out with a hatchet from a block of wood—and her face looked the same way too—that Chris was all right, Chris was very good, he always saw that she got a good chicken and a good price. *Used* to say. Now she said Chris was trying to get rich too fast. She said he was keeping a woman, too.

Elmer ambled around looking at the chopping block and

the blood and sawdust and gave Chris some glances from the corners of his eyes. But Chris didn't offer any penny, didn't smile, didn't nod and raise his eyebrows in silent greetings. So Elmer, who had wised up and no longer looked in the back to see if a woman was being kept there, he now looked at the woman Chris was talking to. She had on a white coat, a long white coat with fur trimmings, and she had one of those things around her neck made out of a fox and the fox's face was still on it and glass eyes, ya know?

"I ain't got nuthin faw ya tuhday Elmer," Chris said.

"I don't need nuthin."

He kept on giving the lady glances and then her mouth went funny at the corners and she moved her head and neck and she gave him suddenly a real dirty look.

"Guh home, Elmer," Chris said. "Go won, guh home."

Elmer had learned that if people, that is, if some *man* said, "Get outa here," you better go right away. But if they said to Go home, Kid, or, Go home, Elmer, then you could go slowly.

Next to the live poultry market (there weren't any baby rabbits here today anyway) was a dull *old* building in which un-fashionable doctors and such had their offices. Doctors. Ladies were always talking about some other lady who had a bump and the doctor opened it up and there was a part of a needle inside, that had "broken off," and (by becoming real quiet, invisible and inaudible) he had by and by learned that what they really meant was a *crocheting* needle: but try as hard as he might he could never learn *how* the crocheting needle had "broken off." Or how it had "worked its way through her system." Or *why*. But he knew it had something to do with babies. Because of the expression when the women talked about it. And in the same building were dentists and corset-makers. And one or two lawyers. Elmer had never bothered to go inside more than once.

Next was the tobacco store with the wooden Indian out front.

In the doorway was the kind of crazy old lady. Some said her real name was O'Shee and some said No that *use* ta be her *old* name but then she'd married some Dutchman name Kleinhans or Kleinhaus or something but he'd died; be that as it may the woman stared from her ruined face as though at the ruins of the world outside almost all the time swaying back and forth and saying, all she said, in a droning kind of voice: Oh Jesus. Oh Jesus. Oh Jesus. And so she was usually called only Mrs. O'Jesus.

In the window of the tobacco store was like a room by itself and there were three men in there making handmade cigars with the funny board with the grooves in it. Well, there used to be, now there was only one man rolling cigars, he was tall as you could see when he wasn't bent over and he had a very large white moustache. *He* wasn't the owner. Elmer went inside. The *owner* of the store stayed mostly way in the back of the store, the big dark old store, playing cards with other men, all smoking cigars. Elmer had heard that thousands of dollars changed hands in some of these games. He thought he would like to see some of those thousand-dollar bills. The owner's daughter, whose name was Hattie, a short and stumpy woman with a shawl over her shoulders, she took care of most of the business, and sometimes Elmer had had business there, sometimes one of his grand-fathers would send him for cigars or snuff or chewing tobacco: and it smelled great, it had a neat rich dark deep great smell and it was interestingly dark in that big old store and the pictures on the cigar boxes were the only bright spots of color, almost. The store didn't *sell* candy at retail but sometimes Hattie would give him a piece, from a bag on a shelf or something beneath the counter with the brass scales where she was usually reading a copy of *True Stories* magazine with photographs showing the stories were really true: as she was doing today. And he got almost to the back of the store before suddenly she looked up and said, "*Yes*?"

He just waved his hand a little as he kept on walking, but she said in a louder voice, "*Don't you go* THERE. What do you *want*?" And as he couldn't pretend anymore that he came to really buy something, he shrugged a little bit and swung around and came back and stopped by the counter and looked at the magazine because sometimes Hattie wanted to *talk* about some story. "What do you think about the rotten way they treated this poor girl just because she wasn't French the way her husband's family was," or something like that, she might say, Hattie. But now he saw that it was an *old* magazine, one they had already talked about, and he wondered why she was reading it *again*.

Hattie said: "You don't want anything, you better go home."

Too bad: because sometimes they'd had real interesting conversations, sometimes she would say, "How come you know so much? Say, you know a lot for a boy your age." And sometimes she used to add to his knowledge some little item or other: like, how a woman if she was going to have a baby she shouldn't sleep with her arm over her neck because a lady did that once and her baby was born dead, strangled by a cord.

But not today.

Sometimes even if he didn't have anything to buy for Grampa or Oma or Uncle Bob, he would still ask for an empty cigar box, and usually get one. Hattie would usually give him one and it smelled beautifully of cedar wood and had such beautiful pictures, men in old ship captain clothes and Spanish ladies and pictures of Hackamack Bay with boats on it and Indians, too. However, by the way that Hattie was now looking down at the *True Stories* magazine he knew better than to ask.

"Well so long, Hattie," Elmer said.

The trolley tracks ran down the middle of the street.

Now in this same block there were two candy stores and in one of them, Bodenheimers, there were trays and trays of penny candies in the glass case just past the cigar-lighter where a tiny blue gas flame always burned inside a brass hood. So sometimes Elmer would buy some chicken corn and candy bananas and some chocolate babies and some candy "fried eggs" in their tin dishes with a little spoon, a tiny tin spoon, to eat it with. Maybe jelly beans or gum drops or licorice whips or cherry whips. And put them in the cigar box and wander off slowly and whenever he stopped he could take out a piece of candy and suck on it . . . *start* to suck on it . . . he hated *hard* candy, the rotten kind in the Christmas stocking, he loved *chewy* candy: and often when the candy had gotten nice and soft Elmer couldn't resist chewing on it and that was the end of that.

Until the next piece.

Coming out of Bodenheimers was a man with a box in his hand and Elmer recognized him because he had come to their door a couple of days ago and said, "I'm a War Veteran selling shoe laces, two for a nickel." Elmer went and asked his mother and she had made an impatient noise and shook her head. Then, after a minute, she very slowly got two cents out of the old jar which still read OR C AC D on its side, and said, "Tell him he can keep this." And the War Veteran looked at the two cents just as slowly and then he said, "Sonny, that's begging, and before I'd do that I'd blow my brains out," and he went away. So Elmer went back and told his mother and she didn't say a word and so he asked if *he* could keep the pennies: and she yelled "NOO!" and dropped them back in the jar.

Often, Old Mr. Bodenheimer used to give him an extra hunk of candy and say, "This is for the baker's dozen, and give your Oma and Opa a *grüss Gott* from me." He'd asked his mother once what the baker's dozen meant and she said, "It's just an expression for a free piece of something."

The door had a bell that rang when Elmer went in and he saw Old Mr. Bodenheimer standing and looking at him and the old man touched one end of his moustache with his finger and he didn't say anything. Elmer said, "Hello, Mr. Bodenheimer" and the old man didn't say anything and Elmer said "*Grüss Gott*," which *always* made Old Man Bodenheimer smile, but he didn't smile and he didn't say anything. And Elmer looked here and there and he strolled up and down the aisles and the old man never took his eyes off him and never said anything and never offered him anything and finally after Elmer was looking at the toys and the games, and then he looked at the magazines, *Ar-*

gosy, Bluebook, American, Liberty, Colliers, Saturday Evening Post, Ranch Romances, Dime Detective, True Story, True Detective Myster-ies, Weird Tales, Amazing Stories, Wonder Stories, Family Journal, American Boy, Boys' Life, The Open Road for Boys, his favorite.

And every time he looked up Old Mr. Bodenheimer was still looking at him; then suddenly he said, "I got to go now."

Surprised, Elmer said, "Where?"

Mr. Bodenheimer got suddenly very mad. "*Where*? Where do you think? Where the Kaiser goes on foot! So, go, now. Go home. Go home, I say, Elmer, go home. Go home."

So Elmer strolled out and the little bell rang again. And he looked back through the last window as he walked past the store and he saw Old Mr. Bodenheimer going through the back door of the store, the door with the white curtains on it, to the apart-ment where the Bodenheimers lived: and the old man was still looking at him.

Bodenheimers had a real good smell too, even though it was too late for Valentines and too early for Halloween masks.

Elmer looked up the street but there was no trolley car in sight. Just delivery trucks and automobiles and one junk wagon and one milk wagon and, turning in from River Street, one big black touring car, a police car. He stopped and watched to see if anyone was going to be arrested. But the car just kept on going.

A sign on the back of another car caught his eye. It said, WASN'T THE DEPRESSION AWFUL?

Next was the pet shop and this smelled almost as bad as the chicken market although differently bad. Pete Miller, a fat man with one bad eye, ran it and he didn't like no kids hanging around if they weren't going to buy nothing; did he make that plain? But he didn't own the sidewalk, he couldn't stop you from looking in the window where there was often a bunch of puppy dogs, more interesting than the inside where there was lots of stuff like dog collars and open bags of dog biscuits which didn't taste like even a dog would want to eat them. "Them's Nellie's pups," he heard someone say. Nellie was a bitch who was part fox terrier and part something else and every so often she would have these puppies and Pete Miller would put them in the window and sell them. Anyway Elmer hoped he always sold them and didn't give them to the Dog Pound. (The Dog Pound was way out by the Pest House, the City of Yokums Contagious Diseases Hospital, out in West Yokums, and the most that Elmer had ever gotten up nerve to do was ride past on the trolley car on a good transfer that he found, and look.) There was no chance of his having a dog. When he was younger they said When you are older. Just the other day he had asked his mother and she pressed her mouth tight and shook her head.

"Well why not, uh huh, please?" he said.

And she said, "No, I said *no* I said *nooo!* I said NO! NO! NO! NO NO NO NOOOO—"

Earlier she had been visiting his grandmother and Aunt Mary on The Other Side of the Family. This *al*ways made her mad.

And as her voice got higher and her face got redder she grabbed the dish towel and clouted him with it and he shoved the kitchen chair out of his way and ran off.

Right next to the Pete Miller's Pet Shop was the other candy store and this one didn't have the nice neat smell of the first one and neither did it have the real rich old tobacco smell either because it smelled of stale smoke, stale *cheap* old smoke, and it didn't really have much candy anyway. Nor did it sell magazines, just scratch sheets and the *Daily Mirror*. This candy store didn't go very far back at all but the *back*, boy did that go far back! And there were always a bunch of men in the back saying things like "Who duhya like inna Thuhyd?" and that meant in the Third race at some racetrack. So everybody knew that "JACK'S PLACE" was really a bookie joint. However it did have a slot machine that gave out a roll of absolutely the world's worst candy, after it showed you pictures of different kinds of fruits; sometimes somebody didn't pull the lever all the way down and if you were the next person, and lucky, sometimes you got not only the candy for free but some money, too.

Very cautiously Elmer went into Jack's.

Very suddenly Jack was right next to him, saying, "Get owda here, *you.*"

It wasn't a very interesting place anyway.

On the other side of this the last block of Valleydale Avenue, on the corner of Main Street, was Berman's Drug Store, and the rest of the block between River and Main was one entire stone wall with one closed iron gate in it. There had been a sloping hill there once and it had been cut away to make the street or anyway maybe to straighten the street. And when they were digging that hill away, guess what happened? Guess what they *found?* Jack Archer's grandfather told Jack, that *his* father had told *him*, they had found HUMAN BONES there when they were digging!

"Cross my heart and hope ta *die*, Elmer! Honest to God!"

And the rest of *that* block, the Broadway and River Street sides, taking up most of the whole block, was the old old Dutch Reformed Church, plus the Sunday school and church offices building and two old houses where some old ladies lived, and a garden. This, what was left of a bluff, had once overlooked the Gristmill River or Hackamack Creek as it was also called, where it widened and used to be pouring down (in the *old* days) in a sort of falls before it flowed into Hackamack Bay which was sort of a part of the Hudson River and sort of a part of New *York* Bay.

But most of that river or creek there had been covered over and streets and houses and warehouses, lumber yards and coal sheds and stores, built over it.

If nothing else happened, Elmer would maybe turn into Main Street and go down to the Bay. That was always interesting.

Berman's Drugstore smelled nice, too. Besides the medicines, besides the soda fountain (delicious sarsaparilla!), there were all kinds of glossy things for sale in glass cases, but mostly for women. Elmer was not interested. He *was* interested in the boxes of fancy chocolates, also glossy, but he had never even thought of buying any of them. Once he and Jack Archer had gone in for some empty gelatine capsules and Mr. Berman had seemed surprised.

"Capsules? What do you want *them* for?"

"To make *jump*ing beans, Mr. Berman! *You* know! You put BB shot in them and you put them on something that it slants just a little bit, and they, like *jump*!"

Mr. Berman had laughed, had sold them some empty capsules for a nickel. "That's all right, I guess. It's supposed to be against the law, without a prescription. But I guess the law isn't going to worry about a couple of jumping beans for a couple of boys."

Druggists had to worry about the law a lot, it seemed. For instance, the angry old woman squawking up at the counter. "I'm *sorry*, Mrs. White," old Berman was saying, shaking his head. "I have known you for years, I know you and your family and I'll be glad to fill a prescription for you. But without a prescription? I can't do it. It's against the law, it's against the *law*—"

The old lady yelling, "*What* law? *What* law?"

Berman: "It isn't the money, I trust you for the money, it's the Harrison Law. The Harrison Nahcotics Act. *You* know that—"

Evidently she did know that, even if she had forgotten it, or hoped old Berman had forgotten it. She made a noise of disgust and annoyance. "*Aaaa*! Harrison Nahcotics! Harrison Nahcotics!" she repeated. The white-haired druggist shrugged, sighed.

"I can't argue with Uncle Sam," he said.

"BuhlieveME, if Uncle *Sam* hadda raise ten children there woodem be nunna dthis nonsense about Harrison's Narcotics! Hah duz Uncle *Sam* expecta woman ta raise ten children if she cann' even put parraGAWric inna milk, ta keepum from *cry*in?"

But the druggist only sighed again and stretched out his hand in a gesture of helplessness. And Elmer, who was trying both to listen and to look at the names on the boxes of fancy candy, *Schraft's*, *Louis Sherry*, must have made a noise then, because then old Mr. Berman looked up and saw him. And he said, not looking angry, but shaking his head very, very firmly, he said, "Go home, Elmer. Go home now. Go home."

By and by it would be getting late. If Elmer got too interested and *was* late, he would really get it. On the other hand, if he got back early, he knew he wouldn't be able to keep from asking, What's for supper? And then, likely as not, his mother would she yell at him! "How do *I* know what's for supper? Whatter ya askin ME what's for supper? Why don't you ask your rotten FATHER what's for supper? Or your GRANDmother and AUNT?" That was the grandmother and aunt from The Other Side of the Family. "Whatter ya eatin MY haht out for?" she would probably yell.

As Elmer stopped and looked back into the windows of Berman's at the two giant jars of red and green—what *were* they?— He heard the sound of the trolley car. He timed what happened next just right.

No sooner had the trolley car come to a stop—it never went any farther than the bottom of Valleydale until it was so late at night that it was early in the morning, really, and the last trolley's time to turn Main Street and go down into the Car Barn across the street catty-corner from the Depot—Elmer was there behind it: and while the passengers were still getting off he had deftly pulled down the trolley pole at the back end from the overhead wire and let its rope snuggle back into the place where it snuggled, and then he ran around to the front end and pulled the rope *there* until the pole rose and then with one quick spark and no more, rested against the wire. The trolley car was now *almost* ready to start back the other way.

As soon as the very last passenger had gotten off, Elmer darted up the steps and into the car. "Hello Mr. Duffy," he said. Mr. Duffy was lighting a cigarette and waved one hand. Elmer sped back the whole length of the car, grabbing with each hand the brass handles on the woven cane seat-backs and push-pulling them clatter-clatter as he passed until he had done the whole car and all the seats were facing the other way. "Thanks, Elmer," Mr. Duffy said. He folded his own little round seat down and made his way back to the other end of the car, now suddenly and again the *front* end, and put the tiller into its socket. He waved his hand again as he opened the door. "Off ya go," he said.

"Ah, cann' I stay on?" Elmer pleaded. "Please Mr. Duffy? I'll get off before ya start, huh Mr. Duffy?"

"Nope, nope. The spotter might spotchez. Off ya go. I gotta getta cuppa *cahfee*. *Come* on." And, once more, he waved his hand.

"Okay Mr. Duffy."

An old man in a dirty overcoat was waiting to get on, and an old woman hesitated on the curb, but Mr. Duffy waved the old man back down. "Notchet. Notchet. We gotta cuppla minutes yet."

"Ah lemme getton ann siddown," the old man said. "Om tie-ud a waitin."

Mr. Duffy shook his head. "Nope. Nope. The spotter might spotchez. I could lose me *jahb*."

The old man looked around in vague and senile annoyance. "Where's the conductor? I got my fare—"

"Conductor? ConDUCtor? Ah, give us a rest, wherea-ya *been*? The Company *fired* ahlla the conductors. E*cawn*amy. An they'll fire *me*, if I letchez—" He didn't finish the subject, the old man sort of slunk back onto the sidewalk, the trolley car door closed as the steps folded back up: all at once. Mr. Duffy half-turned to go into Maloney's, around the corner, a curtain running the whole length of the windows as it had ever since the day when Maloney's, after thirty years as a saloon, had opened one morning as a speakeasy; suddenly the motorman looked to right and left, thrust his hand into some secret place near the car door, the steps descended and the door opened—again the old man and old woman moved to get aboard, again Mr. Duffy gestured down, with rising color in his face: he darted up, closed the door behind him, and, swearing, half-stumbling, half-crouching, trotted up the length of the car, peering under the seats.

"*Out*ta there," he ordered, lurching to halt. "Git *out*ta there! Git ahffa the trolley car! A fine way ye reward me kindness—Guh home," he ordered, chasing the boy ahead of him. "Guh home, Elmer. *Guh home. Guh home.*"

The motorman slapped his money on the bar. "I'm in a hurry, Maloney," he said. "That damned kid—"

Maloney stared at him in rigid and affronted astonishment, as only Maloney could do. "In a hurry fr *what*?" he demanded.

Duffy stared back. "Fr a glass a *beer*," he said. "What else?"

"What *else*? Why, maybe Moxie. Orange *Crush*. Sassperella. — *Beer*? There isn't anny beer."

Duffy stared at him, aghast. His hand twitched. It had been a long, long day. "What in the Hell do ya *mean*. There isn't no beer?"

Maloney shrugged. "Why, what would anny man mean by sayin there is no beer. There is not anny beer, Joseph Duffy. Maybe later. Notchet. Is there maybe somethin else thatchyed like?"

Mr. Joseph Duffy's lips moved a moment. Then the spark seemed to go out of him. "A cuppa cahfee," he said. "But—hurry it up, ah, wouldja. If the spotters spots me absent, I'll lose the jahb."

Maloney's face lost its frozen dignity. His thick eyebrows did a rapid flutter. "*Ah*, no, then: I'll put it in a carton fr ya—lots a sugar—milk— Mind ye don't spill it. Pay me another time."

The day was indeed declining, even though Mt. Hackamack, a sorry substitute for a green mountain, covered its retreat behind a crown of factory chimneys. Often the sunset was spectacular, bloody red from the smoke and industrial dust. Today it was thin and clear. Up and down Main Street, merchants awaited sons, daughters, sisters-in-laws, *some*one to mind the store, so they could be home for supper. For some, to be sure, some few, who had never managed the move away from Behind-the-Store, supper was merely a retreat into the tiny apartment at the rear. For others, supper was on its way to them, coming in a dish or bowl with another dish or bowl turned upside down over it and wrapped in a towel to conserve the heat. "Hold it like *this*," were the directions; afterwards, the towels would be checked to make sure nothing had spilled.

Sundry little dramas were being played out. "Here it is, Pa. You can eat now." "I don't want anything, I'm not hungry, *you* eat it." "Pa, I already ate." "You're sure? Look at me. I don't believe you." "Honest, Pa." A pause. Then, "Come on, we'll split it." "All right, Pa."

Grandpa.
Dad.
Zayda.
Nonno.

And, in between these little scenes, strophe, antistrophe, like the responses in a litany:

Go home, Elmer. Go home. Get out of here. Beat it, kid.
Go home, Elmer. Go home.

CHAPTER TWO

C ity Hall, the City of Yokums, County of Hackamack, State of New Jersey, had gone up during the second year of the Administration of Chester A. Arthur, a stout and tall and handsome man with sandy side-whiskers: but a New *York* State man. Some old-timers around still remembered him as Collector of Customs of the Port across the Bay. New *York* Bay, that is. Yokums had once been a Federal Port in its own right, trans-shipping grain from the Erie Canal barges as far as Europe, unloading Cuban and other Caribbean sugars to make syrup and rum; handling coal from off the Pennsylvania and Jersey Canal onto coastal vessels bound for New England: and everything else under sun and moon to and from and up and down the Hudson, the Sound, and the Bays. Some barge trade still remained, tugboats tugged their tows of sand and gravel and coal. Grain came in, but by rail alone now. Of the forty to fifty packet boats which had once called Yokums "Home," one remained: and it went mostly nowhere. And as for the Port itself, it had been annulled by the stroke of an unfriendly Federal pen. Yokums was now part of another Port Authority: and dust collected in the old Port Offices in Federal Hall on Front Street.

City Hall, however, with its mansarded turrets, was still active enough. People had to be born and die and be vaccinated and get married. They still had to have building permits and business licenses. Streets still had to be repaired. Garbage to be collected. And *sewers* cleaned.

The morning after the previous scenes a group of men gathered at the back door of the City Hall basement. They were hoping for part-time work with the Department of Public Works.

Upstairs, on the main floor, City Tax Assessor Charles Victor Vanderdam, a portfolio under his arm, walked briskly down the corridor and into the office of the Honorable John J. Quoyte, Commissioner of Public Works. One of the women at the desks behind the fence looked up and said brightly, "The Commissioner can see you now, Mr. Vanderdam."

Vanderdam, who had neither asked nor paused, said, "Good," and swung open the gate and went inside. He was a blocky man, blue-eyed and balding, but he still carefully combed his thin, sandy hair in the middle. He wore high collars with rounded "points," and so did that Angel of the Lord, Herbert Clark Hoover. "Morning, John," said Vanderdam.

"Morning, Vic. Well. We're just about ready for the No Man's Land conference, I see." He gestured to a chair. He was large and wide.

Vanderdam ignored the chair. "Yes. But not here."

"*Where*?" asked Quoyte, instantly wary.

"In *Francey's* office."

"Oh. *Oh.* Why, uh, *sure.* Let's go, then." To his secretary he said, on the way out, "Assessor Vanderdam and me will be in conference, Treesa. In the, in His Honor's office."

"*Yes*, Commissioner," said Theresa. She was plump, and a policeman's widow, and as, in addition to her $100 salary, she still had the pension of $50 a month, envious people said that she lived like a king. "A lodda people are after my *job*," she had said once to the Commissioner. "Dthey say I shooden have, like, two *in*comes." "Quit worryin abowd it, willya, Treesa," he had said. And her reply was, "Okay, Honey, that's all I wahned a know."

In the corridor an older man fell into step with them, said, urgently, to Vanderdam, "Cholly, we gotta do sumpin about that as*sess*ment, I cann' *pay*yit!"

Vanderdam, instantly, said, "Heinz, Commissioner Quoyte and I are going to see the Mayor *right this minute* about the assessments problem, and I want you to know and I want to tell you, Heinz, that I am going to do *everything I can* for you, Heinz, *everything I possibly can*. Commissioner, you know H.H. Steinmetz of Wholesale Meats."

Quoyte vigorously shook hands. They paused at the gold-lettered

Honorable Francis F. Flaherty
MAYOR

"Mr. Steinmetz, I will *personally* speak to the Mayor about it," Quoyte said. "Even though such matters are strictly speaking *not my depahtment* but I will *personally* speak to the Mayor about it. As of course so will Assessor Vanderdam, I need not add," he added with some swiftness. The meat wholesaler fell behind, with a faintly relieved mutter. The door closed behind them. Quoyte asked, "He have anything to do with the subject under discussion, Vic?" It was an indication of the difference between the two men that, had Vanderdam asked the question of Quoyte, Quoyte would have answered, "Not a gah damn *thing*," but Vanderdam now merely said, "*No.*"

"Good *morn*ing, Miss Flaherty."

"Good *morn*ing, Miss Flaherty."

A handsome grey-haired woman, meticulous shirt-waist with a small gold watch pinned to it, waved them onward without looking up from her desk. She didn't say anything. She was the Mayor's aunt, and she didn't have to say anything. Miss Florence Flaherty was a career woman, one of the very first local career women, she was immensely capable, she had been at City Hall since before her nephew was born, beginning as a *typewriter* who operated a *typewriting machine*: and it was often said, "*He* didn't get her *her* job, *she* got him *his* job." Which was certainly not altogether true, for His Honor had had a successful career with the Federal Department of Justice (Bureau of Prohibition) "before deciding to enter municipal politics on the local level," as the *Gazette* had once put it.

Vanderdam and Quoyte saw, as they came in, that City Attorney Cornelius J. Flynn and prominent merchant Benjamin M. Rose were already there.

"*Good* morning, Your Honor (morning, Neely, Ben)."

"*Good* morning, Your Honor (hiya, C'nelius, hiya, Benny)."

His Honor smiled at them. It was a warm and winning smile, and they both relaxed in it. "It's all nonsense, isn't it?" the smile asked. "But, ah, what charming nonsense," the smile answered.

"Before I say another thing," Quoyte began. The Mayor raised his perfect eyebrows and nodded rapidly, still smiling. "We just met Heiny Steinmetz outside, didn't we Vic, and I promise him we would, *I* would, *personally* speak to the Mayor about his assessment, *huh* Vic."

"Which," said the Mayor, "we have now done."

There was a general chuckle. Vanderdam said that was all he heard, all day long, Lower the assessments, lower the assessments. Quoyte immediately said that all *he* heard, all day long, was Get me a job, get me a job, get my *son* a job, get my *husband* a job—

The Mayor made a steeple of his long, fine fingers, nodded. "Then you may well imagine, gentlemen, that what *I* hear all day long is a combination of, Reduce the assessments, *and*, *Get* more people *more* jobs . . . There seems a certain paradox involved, could one but put one's finger on it. *Well!*" The steeple vanished, the fingers delved in a desk drawer, the hands came up, there was a small box on the table, and, as the Tax Assessor, the Commissioner of Public Works, the City Attorney, and the Local Merchant looked on, fascinated, the top of the box came off, revealing a quantity of whole cloves.

Said His Honor, "Columbus Day will soon be upon us, my fellow citizens, and we have not forgotten, *have* we, that 'twas the quest for the savory spices which occasioned the discovery of America and the immense benefit to mankind which flowed therefrom. *Therefore.* Have a clove, have *several* cloves, Vic, Jack, Corneel, Ben . . . What? *What?* You don't intend to partake? You don't *use* cloves?" His expression was that of a man facing something very new and very singular; he put his hand up to shade his eyes and his head to one side, the better to examine it.

"Only in *hams*," said Victor Vanderdam. "Or, well, *egg*-nog."

"Or after a drink of booze," said Quoyte. "For the *breadth*."

The Mayor's young and mobile face was now all at once transfigured with a look of delighted enlightenment. His lips opened upon a long aspirate and he pointed a finger at John J. Quoyte, who, well as he knew that this was one of His Honor's games, did not trouble to conceal the pleasure he felt in being pointed out. And, meanwhile, the fingers of the other mayoral hand, not the one holding the spices, felt in another drawer. And came out and set upon the rose-colored, almost desk-wide, spread of blotting paper a bottle of Scotch. And, one, two, three, four, five glasses.

They looked on with pleasurably pursed lips; if Francis F. Flaherty's bottle had a Scotch label, depend on it, it contained *Scotch*. From *Scot*land. And not whatever murky mixture of rot-gut and popskull some cheap bootlegger had bottled with his forged label.

Not a drop was spilled as the glasses were filled.

"I give you a toast from the Kingdom of Kerry," said the Mayor. "—or from *Some*where," he waved the precise provenance of the toast aside as he waved his glass, the others quickly raising theirs. "To wit and videlicet: '*May ye never die till I kills ye.*'"

With, here, a *Here's how*, and, there, merely a pleased little grunt, they drank. The Mayor drained his glass, his eyebrows raised politely, then moved to refill. His associates demurred, a few with firmness, and none, of course, objected to the refilling of his, His Honor's, glass. After a moment, with a very soft smack of his lips, he said, "Well, on to business. Vox populi, vox Dei. Ahmm . . . *Vic* . . . suppose you in your inimitable way, suppose *you* fill us in on the background of the business now before us. *Mm?*"

"Well. *Sure.* Okay. Francey, Jack, Neely, uh, *Ben*, here's the situation. Umm . . ." He paused a moment, let his breath out, rolled his eyes. "Oh. *Yeah.* Lemme get this *map* out." He got it out,

out of his portfolio. "I'll set it here, sideways, so we can all—"
It was a large map, of the sort which ordinary citizens seldom,
and perhaps never, see, but which real estate brokers and tax
assessors use as a common tool of their work. It showed the central part of downtown Yokums, with all the streets outlined in
black: thus far, it resembled any large map of the area. Where it
differed was in showing areas labelled in a different font of type
from that used for the streets' names, and filled in with different
colors; and these areas did not by any means always correspond
to any areas set off by streets. "Okay," Vic began.

They all knew, he told them, that prior to the Revolution
Erry War—

His Honor: "Ah, well, Victor, might as well carry it back to
the Indians. Begin at the beginning, take all the time you need,
there's nothing else to concern us for the next half-hour—except, may God help us, taxes we can't possibly lower and jobs we
can't possibly provide. *Onward*."

The Assessor: "Oh. Well. *Sure*, Francey. Well, the area of the
site of this whole *city*, it belonged to the Hackamack Indians,
whose title, as we say, is extinguished. They *sold* it to the old
Dutch West *In*dia Company, and *they* sold it to Joachim Cornelius
van der Dam, an ancestor, well, sort of, a col*lat*eral ancestor, he
was the patroon, the patentee, as they call it, and *he* sold it to
Oliver *Ed*wardes, who the King or was it the *Queen*? of England,
made him *Sir* Oliver."

At this point Victor suddenly looked up, enquiringly.

The mayor said, softly, "Go on, Vic. The English we will
never forgive. But we have forgiven the Dutch."

Vanderdam, blank, asked what they had to forgive the *Dutch*
for?

With a very light, slight sigh, the mayor said, "For King William III. Of Orange. And the Battle of the—"

"Oh, King *Will*iam's War. French and *In*dian. No, this doesn't
have nothing to do with that." Mayor and Commissioner and
City Attorney exchanged swift glances, looked away. "*Any*way,
the *third* Sir Oliver, he was a Tory in the Revolution Erry War,

so the State Legislature escheated his property. Which was, first the property was leased. To Oliver Edwardes's tenant farmers, and then, in 1786, it was all sold. At auction. And these here," he passed his hand over the surface of the map, indicating the multi-colored areas, "are the people who bought. All the subsequent land titles, come from *their* titles. Paluel Hills, Owen Odell, Abraham Van der Dam, Ezekiel Prince, Jacobus Van der Closter: and *so* on. *Now*."

The Mayor looked at him with great interest. The Commissioner of Public Works looked out the window. Far off, obscured by a combination of early autumnal haze and industrial smoke, the skyline of the City of New York floated vaguely. The City Attorney looked at his hands. The merchant official just looked.

The Mayor poured some more into his own glass without taking his eyes off Vanderdam's intent face.

Assessor: "*That* was when the *trouble* started. *Must* of been some mistake in surveying—"

His Honor: "George Washington wasn't available."

Assessor: "*What? Huh?* Oh. Huh *ho. No* ho ho. George *Wash*ington had *other* fish to fry just about *that* time. No, can't blame it on George *Wash*ington. *Anyway*. So look here. Lemme show you."

He showed where, on the map, the Hackamack Creek (which the local newspapers, or anyway the Evening *Press*, which was fancier, preferred to call the Gristmill River, a name otherwise used for it only where it ran through the fashionable suburb of Gristmill Heights, northwest of the northwest boundary of the really, non-fashionable City of Yokums) flowed into town, open for the most part to the Winds of Heaven—a phrase, however, he did not use—and covered over—at *intervals*—in its course through the downtown area of the city, whence it disembogued into Hackamack Bay. His thick finger, lightly tufted with sandy hair, jabbed into the map to show where the creek was covered over.

"Now the last part, the *last* part where the Creek is still open, see, is here. Right *here*. It di*vides*. And runs around both sides of Turkey *Island*. And joins together. And all *that*. Is covered *up*. And serves as a *sew*er. But. *But*. Right here. Just one block from where we now are gathered, a block from City Hall Square. *East* of it, serves as a sewer, the course of the Creek has been covered over and converted into a sanitary *sew*er system, and *west* of it, it is covered over and serves as a sewer. But right *here*. It is still *op*en—"

"And serves as a sewer," the Mayor murmured.

The Honorable John J. Quoyte said, "Haw haw haw!" and smacked his hand on the desk. "—Scuse me, Francey. Vic."

"Oh, *that*'s all right," said the Mayor, softly. "Go on, Vic."

"'And serves as a sewer,' *yes*sir, right, that is the problem, isn't it? That is the nucleum of the whole, entire *prob*lem. Everywhere where it is covered over, the only way that anything can get into the sewer system is via, the uh, well, the *toi*lets. And, of course, the gratings in the streets. And the *man*-holes. But as to right *here*. Where it is still open, the last *part* of it which *is* still open, well, anyone can just well dump *any*thing into it. Anything at *all*. Of any size whatsoever. Stuff that sewers were never meant to *carry*."

The Commissioner of Public Works said, didn't he know it.

"That's my *prob*lem," he said. "Should be *yours*, Vic."

For a moment his associate looked over, mouth opened but silent. Then he flushed a bit. Then he said, "Well, Jack, you know, Jack, well, it *is* my problem. Over twenty square feet of it. *I* would love to get it on the tax rolls. I would *love* to get it on the tax rolls, Jack. Twenty square feet of downtown Yokums? Oh boy! *Would*n't I love to get it on the tax rolls!"

"Well, why *dont*cha, then?"

The Mayor sighed, raised his eyebrows, set down his glass. "It wouldn't stay on the tax-rolls very damned long, anyway," he said. "Because as soon as we could, we'd con*demn* it, so we could cover it over. No Man's Land, we call it, because we don't know who it be*longs* to—I mean, that *is* what we want to *do* about it, isn't it? Cover it *over*? So as to put an end to this perpetual damned nuisance, once and for all?"

Mr. Benjamin Rose, of the Merchants' Association, nodded emphatically. "I for one," he said, "am very, ver-ry tired, gentlemen, of being referred to as 'The Rose of No Man's Land,' and—"

At this the Commissioner guffawed again, apologized again.

"—and it must be admitted that the area directly behind my place of business doesn't *smell* exactly like a rose," the merchant went on. "And with business like it is, you know, I don't *need* this aggravation, I don't *need* anything extra to drive customers away. Because, you know, besides the *smell*, why I couldn't be*gin* to tell the *loss*es we merchants have suffered from flood damage —"

The City Attorney stifled a yawn, and said, in his own rapid fashion, "Half of the stuff that blocks up the Creek, blocks up the *sew*er entrance, I mean, is thrown there by your fellow-merchants anyway; not*chew*, Ben, I'm sure, but—"

"Ah, come *on*, Cornelius!"

"At least *half* of it?"

But Mr. Rose wouldn't plead guilty even to half. Empty cardboard cartons and waste paper was not the main problems, he said. His fellow-merchants didn't throw mattress-springs out their backdoors. "You wouldn't be*lieve* the, the *stuff* that we find there, day after day, behind our stores," he said, his voice rising.

The Mayor murmured, "Dead horses, Mack trucks, the Cardiff Giant—Yes, Ben. Yes. We know. No Man's Land is open, entirely open, at one end. And just as we can't cover it over with a nice concrete culvert, for the same reason we can't even *fence* it off. And the reason is, it doesn't be*long* to us. To the City, I mean. And we can't determine to whom it *does* belong. For all we know to the contrary," he said, "it might *still* belong to the Indians."

If so, the Indians or their otherwise-derelict guardian spirits were exacting a recurrent revenge via the turbid waters of Hackamack Creek where it ran through the City of Yokums (named, it was generally conceded, for lack of any better ascription, after Joachim van der Dam, the one-time Patroon, or Patentee): a stinking trickle in dry weather, a torrent in wet.

"Don't tell me," Mr. Ben Rose, of Rose's Quality Men's Wear, requested, "that the best legal minds in the City—"

"—Thanks for the compliment—"

"—can't think of *no* way to do something about getting *No* Man's Land covered *over*?—once and for *all*?"

But it seemed that they could not. No way seemed open to condemn the ownerless piece of land. The law was the law, good, bad, indifferent, or an Ass: and the law kept coming back to the same section of the circle: the City could not act against a piece of land. It could only act against an owner. And *this* piece of land, certainly owing to an oversight almost a hundred and fifty years old, had no owner.

And therefore the City could not act.

"Not in any permanently effective fashion," the Mayor said, suddenly throwing his eyes up to the Seth Low clock on the opposite wall. "But that doesn't mean we are going to allow that damn creek to build up a damn *delta*, for crying out loud! You've got a flood, filth, and flotsam problem in your backyards there, Ben, again, have you?"

Mr. Rose, who had taken off his glasses, put them back on again. "*Worse* than ever! Worse than *ever*! I'm ashamed to *see* some a the things that people flush down their toilets and which wind up washed up on the back porch of my *store*—"

The Mayor murmured, "Sold for prevention of disease only; WELL." Suddenly they were all standing up. "The Commissioner of Public Works will get a crew down into that sewer within the hour, won't he, Jack?"

The Commissioner of Public Works said, "Within the *half-hour*—"

The Assessor said, rather vaguely, "Maybe the *State* could do sumpthing about the legal problem. Mr. City Attorney?"

Mr. City Attorney pulled his nose and pushed his lips out. "You *may*, *have* something there, Victor. If the sovereign State of New Jersey—" They were all on their way out of the Mayor's office by now, the Mayor acting as cheerful shepherd. "—escheated the Estate of Sir Oliver Cromwell, may he burn in Hell, or whatever his name was, oh I beg your pardon, Miss Flaherty—"

"No pardon is necessary, Mr. Flynn."

"—then it seems to me (thank you Miss Flaherty) that if the sovereign State of New Jersey failed to sell off those twenny square feet consisting of ten square feet on either side of the Creek, then those twenny square feet, eck cetera eck cetera, must still be*long* to the sovereign State of New Jersey: in which case—"

But the Mayor had the last, and reluctant, word.

"Which case is that this City is still under a Republican administration," he said, "whereas the sovereign State of New Jersey is under a Democratic one. So we can alas forget *that*. Until either the State goes Republican or the City goes Democratic. *Or*," he added, with a quirk in his voice and a quirk on his face, "Colonel Corbett succeeds in bringing back the Bull Moose Party—"

They had all laughed, and were all gone in another moment. Even Miss Flaherty had smiled. Briefly.

The Mayor turned and went back into his office. His aunt was already there, busy at his desk; then, her hands full, she moved on back into the tiny washroom. "Ah," said her nephew, over the sound of running water and clattering crystal; "the medicine glasses. Thank you, Miss Flaherty."

Miss Flaherty did not say You're welcome Your Honor. She did not say anything at all. And this time she did not smile.

"Treesa," said the Honorable John J. Quoyte, "tell the Assistant Comishner to get a crew a *men* to clean out the *soor* there, below No Man's Land. Tell um, Right *Now*."

"Agnes," said Assistant Commissioner of Public Works Kendall S. Diedrick, "tell Deputy Commissioner Bradlaw to send six men a clean out the *soor*, y'know, down by what they call *No* Man's Land? Tell him, Not tomorrow: *Now*. Tell him, he has any questions, call *me*."

Deputy Commissioner Bob Bradlaw had a question. "Uh, you any particular man you had in mind to *fore*man this crew, Commissioner Diedrick?"

The foreman would draw extra pay.

"Goddamn it," said Assistant Commissioner Diedrick, "do I hafta duhcide *every* goddamn thing in this depahtment by myself? NO, I haven't got no particular—" His voice dropped. "Yeah," he said. "Sure," he said. "Whatta bout . . . Joe Horvath?"

For a moment the Deputy Commissioner was also silent. Then, his own voice lower than before, he said, "Iddle be a pleasure."

CHAPTER THREE

The Civic Club was at monthly lunch, each member and each guest wearing a convenient name badge. "Bob" Harlow (insurance) was honored to find himself sitting across from "Jake" Houghtailing (U.S. Senate). And though of course he knew this distinguished gentleman very well, the name-badge nevertheless attracted his attention. And so, after a while, he spoke up about it.

"Say Jake, I mean, uh, Senator, no offense, and uh—"

"Now Bob," the legislator said, with a genial smile containing some elements of equally genial reproof, "Jake will do perfectly well. Jake will be just swell. Besides: do you want to risk the fifty cent fine for not calling a fellow-member by his first name?" And he chuckled. Harlow chuckled, too, but he seemed hesitant how to continue. So the other said, cheerfully, "Come on now Bob. Drop the other shoe."

"Well, yeah, uh. Uh. Didn't you used to spell your last name H-o-t-a-l-i-n-g, same as all the others?"

The senator nodded vigorously. He was a big man, in body as well as political stature. "But don't say, 'All the others, Bob,' say, 'Most of the others.' Yes. Sure. Certainly I did. And you put your finger on as to why I changed it back to the old, original form—"

"Oh I didn't know that. The old, original form, huh."

"Absolutely. But, as I was saying, *no*, as *you* were saying, Bob: 'All the others.' Do you have any idea how many other people there are who spell their name H-o-t-a-l-i-n-g? Well I don't myself. But I can tell you, lots and *lots*. Why there used to be anyway four Jacob Hotalings that I *know* of in this county alone, as well as who knows how many up in Bergen County and in fact all along the River, on both sides. And just as I was getting ready to hang up my shingle as a brand new lawyer, I picked up a newspaper, in fact I can tell you *which* newspaper, it was the old *Jersey Whig-Democrat*, you know, the one that wonderful old rascal X.X. Bixby put out, as we used to call him, *his* real name was actually Alexander Dexter Bixby, had his place out on, *way* out on Principal Street, between the Glen and the Swamp: well: And low and be*hold* what did I see under 'Criminal Reports' but the word *Arrests: Jacob Hotaling, teamster, charged with stealing three chickens*—"

Everybody at the table burst into hearty laughter.

The senator, who had joined in the merriment, wiped the corners of his eyes and his dark lips with his napkin, and continued his narrative. "Well, I said to myself, 'That does it, Jacob, that does it.' And I folded up the paper and I went down to the courthouse and had the spelling changed to what it is now and used to *be* before the original Houghtailing, or, rather, I suppose his children and grandchildren, they started changing it and abbreviating it. Now, mind, no matter how they spell it it is a fine old name and they are all fine people and they are all of them my own blood kith and kin, cousins one way or cousins the other—"

Rather boldly, Bob interjected, "And they can all vote, too, hey Senator?"

"'And they can all *vote*, too,' yes, right. Give that man a good five cent cigar."

After the laughter was dying down, up spoke someone else, who was it but Mr. H. Prester Jones, the antiquary and antique dealer and director (part-time) of the small local museum. He cleared his throat and said, "Well, yes, Senator, I well know the problem, because after all you may have noticed that Jones is not after all a very uncommon name—"

"Haw haw haw!"

"Although of course there is only one way to spell it, I thank heavens," he said, in his wry, dry, funny way. "*But.* Isn't there a school of thought, sir, which holds that your family's name ori-

ginally *had* no 'g' on the end of it and the 'g' was added after
the assumption that a 'g' had been dropped, as in readin, writin,
and arithmetic? So that therefore the original form of the name
would have been with*out* a 'g'?"

The senator had pursed his lips and raised his eyebrows and
said, "Well, I can only quote my estimable Hebrew friend Mr.
Izzy Feinbein—'*Now*, he tells me!'" And of course everybody had
laughed heartily. "Laugh your troubles away," the old saying has
it, and in those days of gloom and pessimism and so-called "depression," a good laugh was heartily needed.

The senator, as he was always called, the other senator from
the state being referred to by his full name, *the* senator being
understood as indicating Jacob Houghtailing,—the senator was
after all an educated man, he had been to college in addition to
having merely "read law" in the offices of old Lawyer Bremen;
and this plus many years in Washington had rubbed the rougher
edges of the local accents from his speech, but he could slip back
into them when he wanted to. Did some committeeman in some
smoke-filled room hem and haw and beat around the bush, the
senator would lift his heavy face and give him a heavy-lidded
stare and bid him to "Either shit, er git awf dthe pot."

But of course there was none of this when he, for example,
made one of his famous addresses on citizenship to the as-
sembled students of the local schools, nor when he addressed
the Civic Club. And as for his justly-famous and often-reprinted
speech at the Flag Day Dinner which the Junior Chamber of Commerce gave in 1925 (inviting, with laudable attention to The Future Leaders of Our Community, two outstanding seniors from
each of the City's two high schools, *plus* Simpson Trades School),
why, let Alton Ahearne, one of the young men from Central High
say what he said then.

"When I heard the senator say, 'When I consider the infinite
riches and the infinite resources which our American way of life
offers to each and every one, to one and all, I say unto you young
men—and, yes! you young women, too!—say unto all of you,
'You can *have* no *right* to *be* poor!'" Alton recalled; "when I hear

him say this, it was like a, now, thrill, run right through me."

And the senator, though certainly a one-hundred percent American, was certainly a friend to those still undergoing the essential process of Americanization. Some called them Foreigners, some called them Immigrants. And some called them Minorities.

Yokums had a number of rather interesting ethnic minorities, except that, of course, hardly anyone was really very interested in them. A common question was, "What nationality are you?" The answer, "I am an American," was not invariably acceptable. In fact, it very seldom was. The law of the land, the entire school system in its intent and purpose, said that everyone, once naturalized, was an American—and that, of course, should have held true for the American-born children of those born subject to alien princes and potentates. In everyday usage, however, the title of *American* was reserved for people of northwest European descent whose progenitors had migrated, say, prior to the War of 1812. Charles Victor Vanderdam, for instance, did not think of himself as or describe himself as, nor was he (usually) referred to as, a Dutchman, or a Hollander, or (to be in the local idiom more precise) a Holland Dutchman. The Vanderdams, Vander Dams, Van der Dams, van der Dams, Van Dams, van Dams, had moved from Bergen-op-Zoom three hundred years ago—But Francis F. Flaherty, whose grandparents, seeing the handwriting on the walls of the potato-shed in the starving suburbs of Skibbereen, had taken, first, the few gold coins saved up since before the Flight of the Earls, and, next, passage on the first ship out—a passage which landed them on the Old Wharf in Hackamack Village—Francis F. Flaherty was still, despite three generations and family service in three wars, an Irishman.

Besides such standard Nationalities as the Irish, Scotch, Germans, Italians, Polish, Jewish (Ben Rose, without heat and without hope, would insist that this was his *religion*: to the world at large, however, it was also his nationality, and all the insistence in the world *vet gurnisht hilfen*), Yokums also contained sizable numbers of such lesser-known kiths as Azerbaijanians and Slovatchkos. The Azerbaijanians said that they were *Assyrians*, "You know, like in the Bible, only *Christians*." The Catholic majority in Yokums did not know, had a vague notion that the Bible was somehow connected with the Freemasons and the fez-wearing Shriners, referred to the humble and hardworking posterity of Prester John as "them Arabs." The Slovatchkos, whose homeland, sundered by the break-up of the Scythian-Pannonian-Transbalkanian Empire, was now divided between two other—and larger—nations, usually said that they were Ukrainians, on the assumption that perhaps the rest of the world had at least heard of the Ukraine—an assumption not always by any means justified. The Ukrainians themselves were inclined to deny this, but nobody listened, except, perhaps, other Ukrainians. The Assyrians were mostly housepainters. The Slovatchkos were mostly drunk—

Some nations, seemingly, last forever: who would expect to find the seed of Assurbanipal painting the side of a Ford agency in New Jersey?—as much expect to find a mastodon in Palisades Park. Other nations fade away barely noticed: who remembers the Livs of Livonia, or the Morlocks of Istria? Outnumbered and out-noticed by the Slovacks and the Slovenes, unrepresented on maps of postage stamps, some odd and uncharted tide had brought more Slovatchkos to Yokums, N.J., than to anywhere else in the New World: and in the drab rookeries of the neighborhood known, archaically, as The Swamp, they were for the most part content to be as unrecognized and unrepresented as anywhere else. "For the most part," but not for every part. Joe Horvath recognized them, and, insofar as they were represented at all, Joe Horvath represented them. On the ground floor of a five-storey walk-up tenement on Freylinghuysen Street at the corner of Principal, next to a tiny grocery store which seemed to deal chiefly in headcheese, dingy small potatoes, and spotted bananas, was another storefront. And on the glass window of it one could see, if one looked, and few did, the words, the brave, mysterious words,

Fourth Ward Glagolitic Slovatchko-Ukranian
Improvement Association
J. Horvath, Pres.

This constituted the sole incorporation in America of the former inhabitants of the so-called Glagolitic Alps. If they needed help with their citizenship papers, if they required to be bailed out of jail after a Saturday-night brawl, if they had to fill out forms to bring family or friends to America, Joe Horvath it was who helped them. Joe Horvath it was who calmed fears that the truant officer was really readying a roster for the purpose of forced labor or conscription. It was Joe Horvath who rolled up his sleeve and let the doctor vaccinate him in order to show that the act was not after all invariably fatal; after which the Slovatchkos, albeit still trembling, suffered the same arcane ritual to be performed upon their children, supported by loud roars (from Joe Horvath) of the age-old cry, "*Courage! Courage! —and confound the Turks!*"

It was also noted that in his capacity of notary public, an office held in immense awe by the Glagolitski, he would often let the beshawled *bobba*-women off without paying anything; as for those men who "were working every day," he would likelier say, loudly—he usually said everything loudly—"You are a rich man and should have the *gold* seal on your papers; that is another twenty-five cents piece!" And his command of both the dialect and of English, his status as a highly active member of the American Legion and the Veterans of Foreign Wars, "three wound stripes and President Hoover himself sent me this medal with the Purple Heart," his relentless benevolence in pulling-pushing-prodding-dragging his Slovatchko people first into citizenship and second to the polls, finally received recognition and reward.

Among those also appointed by the new City Administration was Mr. Joseph L. Horvath, as Assistant Deputy

*Commissioner of Public Works. Mr. Horvath is active in
veterans' affairs and is a co-chairman of the Americanization Committee.*

—the Yokums (N.J.) Daily Press

They didn't know how to spell "Slovatchko," anyway, on the
Yokums (N.J.) *Daily Press. Or* "Glagolitic."

Joe was a successful politician, then. But he was not really a
highly-successful politician. His reluctance to suffer fools gladly,
if at all—his unwillingness to admit that his status was as low
as most of the City Hall regulars thought it was—and, also, his
tendency to become restless when called bad names—all stood
in the way of his career.

"He *come* around," went a typical complaint, from a citizen
with a bandaged face, "he *come* around with this bunch of Bo-
hunks and he says, now, he says, like, he says, 'We got too many
gahdamn complaints that *rats* is breeding in the backa dthis
warehouse, and besides, it's a hazard to navigation,' or sumppin.
An *I* says, *I* says, I says, 'Say, don't tell *me* what ta do on my own
proppity, you Hunky son of a bitch.'"

City Official: And so then what happen?

Bandaged Citizen: An dthen he *hit* me, he musta hit me about
tenner twenny *times*, an I like slipt an fell, an dthen he, now, he
grabba hole a me an he pull me back upta my feet and he hit me
again about tenner twenny *times . . .*

City Official: You are certainly entitled to press a charge
against him. You want to press a charge against him?

Bandaged Citizen: Say, I ain't *crazy*, ya know.

Also, to tell the Commissioner of Public Works, whose
difficulty with the written word extended to locating anything
printed on a map, that he (the CPW) couldn't find his own fat ass
with both hands in the daylight with the lights turned on, indi-
cates a certain lack of what is generally termed tact. Also—

Assistant CPW Diedrick: Say listen here Joe Horvath don't you
talk that way to me, I'll get around to issuing that order when I
good and well feel like it, I don't take no orders from you—

Assistant DCPW Horvath: If your second cousin wasn't a Congressman you'd be taking orders from the negro who shovels out the shit in Feinbein's stables, that there hole in the street by the fire hydrant on Rupert's Road is deep enough t' drown *babies* in it al*ready*, you nipple-headed numbskull. (etc., etc., etc.)

Still. Still. Fifteen hundred and thirty-five votes, delivered like clockwork. *Plus* "active in veterans' affairs." *Plus* the great interest of a certain U.S. Senator in the work of the Americanization Committee, on which Horvath was "active" as well. No. Horvath could hardly be fired, with the Depression deepening and the Democrats coming to power everywhere.

What they *could* do, however—

"Hey, *Hor*vath!"

"Whaddaya want."

"I wahn chew ta take a crew a six men and clean out that damn *soor* there, juss buhlow *No* Man's Land. Right *now*." Bradlaw eyed big Horvath half-truculently, half-warily. But Joe merely smoothed his moustache and shifted his cigar. His next words echoed those of the ACPW a moment earlier.

"Iddle be a pleasure," he growled. And he turned on his heel.

"Never give the bastards the satisfaction," was his motto.

Later. Commissioner Quoyte checked with his Assistant. "Ya send some men down ta clear out there, past No Man's Land?"

"Yes, John, as soon as you *said* to, John."

"Whodja send in chadge?"

"Joe Horvath."

Quoyte guffawed. "See how he likes *that*," he said. "Huh?"

"Yes, John."

"Lotsa rats, huh?"

"Yes, John."

"*Lotsa* rats!"

◆ ◆ ◆

There were, indeed, lots of rats, and one of them, a huge great-granddaddy of a rat, leaped out of the tangled mass of rubbish which packed the lower part of the conduit and jumped at one of the men. The man screamed, tried to flee, his rubber boots slipping on the slimy surface beneath his feet. For a second, panic threatened. Then there was a sharp report which echoed and re-echoed, the rat fell writhing in the filth and muck and was immediately stomped to death by Joe Horvath, who had shot it.

"I seen bigger ones in France," he growled. He waved his revolver in one hand and his lamp in the other. "Come on, come *on*, what're you waiting for?"

The answer—as the frightened DPW crew huddled fearfully together—came from the shadows surrounding them. As the last echoes of the shot died away, a chorus of squeaks and scrabbling sounds came from the darkness. Just outside of the sharp circle of the beam of light, grey forms darted, red eyes gleamed. "What makes them darn rats grow so *big*?" someone muttered.

"Dthere must be *mil*lions of um!" another protested. "Dthey bitecha—y' could get hydrophobia!"

"*I* bitecha, y'll get worse than *that!*" Joe Horvath threatened. "Let's *go!*" He shined his light around, muttered disgustedly, "Look at all this junk—bedsprings, old mattresses, auto seats and auto springs, Christmas trees—at this time a year!—boxes, crates. No wonder the Creek backs up—no wonder it smells bad. We got to get this *crap* outta here. We *don't*, well, they'll give us all the bum's rush and get some people down here who *will*. So let's *go*." He gestured to the men. They moved forward slowly—but they moved. Partly it was Joe Horvath, partly it was the gun, partly it was the reminder of the possible loss of their jobs. If you had a job then, oh boy did you take good care of it . . . *if* you *had* one.

Horvath moved along, holding his revolver on the ready. He muttered into his cigar, gnawed his moustache. The place did really remind him some of the trenches in France, twelve, thirteen years earlier. It seemed an odd reward for it all. But a man was so lucky to have a job nowadays, any job at all. Business and industry in Yokums, like anywhere else, were hard hit. The Federal Ironworks Company and the Alonzo Jones Woolens Factory, both traditionally among the Big Three of local employers, were laying people off. And even Standard Syrup Refining, the richly famous and legendary "Sugar House," was reportedly not doing so well; and had not taken anyone on for a long time. Not even the dead and the retired were being replaced.

The campaign which had as its total slogan, "Repeal the 18th Amendment," was still in the future, although *Repeal*, like *Prohibition*, had become a proper noun. Business was in general not doing well. But bootlegging was doing well. *Damned* well. However, not everyone had the good luck to work for a bootlegger.

Or, for that matter, to work in the sewers.

Joe Horvath's voice, which had died down into mutters, now exploded into a shout of disgust. "Who in the Hell threw *this* into the Creek? And what in the Hell *is* it, anyway?" This looked like it was a pipe or hose of some kind. It was about four inches in diameter and was tightly bound around with wire. "Copper wire," Joe observed, thoughtfully. "No, y'know, *no*body would throw away this much copper wire . . . Where's the end of it?" He flashed the light backwards, then forwards. But the hose seemed to have neither beginning nor end. "That's a funny thing," he muttered. "A damned funny *thing. . .* "

One of the men suggested, diffidently, "Maybe you look in chart, Joe—dem maps you get from City Hall? Maybe is sup*pose* to be pipe here, huh?"

Joe gave his head an emphatic shake. "I know what's on the charts. And there's no pipe supposed to be there. *Here*. And we can't get any of all of this junk out until we get *it* out, either. All right," he said, abruptly, making up his mind. "Let's all grab ahold, and when I give the signal, I say 'pull,' we *pull*." The men laid aside their tools, wiped their hands, seized the funny-looking pipe—or hose, or whatever it was. "All ready? Get set—"

"Pull!"

Mickey Kelly was breaking in a new helper, Patsy Lo Moto. "Boy, yer lucky ta be gettin a job like dthis," he said, with a side-wise jerk of his head, as though he didn't entirely understand it or entirely approve of it. "Gee up," he said, to the two fat horses drawing the green wagon with *Feinbein's* Market painted on the sides in elaborate letters. He flapped the straps so that they rose and fell on the horses' backs.

"Geeze, I *know* dthat," Pat said, rolling his own head from side to side, and pressing his mouth thin. "Cha don' hafta keep *tullin* me, I *know* wit."

The hill rose in slow folds. A few of the huge trees had already begun to turn color. The big houses, some of them fifty years old, were set higher up and back from the road, Upper Bluffs Avenue. The Hackamack Bluffs were by no means the Palisades, but they were not only the best that Yokums had to offer, they were *there*. In Yokums. And gave a very fine view of the Bay, the Meadows, the Hudson River and New York Bay and even of New York City itself.

"Aldthough I dun*no*, dthough," Mickey shook his head again, and his red curls bounced; "summa dthese *rich* people—"

"Huh? Whudda *bowd* um?"

"'F dthey don' staht payin their *bills*, boy . . . I dunno how Izzy's gunna be able ta stay in bizness."

Pat said, "Jesus," very softly.

"An a*nud*da t'thing. —*Gee* up!— Dthe only t'thing I doe' *like* about dthis job, he still uses *hawsses. Crazy* abowd um! —Ohwell. Huh? Oh yeah. A*nud*da t'thing about dthis job, he ahlweez letsya take home the stuff it isn't strictly fresh no maw. Dthese *rich* people, dthey don't ahlweez have the money to pay their *bills*, but if by some *ac*cident it isn't strictly fresh, *boy* yawda hearrum complain."

"Yeah…"

The road turned. Looking down, they could see the whole of downtown Yokums spread out, with the narrow and winding streets laid out long before there were either automobiles or trolley cars. "Yeah. Somebuddy says ta him, I doe' wanna mention no *names*, somebody says ta him, 'Whuddaya givin it a*way* faw, Izzy. Make the people *pay*faw it, fthey doe' pay faw it, t'throw it inna *gah*bage!' An he says, 'God should strike me dead, foyst.'"

"Yeah. . . " Pat nodded, slowly. His face suddenly brightened. "Bet I cn tullya *one* rich customer who I bet dthey always pay on time!" he said, emphatically.

"*Yeah*? Who's *dthat*?" There was a touch of sarcasm in Mickey's tone: look, this new guy trying to tell him the business.

"Dthe Stoltzes," said Pat.

"'Dthe Stoltzes'? Who's *dthat*? Which Stoltz 's ya *talkin* about?"

Mickey feigned ignorance, wonder. But Pat knew he knew. "*Dutch* Stoltz!" he said, excitedly, a touch of red in his cheeks. "*Al*bert Stoltz! Huh? Am I right? Huh?"

Mickey smiled crookedly. "Ah, I knew who ya meant, ahlright. Yeah. *Sure. Dthey* pay. On the button. 'A pleasure doin business vit you,'" he mimicked their employer's accent.

Pat snickered. "I never wuhyked fuh no *Jew* before. . . ."

Mickey gave his head another rolling shake. "Lemme tullya. Ya lucky ta be wuhykin f' *any*body, nowadays . . . boy. . . "

"Ahright," Mickey was suddenly business-like, unsmiling; "fuhyst stop's right around here, dya know who's the fuhyst stop. Ya *dunno*. Okay, look at dthe *tick*ets." Rather nervously, Pat consulted the thin sheaf of order-bills. "Ah, ah, om, om, *Walley*?"

"Whaddaya *ask*in me faw? Whaduzzit *say*?"

Pat swallowed. He and Mickey had been boys together, they had for a while attended the same public school, old Number 5, together, having, as it happened, both been kicked out of their respective parochial schools the same year and not allowed back till later; they had played ball in Poulson's lots, and they had even showed each other what they had, in the bushes behind The Lots (Mickey was longer, Pat was bigger)—but now he suddenly remembered that Mickey was the boss and he was only the helper. "Om, it says, like, 'Walley, 329 U.B.'"

"Dthat's right," Mickey said, suddenly becoming friendly again. "Walley, William H. Walley, 329 Upper Bluffs Avenya. Hey!

I'll betcha I cn tullya ex actly what he's gunna say! How bowd it? Ya wanna bet? Egg, zack, lee whut he's gunna say. It's a bet, yeah?"

Pat was leery. How could he hope to win? "Naa. I doe' wanna bet nuthin."

"Ah, *come* on, *come* on. We bet a treat at Bodenheimer's. A cole drink. Ya cn risk t'three *cents*, cantcha? O*kay* . . ." Mickey turned the horses into a gravelled driveway, and he gave a snort of laughter. "But, listen, don' let *on*, now. No laughin, not even no smile. Ur I swear ta God I'll tell Izzy on ya. O*kay*? Okay. He's gunna say, Ol Man Walley's gunna say," he cleared his throat and assumed a different expression of face and of tone of voice. "'Hello Boys, the housekeeper's busy right now so I'll take care of this.' Wait. Ch'y'll *see*."

Someone working in the garden disappeared as they drove up. The order was in three bags and when Pat moved to take two, Mickey shouldered him away and took the second bag himself. The green feathery tails of carrots tickled Pat's nose, and he could smell scallions, too, and the earthy scent of potatoes. Mickey rang the bell at the back door, which was level with the ground; Pat wondered at the absence of a back porch, the old wooden houses in Italian Heaven, up on Goat Hill, they weren't fancy like this, but they at least all had back porches as well as front ones.

The back door opened. A middle-aged man in vest and shirt-sleeves, gold eyeglasses on his nose with a little chain, looked at them with a set little smile. He said, "Hello Boys, the house-keeper's busy right now so I'll take care of this."

"Yessir."

He took the bags one at a time and closed the door behind him each time. Then he came back, Mickey handed him the bill and he put it into his pocket without saying anything and he took out a coin and handed it to Mickey, who said, without look-ing at *it*, "Thank you Mr. Walley." Mr. Walley nodded, did not look at them again, and went back into the kitchen.

Not till they were a ways down the block did Mickey say, "Ya see? Whaddid I tullya?"

"Yeah. . . "

Mickey opened his closed hand and showed a nickel. "Can ya beat that? Boyyy . . . Never mind the bet," he said. "I'll treat *chew* . . . 'Housekeeper,' didja getta loada that? There hasn't been no *house*keeper dthere for, oh, four? five? munce. . . "

Pat snorted, smiled. "Hoccome his *wife* doesn't come ta dthe daw, then?" Mickey it was who snorted then. His *wife* (Mickey said), his *wife*? She was probably lying down with a book and a bottle of smelling salts. Then they both laughed.

The Stoltz's house was not strictly speaking the next one on the route this morning, but it was the next one they were going to stop at inasmuch as Mrs. Stoltz had called and asked if they could *pos*sibly? because she wanted to get dinner on *early*? And, of course, it turned out, of course, that they could, possibly. In fact: *cer*tainly.

Street numbers in Yokums did not start in a One Hundred block and change every block in units of one hundred more, they started at Number 1 and continued until the number of houses reached 100, as many blocks later as might be; then they began again at 101. The house numbered 453 was like any of the large Queen Anne style houses on Upper Bluffs Avenue. Mr. Dooley had once said that the Victorian Age might as well have been named after him, because "I had as much to do with it as Queen Victoria." In this case he had more to do with it than Queen Anne, whose famous death had occurred almost two hundred years before any houses in that style were built. There was a porch, called the front porch, which actually ran around three sides of 453. There was a turret which constituted a half-floor above the second floor, there were bay windows, niches, gingerbread of a subdued sort, and a sort of balcony outside of one room on the second floor. A double-flight of stone steps, walled on each side with stone, led up to the front door. Unlike a few others, 453 had no hitching post but a carriage block was still there, half-sunken into the earth between the stone curbing and the slate sidewalks. All the windows had window shades and lace curtains.

Most of the U.B. Avenue houses had a garage half-set into the hillside; but at this one and only this one, the garage was no longer a garage, it was open at the back and the driveway ran right through it. A heavy-set man with a grey suit and a grey face got up from a kitchen chair as the wagon approached. The wagon stopped. Mickey said, "Hiya, Tully."

Tully said nothing at all in reply; what he said, looking at Patsy was, "Who *zis*?"

"Dthis is my new helper, Patsy, ah, *Pat*—"

Tully did not wait to hear Pat's last name. He peered into the wagon. "Hoccome ya got so much *stuff* in here, *dthis* time?" he asked.

Mickey hastened to say, "We was *ass* to. Mrs. *Stoltz* she call up ann she ass us could we come uhyly. Ya cd *ass*ter."

Tully had perhaps never read George Eliot's comment that "The rude mind with difficulty associates the ideas of power and benignity," did not show any signs of asking anybody anything else; he gave his head a slight—and slightly contemptuous —jerk towards the rear: Mickey, in a tone more subdued than usual, said, "*Gee* up!" and the wagon rolled on through and up and around and into the enormous backyard, at the other end of which was a new building: the true garage. A stooped and grey-haired man was bent over the flower beds. Mickey recognized him as *the* professional gardener of the classy Upper Bluffs, "Uncle Will," he was called, and he made a lifetime career of being "A Yank, y'know, a Yankee, a *real* American!" Uncle Will belonged to the United Order of American Mechanics as *well* as the Masons, and during the last month and a half of the year 1928 he had staggered, drunken and victorious, up and down the city streets calling out over and over again, "What did AL SMITH telegraph the POPE after the ELECTION, huh? *Huh*?" And, throwing back his head and opening his mouth wide enough to show all his horrid teeth, Uncle Will would shout the answer: "Un-PACK!"

Mickey, seeing him, renewed his hopes that someday the old

bastard would stagger near enough to Feinbein's horses. The gardening business must be very bad indeed for Uncle Will to be working *here*.

Suhyvim right.

Stoltzes' orders filled quite a number of heavy brown paper bags and several baskets. The back door was opened by a wide woman with a pudding face and blueberry eyes; this was the cook. She exclaimed her satisfaction at seeing, not Mickey and Patsy, but the order, and was gesturing directions when someone else, unseen at first behind the not-yet-taken-down screen door, "Oh, is that the de*live*ry man? The fruit and *vetch*tables? Oh, *good*!"

Mickey, grunting slightly under the weight of a basket of fruit, said, "Hullo Mrs. Stoltz."

"Just put it down *here*. Hello, Mickey!" Mrs. Stoltz was not exactly *good*-looking but she was not *bad*-looking either, her hair was elaborately waved even though she was wearing a cotton-print housedress, she wore gold-framed eyeglasses and, as she smiled at them without artifice, the gold of a back tooth glinted briefly. "Oh, do you have the *cook*ing apples?" she asked, somewhat anxiously. "The *sweet* butter?—oh no, that's the *dairy*," she laughed at her own mistake. "I'm so anxious to get my *pies* started! Mary makes *won*derful pies," she added, in an aftertone, "but she's going to have so much to *do* today, so *I'm* going to make the pies!" And she chattered on; Mary, meanwhile, checked out the delivery not only in general but almost in every particular, as she always did, but had never found anything really wrong. Satisfied, finally, that there were no worms, weevils, or rotten or bruised spots, she gave a tiny grunt. Then she took up a bowl from a shelf and they could hear the clinking of coins.

"No, give them a dollar," said Mrs. Stoltz. Mary looked at her mistress, she did not say anything, but she did look at her. "No, give them a *do*llar," Mrs. Stoltz insisted. "No, Mary—a dollar *each*!"

Mary said, "*Yoy.*" But she gave them the dollar each.

And suddenly there was someone else in the kitchen.

"Albert!" exclaimed Mrs. Stoltz.

Someone else was with *him*, someone with a red and puckered face and the expressionless expression of Tully; but neither Mickey nor Patsy had eyes for *him*. They had eyes on the big one of the two: in his tan, obviously custom-tailored, double-breasted suit, and the tan fedora hat which had never even so much as sat on a block in Danbury, Connecticut. His rectangular face, his slightly dented nose, his big jaw, running slightly—*very* slightly—to a jowl.

"Albert, the fruit and *vetch*tables are here, and as soon as the *dairy* brings the *butter*, I'm going to start the *pies*—"

He said, "Whudja givvum, Flossie?"

Mickey and Patsy looked, looked down, swallowed. He was going to growl "*What?*" and he was going to be *mad*, and—

Mrs. Stoltz said, "Why . . . A *dollar*? *Each*?"

The big man smiled a brief and one-sided smile. Thrust his hand into his pocket. (A, a *gat*?) Brought out a wallet. Diamond ring glinting on his fist. *What* a fist! What a *wallet*! Peeled off two more bills. "Since ya catch me at *home*," he said, "so here's *suh*mpn a remember me by." Abruptly turned to his wife. "How about d*the meat*?"

"It's *here*, Albert. It's *here*."

He nodded. Again the brief one-sided smile. He swung back and faced the delivery men. For a moment it was as if he had never seen them before. Then he said, almost indifferently, "Give um a bott la beer, too, Mary."

They were sure, afterwards, that they *had* thanked him. But they did not remember having done so. One minute Mary, with not so much as a grunt, let alone a *Yoy*, was shoving the bottles into their hands. And the next minute they were out in the rear yard again.

The two of them climbed up into the wagon and placed the now-empty baskets carefully behind them. Uncle Will looked up briefly, his long grey moustaches bobbing, then he bent to his work again. "No Irish need apply," he said, if not loudly, distinctly. And, "'*Pasta fazul'*. . . "

"*Gee*-up!" The horses trotted heartily down the slope. "*Bye*, Tully!" Tully scorned to acknowledge. After a minute, Mickey said, "*Dthat* Proddissint *bast*id. . ."

Patsy, slightly surprised, said, "Who, om, *Tully*?"

"*What* Tully? *Ide* a know *whut he* is. I mean, the, uh, *gahd-nuh.*"

"*Dthat* ole son of a bitch. I'd like ta meetum in Italian *Heav*en, some dahk night," Patsy said, broodingly. Then a brighter thought occurred to him—or, at any rate, one equally bright—and he took the two bills out of his shirt pocket and smoothed them, the ONE an ordinary one, wrinkled, grudgingly doled out by Mary; but the FIVE! the *five* smooth and crisp and even . . ."Hoddaya like *dthat*!" asked Patsy, exultantly.

Mickey swung his head, rhetorically, from side to side. "Lemme tullya," he said. "Lemme tullya. Ya deal wit nice people? Dthey treatcha *nice*!"

Patsy digested this, nodded slowly. Then he asked, hesitantly, "An, ah, how about the, om, *beer*?"

"Nuthin but dthe best," Mickey said, emphatically. Then he suddenly looked over at his helper. "Oh. Y'mean, *now*? I wooden, fi was you. Not me. Om gunna take it home wit me. You cn do wutcha like. But. Summa dthese people? Dthey smell it onya bret? Next t'thing ya know? A com*plaint*. Cha gotta good job right now. Don' *rune* it. Cha cn *live*, almost, on whatcha get fa *nut*tin."

Patsy slowly nodded his agreement. Clop, clop, went Dapple and Beauty. The beer, in its nice squat brown bottle, with the cold drops oozing down its sides, looked very nice. It looked *very* nice. But— Then a sudden thought came to him. "Say, I wonder would he gi' *me* a job?" he said.

"Would *who* give yuh job?"

Patsy clicked his tongue in faint annoyance at having to explain the obvious. "Dthe Big Dutchmun. I wonder would he gimme a *job*. *You* know who I mean."

"Dutch Stoltz."

CHAPTER FOUR

Mrs. Mary Mabel Moomaw would have, in the last two previous centuries, have been called "a fine figure of a woman." But fashions had changed. Down throughout the year 1919, women were still being admired for having large bosoms, slender waists, and large lower sections tapering to the feet. These lower sections presumably consisted of such items as hips, buttocks, thighs, and legs; but, insofar as public illustration failed to indicate the contrary, possibly they consisted of one solid, undifferentiated block—And then, suddenly, Something Happened, it is not known exactly what, let alone why. Millions of women, most of whom were built more or less the same as Mary Mabel Moomaw, had fought, and fought fiercely, for Country, Flag, and Family: and, finally, having achieved the first fruits of victory in the form of the 18th and 19th Amendments to the Constitution of the United States (guaranteeing, first, that the manufacture, sale, or transportation of intoxicating liquors within, the importation thereof into, or the exportation thereof from the United States and all territory subject to the jurisdiction thereof for beverage purposes is hereby prohibited; and, second, that The right of citizens of the United States to vote shall not be denied or abridged by the United States or by any State on account of sex), suddenly found —and found almost overnight—that the female body forms which had in large part achieved these victories were no longer deemed fashionable *at all*.

Instead, the boyish look had become the thing. The veil had, so to speak, been stripped from off the form of desirable Ameri-

can Womanhood, and what was revealed underneath was an absolute absence of prominent breasts, hips, bellies, and buttocks.

It was all most unfair. Wasn't it?

But Mrs. Moomaw had not yielded. Not for her the slender-
izing diet, the rusk and the cup of broth, the grapefruit; the
breastband or bellyband. She eschewed them, as she did alcohol in all its forms (her Church, having learned that wine, in
Biblical times, owing presumably to a secret known only to the
Ancient Hebrews, *did not ferment*, administered the Lord's Supper in grape juice). Not for her, either, was the short skirt or the
short sleeve, the cloche hat. Did not such things go hand in hand,
not to say arm in arm, and—but here one had to draw the line in
speaking of them—hand in hand, then, and arm in arm with the
fast car, the fast dance, the fast cigarette, the fast hip-flask, the—

Well.

Yes. Certainly.

If Mary Mabel Moomaw did not weigh any more in, say,
1930, than in 1920, she certainly did not weigh any less. And
if her skirts and coats and sleeves were not any longer than in
that year of grace, they were certainly not shorter. Nor her hats
smaller.

Her principles were just the same, too.

"Now, I hear people saying on all sides, that Prohibition has
been tried and that it is a failure and so that therefore it should
be re*peal*ed," she was saying that morning. A faint hissing was
heard, the people in Mrs. Moomaw's office glanced up, startled,
saw that it was her assistant, Birdie Shallot, who was now smirking her crooked little smirk; saw, too, that Mrs. Moomaw smiled
indulgently, decided to smile also. "And we needn't have to look
very far to see what are the *sources* of this propaganda, because
the Liquor Interests have never actually and genuinely re*pent*ed
their systematic *pois*oning of the people, no; they are *still trying*.
And so, er, as I, when I hear people saying on all sides that Prohibition has been tried and it has proved to be a *fail*ure and so
that therefore it should be re*pealed*, I say: *No*. On the *con*trary. It
has been found *dif*ficult. And so it hasn't ever really been *tried*."

There was an outburst of approval, and everybody, with little goggling looks of guilt, hushed themselves and waited for her to continue. But she, with her invariable and innate courtesy, was waiting for the newspaper reporter to finish writing down the epigram. His name was Bill Bomberg, and, contrary to what the *movies* would have you believe, the *talk*ies as they were rapidly all becoming, he was a perfectly well-mannered young man. Used no offensive "slang." Had neatly hung his hat on the hatrack. *And* had been wearing it the right-way forward, for that matter. True, he did have a press card in the band, but, well, that was sort of necessary, wasn't it, it was sort of like a badge, wasn't it; and, anyway, only a part of it was sticking out from the hat-band. A *lit*tle part. Mrs. Moomaw not only gazed at him patiently, because she wanted everything to be just right; but also she gazed at him with just a touch of something like esteem. The late Mr. Moomaw had been just such a "dark and handsome" man, with just the same touch of color in his cheeks; and if he (Robert Henry Moomaw, A.B., Deceased) hadn't been exactly, well, *tall*, what of it? Neither was this young man journalist your big and gangling type. He was average in stature, and, Mrs. Moomaw reflected, employing in her thoughts another out-of-fashion phrase, he was well-made.

And then, just in case anyone should think that she was gazing upon him with perhaps more than necessary interest, she gently allowed her gaze to move out the window. Somewhere in the middle distance a man on a horse, there, you didn't often *see* that nowadays, whoever he was, she saw him fairly often. The only one in *years*, though. Well, much as one liked to sing about Over The River and Through The Trees, still, you can't stop Progress. And as she thought about Grandmother's House, her stalwart face, sometimes known to look, well, *grim*, from the years of Struggle against the Poison Trust, her face relaxed still more. Had you known her in olden days and former times, it would be easy to overlook the lines around the mouth, the double-chin, faint perhaps but perceptible moustache, and grey hairs; and see once again the Mary Mabel Moomaw of Morristown, of whom many *many* people still said (in Morristown), "Let them say what they will, she stands up for what *she*, *believes*, *in*, and let-*me*-tell-*you*: she was so *pop*-u-lar when she was a girl!"

Well well. Be that as it may. Also present was Birdie Shallot, Assistant to Mary Mabel Moomaw, Regional Director of the Northern New Jersey Region of the National Family Temperance Union, and also a stalwart in the fight to secure the Vote for women under federal law—and everything that went with it. And much, *much* was to have gone (or, perhaps, rather, come) with it. A newer, purer day for American politics, for one. Mary Mabel was a widow, but Birdie had never married, she had not only given up marriage, she had also given up a wonderful career in Education, she had simply *walked away* from her job at old Number Five School, because she had *seen*. What liquor *does* to people. The neglected children. The haggard and desperate wives. The drunken husbands and fathers. Where had the children *learn*ed that awful language? Why from their fathers and their older *broth*ers that was where. Who hung around the sa*loons*. The so-called *speak*easies, they called them today. Often Birdie could not sleep, she simply could not *sleep*, she rose from her bed on the third floor of the Women's Residence of the N.F.T.U. Building on Lower Bluffs Avenue (where, for a very reasonable sum, people—anyway, women—anyway, women without husbands and children to care for, could find decent lodgings away from the vile sights and sounds of the hotels), and she walked the floor, Birdie walked the floor, wringing her thin little hands and sighing and sometimes even sobbing. Till, finally, Mary Mabel would come and knock softly—oh, Mary Mabel knew! However softly Birdie walked, Mary Mabel had a way of knowing. And they would kneel and pray together, oh so very softly, so as not to wake the others.

And also present, and, certainly, knowing nothing of it, being a man, and a married man, although mind you a very *nice* man, was Mr. Hubert Harrison, a government inspector. "Of course," said Mrs. Moomaw, seeing that the reporter had finished his writing down; "I don't address these remarks to *you*, Mr.

Harrison."

"I preciate that," he said, nodding seriously. "I preciate that, Mrs. Moomaw. Because if there is one thing we do, that is we do try. And, I think I can say: suc-*cess*-full-ly." And he nodded again.

"Oh I am *sure!*" Mrs. Moomaw turned to her colleague, Regional Director of Southern New Jersey Region, N.F.T.U. Director Sarah (Mrs. Charles R.) Cambell Sturt. "Last year, Mrs. Sturt," she said, "Mr. Harrison took us all on a tour of the Cereals Plant, you know—"

It was at once made clear that Mrs. Sturt did not know and did not know that she did not know. "Breakfast foods," she said.

"—National Cereals," Mary Mabel continued; she would make it all clear in her own way in her own good time, "operates the only, well, it is, well, what it *is*," she cleared her throat; "it is a *brewery*." Mrs. Sturt's jaw opened, sank. "A *legal* one. The only legally-operated brewery in the *State*. It operates under Federal permit and Federal supervision," she slightly indicated Mr. Harrison with her head and hand. "It makes malted beverage—what is generally termed '*near beer*.'" It was clear that she did not care for the phrase. She cleared her throat. "Many people are still of the opinion that *any* kind of beer is good for the health, oh, for example, that it puts on weight, it helps people put on weight, who are, ah, threatened with, ah, ah, con*sump*tion;" she liked this word even less, her voice sank as she said it.

Mrs. Sturt received this with a downward turn of the lips. "Isn't that nonsense!" she declared. "Why what *is* beer, ittis malted *grain*, is it not? Well, what is the matter with good old-fashioned home-baked *bread*? And malted *milk*? For that matter. . . " Her voice trailed off, she waited for Mary Mabel, whom she had, albeit with the best intentions, rather crudely interrupted. Mr. Harrison, though, who after all, had *not*, now spoke up heartily.

"Gree with you a hundert percent!" he boomed. "But after all, I am jist like a sojer, I am like one of Uncle Sam's sailor-boys, and I jist go whir I'm sent; that right, Miz Moomaw?"

Mrs. Moomaw nodded gravely. "And speaking of *that*. Not,

oh, more than two *weeks* ago, I was approached by one of our own dearly beloved old boys in blue of another era, old Daddy Wilkerson, as we call him, a veteran of the G.A.R. And he said to me, and oh I just wish that *everybody* could've *been* there to've *heard* him, he said, 'Mrs. Moomaw, we fought the wrong people back there in 18 and 61,' he said, 'we should of fought the Liquor Interests!'"

Everybody agreed with this rather moving sentiment, except that the reporter's pencil was scribbling it down too rapidly to allow him to speak, or, even, nod. As soon as he had finished, though, Mrs. Moomaw, this time without interruption, described the conducted tour of the legal brewery, how the grain was malted and mashed and cooked, and so on, and—yes! —turned into *real beer!* "Because, you can't, it seems, you can't *make* near beer from the start, noho: you have to make real beer, and *then*. You de-nature it. Yes! After it's made, they take *every drop of alcohol, out* of it, or, well, they do, they are allowed, they are obliged to leave a very little, which is unavoidable and in fact they assure me quite harmless, maybe oh one percent."

Mr. Hubert Harrison nodded, and rubbed his hands together grimly, then he punched one fist into one palm. "And that's *whir I* come in," he said. "Me and my boys. We stand guard there, ladies—and Mr. Bomberg—we stand on guard twennyfour hours a day. We have are scientific aquipmunt, and we ah *test*, every drop of beer that goes inta thuh bottling plant. Because, oh, it's not that we don't trust the mannafckchers, no, *we* trustum. Not trust Prafessor Brower, the ah *head* a thuh place? Why a mannud hafta be out a his *mind* not ta trust Prafessor Brower, man's reppatation is as clean as a *saint*. But that is the *law*. And we en-*force* the law. And if thuh resta thuh forces a lawn order would jist do thuh, um, *same*, why there jist wouldn' *be* ahlla this *rum*running, although, mine jew, I take ahffa my hat ta thuh *Coass* Guard. Neither snow ner rain ner frost, cha know, keepsum from patrolling aginst them *rum*runners. —Foreign ellamunts, mostly," he wound up, with a nod and a cough.

Mrs. Moomaw said that the matter couldn't be allowed to be

left entirely in the hands of even such devoted public servants as the Coast Guard and the government inspectors. Who had their hands *full*, she had no doubt. There *was* a time when a citizen had a right to believe that the *police* would be sufficient to enforce the law. (Mr. Harrison, Mrs. Sturt, Birdie Shallot, all pressed their lips together and shook their heads from side to side. Mr. Bomberg wrote rapidly on his pad.) But as was only too well known, some of the police, well, they just looked the other *way*. "The National Family Temperance Union worked for almost a hundred *years* to get these so *dire*fully-needed laws on the lawbooks of the land; the N.F.T.U. and the Anti-Saloon League, and of *course* the churches. *Most* of the churches," she amended, not without a trace of sorrow. —The total non-cooperation of the Catholics, well, that was to have been expected: but wouldn't you have thought that the *Luther*ans, after all they were the *first* of the Protestants, weren't they? Wouldn't you have thought that *they*—? But no. No. No. No.

With no more than a faint shake of the head as all this rushed through her mind, Mary Mabel went on, "And the N.F.T.U. stands like a *rock* against Repeal. But all of this is not enough. We of the N.F.T.U. and all our members, we have to keep our eyes open around the clock. Every violation of the Volstead Act that we see. We re*port* it. We *must*! But, oh, sometimes it is just *heart*. Breaking. To see. What goes on." Mrs. Moomaw again shook her head, and, taking out a handkerchief, pressed it to her eyes.

Birdie, who had leaned over, with a most sympathetic gesture, suddenly drew in her breath with a sharp sound. "She means about the lady with the little boy! Don't you, dear?" Mary Mabel nodded. She moved her hand to indicate that her secretary should speak for her, so Birdie, with an introductory smacking sound, began to do so.

About two months ago, was it *two*? Yes. Two months ago, one of their members, Mrs. Shinwell her name was—Mary Mabel, at this point and from behind her hankie, said distinctly, "Mr. Bomberg, I don't want you to write this down, please," and the reporter obediently set down his pencil. —Well, this Mrs. Shinwell, she came in and she said that she had observed that a small delivery truck was making a delivery to an apartment house in a working-class section of town and that she was *absolutely certain* that it contained *beer*! How could she be so absolutely certain? Well, within just a few minutes after the man who was making the deliveries had gone about his nasty old business, people came out and sat on the porch of the second floor apartment and they had *glass*es and they had *bottl*es and they poured this darkish substance out into the glasses and they sat there drinking it, oh just as bold as brass. And when she said *"people"* she didn't mean just *men*. Which would have been bad enough. *No.*

Women and even young *chil*dren were allowed, even encouraged to partake!

And when they observed good Mrs. Shinwell looking up at them, her face constricted with horror, and they made scornful movements of their heads at her, and insulting gestures.

Mrs. Shinwell did her duty, and she reported it of course to the police. Who said, "Yeah, yeah, okay. Okay lady. Okay." And of course, well, nothing was done.

Upon the advice of Mary Mabel Moomaw, Mrs. Shinwell kept a sharp eye out for those bootleggers and observed that the man always came on a weekday afternoon, between two and three p.m. in the afternoon. And so she, Mary Mabel Moomaw, she contacted the Bureau of Prohibition office *and* the Sheriff (dear old "Charley" Shurt) *and* the State Police. She had the license number of the truck! A description of the *man*! And *she* laid down the *law* to them: and *they, listen*ed! Did the man make his very next delivery?

He did *not*!

But only a few days thereafter, while Mary Mabel was going about her business buying a nice leg of lamb at Schultz's, for the Sunday afternoon dinner at the N.F.T.U. Residence Hall, up came this perfectly strange woman to her and began to shout and scream a*buse*! This woman said that her husband had been out of work and that after a while he had found work (as *she* put it) "delivering for the Dutchman," and then the police had arrested him and that as a result there wasn't enough *food* to put on the *table* and that her little boy needed shoes and there wasn't even enough money to get *shoes* for him! And she blamed poor dear Mary Mabel Moomaw for this! She. *Blamed*. Mary. *Mabel*!

"I *told* her," said Mary Mabel, still from partly behind the hankie, "that we would *glad*ly provide a pair of shoes for her little boy if she would only give me his size, because we have The *Fund*, you know, for the innocent *victims*. Of the *Liquor* Traffic. But oh this only seemed to add *fuel* to the fire. And she became absolutely hyst*eri*cal and I am not sure but what she hadn't been drinking her*self*. And, oh, the *names* she called me. Names I can't repeat. Some of them beginning with *B*."

Little Miss Shallot, her eyes bitter, said, "And other letters, too."

But Mary Mabel Moomaw was made of pretty stern stuff. She had known dear old Mrs. Nation! And she was herself after all *an old suffragette*! And it didn't matter *who* the bootleggers, the rum runners, and the rest of the Poison Trust and the Liquor Interests got in cahoots with to try and stop her. "We will *never* surrender," she said, rubbing her nose. "We will never sur*ren*der. Never. Never.

"*Never*."

CHAPTER FIVE

Not all of Gristmill Heights, to the north of Yokums, was actually very high. The original mill itself, long gone, leaving not so much as a tumbled wall to show where it had been, had been at the foot of what was then called, simply, Big Hill. Even old Joachim van der Dam had once been young, and here, in the full vigor of his youth, he and his two White servants and one Black servant had built the wall which first impounded the Hackamack Creek after it raced down the Hill; had been the first to put its once-free waters to toil for men, had turned it in name and in fact into the Gristmill River. And here they had ground the first grain of the first colonists, poured the meal into deerskin sacks, and laden the sacks aboard an incredibly small, incredibly slow sloop, and by oar and by sail and by tide and by guess and by God had gotten it across the lesser river and the two bays and the greater, or North, or Hudson River: and to the walled townlet of New Amsterdam.

There was no New York, no New Jersey, then. Just New Netherlands.

And the next rains had washed away the mill-wall. And they built it up again. And the rains washed it away again. Well—not exactly the rains. The rain-swollen waters of the small river. Van der Dam could not in any way control the rains. Nor could he control the Hackamack itself as it poured and tumbled down Big Hill. But he was after all a Holland Dutchman and the Holland Dutchman have controlled the sea itself. That next summer, although the few farmers raised despairing faces to the sullen sky, sky from which no rains fell at all, Joachim van der Dam and

his (by now) three White servants and two Black servants and
an Indian man and woman whom he had enticed to unaccus-
tomed toil with promises of rum and a red blanket and an old
flintlock musket and an eelskinful of gunpowder (and he did
keep his promises, too)—they had all them with backbreaking
labor diked the almost dry bed of the Creek at three places in its
lower course between Big Hill and Hackamack Bay. Diked it and
sluiced it: when the next heavy rains fell, van der Dam, racing
on horseback from one to another of the sluices, opened them
enough to let the brimming waters run off before the pressure
of them could burst the dams. And, as the rains slackened, had
raced back again and closed the sluices, leaving enough water
impounded in and for the new millpond to turn the new wheel.

It turned for decades, till both van der Dam and the wheel
grew old: the *Engels* came. Across the Hudson, Oude Piet Stuy-
vesant stayed on. But Oude Joachim did not. The *Engel*, the *Eng-
lander*, Oliver Edwardes, offered him money enough to buy the
yellow brick house and warehouses by the canal basin back in
Bergen-op-Zoom in Old Netherlands: and more was left, as Joachim had cannily calculated there would be: and he kept the
silver and the gold in an iron chest under his bed there, when he
wasn't trading with it, and he traded with it carefully: and, after
the end of his very, very long career as a trader and the years
after that when he did no trading at all for reason of very old
age, there was still something left when his nephew and niece
opened it to see how large a tombstone they could prudently
erect for him: it was not a *very* large tombstone.

But, of course, large enough.

One of the White servants whose labor had helped dig and
dyke was from the upper Rhine. He had drifted far with the tide
and he considered that he had now drifted far enough. Having
served his time for Joachim van der Dam, this man made treaty
with the patroon for a tenant farm. He had helped grind the
grain, now he helped grow it. The farm was near the first mill,
down in what came to be called The Glen. The farmer's name
was Hendrik Bomberg. He had long had his eye on the daughter

of another servant, from the Brabant, her name was Marguerite, she was called Greet, and she had wide hips and heavy breasts; they married. By favor of the wide hips she gave easy birth to eight living children and by favor of the heavy breasts she had milk to keep them live. They grew up in the faith of the Living God according to Doctor of Laws Johannes Calvin; they did not clearly realize that he had been christened *Jean* in Paris, they rather thought that he must have been the *predikant* of the great Dutch Reformed Church in Amsterdam—The farm grew wheat and rye and corn, in the kitchen garden was cabbage and potatoes, poultry in the coops, and fish for the fishing of them: although the rent was high.

High rents, five sons of the eight children, and not five more farms available. Not even *four*—

The first William Bomberg had actually been *Willem* at first. He took the wherry from Weehawken and apprenticed himself to a baker in Canal Street. It was almost ten years before he returned.

Two hundred years and some years later, there was still a

Bomberg
Baker

in Yokums Glen.

The youngest Bill Bomberg could remember chiefly that his father always smelled sweetly, more than he could have said for every father, that he worked at night and slept in the morning. "Get up quick and go for the doctor," Bill's mother said to him that one time, the dawn just brightening outside.

The War was on, flour was high, eggs were high, sugar was being hoarded (by some, though never, you can bet your bottom dollar, by *Bomberg, Baker*), and high, too, were the wages asked by the only available journeymen. The ovens were never heated again. Bread and cake (by firm family acceptance, unspeakably inferior to that which they no longer made themselves) came in by wagon from *Semmil's*, in Yokums, barely warm. Daisy Bomberg filled the empty spaces in the showcases with candy and fruit, and put a few items of grocery on the shelves.

They made out.

One day: Miss Peterson the English teacher, in the store buying her regular two sugar-buns: "Mrs. Bomberg, do you intend William to go into this business with you, when he is older?"

"Not if *I* can help it!" said Daisy, crisply. "Something else?" *She* was referring to Miss Peterson's order, Miss Peterson sometimes took a raisin-bread or a Mackintosh apple. Miss *Peterson*, however, chose to interpret the question differently.

"Yes, I *do* think that he should do something else," said Miss Peterson, "and I am *so glad* that you agree with me: *I* think that he should go to *college!*"

Afterwards: "You could have knocked me over with a feather," Daisy said, pouring condensed milk into her tea. "*She* thinks that you should go to college! Does *she* think that *she* is going to pay for it?" Daisy's own idea, unvoiced, was that her son might get, eventually, on the strength of the old family connections, a job selling bakers' supplies.

"I could work my way through," Bill suggested, dipping a day-old cruller into his own cup. And was surprised at his own say-so.

"You *could*?" his mother asked, with great simplicity. "*Oh.*" After a moment she said, "*I* didn't *know* that." And, next, "Well," and that *Well* implied more than mere consent, it transformed the possibility into an all-but-accomplished fact; "Well, what would you study there in college?"

Bill rolled the semi-dissolved cruller around in his mouth, considered the question. What indeed. The answer came to him while he was swallowing. "Journalism," he said.

Daisy frowned very slightly. She lifted her cup from the saucer and tilted the spilled tea back into her cup. "*Jour*nalism. What's *that*?"

Girls were expected to be at home, but boys were allowed

to hang around. Some boys hang around their own homes, anyway; some around their father's or family's place of business. Some hang around pool halls or public libraries. Wharfs. Boats. Garages. Candy stores. Billy at one time used to hang around a small dry cave in the upper Glen, still entirely wild in those days. He had for some time believed that no one else ever knew it was there; then one day, digging idly with a stick, he found part of an old spoon with its small bowl so different in shape than those of his own day that he took it into old Mr. Jones at the Museum. Who said that it was pewter, and "Certainly colonial, perhaps even Dutch colonial; where did you find it, young man?" Suddenly alarmed lest a troop of archaeologists descend upon his hidey-hole, Billy muttered, "Oh, just around…somewhere." And, with a hasty thank you, took his leave. He dug some more, but never found anything else. Mostly he spent his time there just sitting on the floor of the small cave and hugging his knickered knees with his arms and just looking at the screening trees and letting his eyes go blurry and his mind go limp. With this assistance he soon was able to see, again and again, the canoes of the Indians, the Canarsies and the Nepackamacks and the Hackamacks and all the others, going up and down the wide and narrow waters: and, finally—though with a finality which he little realized—the white sails of the *Half Moon* bellying in the breeze. Tarry a while, Hendrick Hudson. Don't be hasty to depart. What awaits you from your own countrymen after the Safekeeping Service in St. Olave's Church and the longer voyages farther north by far?—death, Hendrick Hudson, death at the hands of the English, in the ice-studded waters of the Hudson Sea. . .

One day Billy climbed there, and lo: all had been changed! The cave was swept clean and furnished with an old red rug on which were a stool and a broken but usable chair and a kerosene lamp and a quilt which was almost if not entirely covering a mattress: and other stuff like that. And there was a green canvas flap which was capable of being let down to cover the "door" of the cave itself.

Also there was a boy named Adam Van Dam and a girl named Ella Stokes, who were maybe two years older than he was. And whom he really did not know at all well. Mixed with the shock of seeing Others in his own secret place was the thought that since they weren't friends and that since he was younger, and right that minute uninvited, too, though in their pre-empted place, that they would say something like, "Get out of here, Bomberg!" and, or, "Beat it, kid!" But they did not, not at all; in fact they were nice to him. They even showed him a real Sterno stove they had and a frying pan and some bacon and potatoes. "Gee this is real nice," Billy said, savoring the new atmosphere. "It's like a sort of play house, huh."

Ella said, nodding her head quickly and bouncing her taffy braids and smiling, "Uh-*huh*!"

Adam's sleeves had been cut off at the shoulders, and his pants cut off just below the knees; it was to be decades before Bill Bomberg saw anyone else dressed in that sort of home-made comfort. Dam was ahead, he was way ahead. And now he rolled over and, supporting himself on his elbows, said to Ella, with a grown-up grin, "Yeah. Let's play house. Momma and Poppa."

And Ella, to Billy's astonishment, punched Adam on his naked arm. "Oh you shut up!" she said.

Not long afterwards, and having been administered an oath of secrecy, Billy learned what Dam had meant and why Ella had been angry at him for saying it then; and he learned what they were really playing together, Adam and Ella, and then they let him watch them play it: and then they let him play it with them. Smick-smack. And so he learned a *lot* of things and as far as he, Billy Bomberg was concerned, it could all have gone on forever: but one day, almost like a blow on the head, the secret cave was empty of everything. And of Adam and of Ella, too. Nor did he see them anywhere around. There was a girl named Olga, though, who had reddish hair and mottled arms and whom he had a couple of times, earlier, seen jumping rope with Ella while they sang

Doctor, Doctor, can you tell?
What will make poor Lester well—

—so, seeing this girl on the street, and surprised at his own boldness, he just walked up to her and asked, "Say, is Ella sick or something?"

"'Sick'?" Olga stared at him. "What do *you* know about Ella being sick?" He stared at her, stunned by her angry voice. "Sure she's sick! She's a *whore!*" said Olga.

"She *is not!*"

Olga put her hands on her hips and glared at him. "She is *so!* A girl under sixteen who has a baby is a *whore—*"

"She didn't have any *baby—*"

Olga's face turned absolutely red with rage. "Well, she's going to! And they put her in *jail!*—Much *you* know!" And she turned and stomped away. Looking after her, Billy felt sick himself.

And then, all in a rush, he heard that: Adam was in jail, too. Adam was not in jail, nobody was in jail, Adam had run away from home. No. Adam had joined the Navy. No: Dam's father had shipped him off to his, Adam's father's uncle, in Detroit, Michigan. And: Ella was not either in jail, exactly, Ella was in a *home*, sort of. No: Ella was with her older sister (with her aunt) (grandmother) in Jersey City.

Also: Ella's brother, who really had been in jail, he had a *gun.* And if he ever found Adam, he was going to kill him.

After that, Billy never went near the Upper Glen again. In fact, he avoided it by a mile. The Upper Glen lay north of his house, Billy never again for years went north of his house, the old apartment over the old bakery; Billy went *south.* And as far south of home as he could conveniently walk and still be home in time for meals or to help out in the store (though much helping out was not needed, business was never *that* good). And still, he was from time to time sick with fear that Ella's brother, whom he had never knowingly seen and so did not know what he looked like, even, might somehow know what he, Billy Bomberg, looked like: and track him down: and kill him . . . And yet with all of that, it was another five years before the thought actually occurred to him: Jesus Christ! Suppose that was really *my* baby, *not* Dam's?—and the same wave of sick feeling, but this time mixed with shame and contrition instead of fear, rolled over him: and he missed them both intensely. He wanted to say to them—ah, but, he had no idea where either of them might be. None whatsoever.

As far south of his own home as he could conveniently walk and still be back home in time for whatever, was a part of town even then run-down and shabby. And, walking down a sidewalk that still had the old-style wooden awning from the building right to the curb, one Saturday morning he heard someone call out to him, "Hey brother, hey boy, could y' come in here, buddy, and hold onta this duss-pan for me, and I'll give y' something."

It was an old man with a big grey walrus moustache, and a broom in his hand. Billy of course went in and held the dust-pan for him, because the old man said he had lumbago and it gave him Hell to stoop. As for what he was going to give him, Billy was merely curious, because if it was money he intended to refuse it, having been well-trained that he didn't have to get paid just for doing people little favors: especially old people, because, "Someday you'll be old your*self*. And you'll *see*," his mother would say, in an accusatory voice which was entirely without any basis at all. In this case.

The floor of the sagging old grey-wooden building had not been swept in quite a long time, and, besides the usual dust and dirt, was deep in paper. "Oh God," the old man groaned, in an almost weeping tone, as he plied the broom. "What have I done to deserve such agony? Speak, Lord, for Thy servant heareth!" Then, being evidently unsatisfied with the terms of the reply, and lowering his face and voice, in a moment, "Shit, piss, and corruption . . . Lived too long, is the truth o' the matter. All my bones broken on the rack of time and ancient age. . ." Then, his voice, which had first ascended to an almost-old-womanish tremor which quavered with pain, the old man's voice suddenly became very deep. "'Build *thee* more stately chambers, O my soul,'" the old man's voice intoned; "'As the swift seasons roll. . .'"

Not understanding, but very much impressed, Billy looked up. "What?" he asked.

"Chambered Nautilus."

Billy, still in ignorance, asked again, *"What?"*

And the old man stopped the broom, flung him a look of deep astonishment, mingled with disdain. "'What?' Why, boy, what do they *teach* you, what do you *mean*, 'What?' What do they teach you in the *schools* nowadays? I say, The Chambered Nautilus: and you ask, *What*? Why, have y'never heard of either the mollusk *or* the poem? *Je*-sus Christ! I have lived too long!" And he threw out his arms, the broom dropping unnoticed to the filthy floor, and turned his gaze again to the shadowy ceiling. "Take me! Take me now! Take me to the bosom of Abraham, O Thou great Jehovah! *Now*! I live in an age of illiteracy and of illiterates . . . and upon the sufferance of imbeciles. . ." Covering his face with his hands, he tottered off and let himself fall down into a chair. The chair was of an age with himself, and let out an alarming creak. But it held.

Afterwards, Billy having finished sweeping the floor all by himself, the Something which he was given consisted of a huge mug of excellent coffee, with a heaping spoonful of damp brown sugar, and a big splash of booze. It was not refused.

This was Bill Bomberg's first meeting with the great, venerable and perhaps (some said) eccentric Alexander Dexter Bixby, Editor of the even more venerable *Jersey Whig-Democrat* ("Published weekly, quarterly, and semi-occasionally, young boy Billy."); sole proprietors, Bixby Brothers, Job Printing (his twin, Praxilites Baxter Bixby, had been dead for decades): and friend of Whitman: "A great man, my boy Billy. A *great* man! Shakespeare had predecessors, Petrarch had antecedents, but Whitman sprang up out of nothing and nowhere! Whitman, my child, was the truest original of all the ages. Whitman? Genius. Whitman was joy. —And as for the rest of the story, well, if he liked to play Drop-the-Soap in the showers with an amorous horse-car conductor, why, that was *their* business. (Their soap, too.) —B'sides, in the manner of a Scotch jury, I ruhgard thuh matter as, Not Proven.

> "Long enough have you dreamed contemptible dreams!
> Now I wash the gum from your eyes,
> You must habit yourself to the dazzle of the light and of every moment of your life!"

"Well, they say the farmers all *swear* by his paper," Mrs. Daisy Bomberg commented once, to her sister Mary.

"Yeah, but how many farmers *are* there, any more?" was Aunt Mary's question. No answer required.

And, later some years later—well, two and a half years later, Bill had walked boldly into the *Press* office in Yokums and asked for a job. Alas that the one man he chose in his ignorance to approach was Peter S. ("Pickle") Pierce, noted on the staff: but not for any kindliness of nature.

"Oh *yeah*? Doing *gwhat*?" was Pierce's genial question.

"I can set *type*—"

"What? On a linotyper?"

"No! By hand!" And he could, and fairly well, too. Old XX had taught him. And now old XX was dead. And his niece had sold out everything. And so, so much for any half-formed visions of Bill Bomberg, Boy Editor.

By *hand*? Haw Haw Haw.

Haw.

"Say listen kid, we publish a daily noozepapa' here, not Poor Richard's Almanac!" And then Pickle Pierce, working rather extra-hard at being offensive, said, "Ann what else can ya do by hann? Huh?" And had made a gesture easily recognizable as indicating masturbation.

There had been other girls since Ella, but there had not been *many* other girls since Ella. The last time, old XX Bixby was still alive, very much so, and, having collected (in produce) his sub-scription from one of the farmers out on the Old Pike Road, was sitting in his buggy out front, talking politics. Bill, under guise of "getting a drink of water," had gone out back—yes!—there he'd been, in the barn, with the farmer's daughter!—in the best Old American tradition: but that had been three months ago. "It doesn't stand up very often anymore," XX said once; "and when it does, I tell it to stand down"—but that hardly works in one's teens.

So, in addition to the disappointment at in effect being re-fused a job, plus the chagrin of being made to seem a fool for asking, there was of course enough truth in the crude gesture to make him mad. He drew back his own hand, a rather big hand for his size, and rather a big fist it made, too—Pickle Pierce jumped, then, quickly attempting to cover that up with a display of courage—

"Oh a *tough* guy! *Huh?* Okay kid, let's *see* how tough y'are!" The man started to take off his coat. And another man, older, though not *old*, with a "Now, now," and a "Come on, now," smoothing and soothing it out: and a third man, the phone ringing just then, calling out (perhaps not truthfully), "Hey they wantcha up*stairs*, Pick—" and Pierce putting his coat back on and going off, still defiant, aggressive, talking threat over his shoulder as he walked away—

The peacemaker was Peter Fogarty, the major news reporter on the *Press*, and he walked Bill out to The Coffee Pot and by gentle conversation calmed his angry heart down and drew his story out of him. Old XX Bixby! There was an original for you! (The very word which Bixby had used about Whitman!) One of the last of the noble old Romans! *Yes* yes. *Well* well. "But, alas, the truth be known, there isn't so much as an opening for an office-boy," said Peter Fogarty.

"I don't want to be an office-boy—"

Fogarty, who had raised his cup, set it down again. "Well, Mr. Bomberg, you can't, you really can't expect to become a newspaperman just like *that!*" He snapped his fingers. The

Greek counterman jumped, came quickly with the white en-
amel coffee-pot, looked up in surprise as Bill and Peter burst out
laughing.

"But I *am* a newspaperman, Mr. Fogarty. Isn't the—wasn't
the *Whig-Democrat* a real newspaper? —Only it was *small—*"

Fogarty was a gentleman. He did not laugh. For a moment it
seemed as though he were changing the subject. "Have you ever
read a book by a man called H.G. Wells? *The—*"

"*The War of the Worlds!*" Bill's face burst into a grin of pleasure. "Yeah! Wasn't it *great*?"

"Oh, it was! It was indeed. But I had in mind another one,
The Time Traveler. Have you read that one, too? You have. Well.
Now, well, how am I to put it? Working for old XX Bixby, Mr.
Bomberg, working on the *Jersey Whig-Democrat*, you, I suppose
you don't realize it, but that has made *you* a time traveler. Don't
take offense, now, but, well, by the standards of 1885, *yes*: the
Whig-Democrat was a real newspaper. But, ah. By the standards
of 1925? I am afraid *not*. Oh, I will certainly not deny that you
have had experience. *Val*uable experience, too. You say that he
taught you more about history and poetry and other literature
than you learned in school, and I be*lieve* you. And you can set
type by hand and operate a flat-bed press, and all *that*.

"But. There is a forty-year gap in your experience. And you
will have to close that gap, you see." And he, Peter Fogarty, had
talked to the point and he had mentioned a number of possible
ways of closing that gap.

And one of the suggestions consisted of the words, the *Col-
umbia University School of Journalism*.

Bill, Senior, and Daisy, although her actual maiden-name
was Van Horn, had been (as she put it) "fifty-second cousins." In
fact, she, too, was a descendent of one of the eight children of
Hendrick Bomberg and that same Greet who had come over as
a child from the Brabant. And so was Hank Hotalin, who, long
years gone, suddenly appeared one day in the bakery (as it was
still called), demanding a fresh roll. Young Bill was there, helping
out.

"Forgotten my ugly face, Daisy?"

She stared. "Oh my *God*," she said. "*Hank*!"

The two of them hugged across the counter. "You must be Billy. Don't mind us, Billy, it's all right, your Ma and me, we are related, about fifteen miles back on my mother's side."

"Oh Hank, For God's *sake*."

Later: "Yeah, Bill, your Ma and me, we were kinda like childhood sweethearts, then your Pa he beat me out, he ast her *first* to go on the Dayline excursion—"

"Oh that's *right!*—"

"He hadda new store hat—"

"Oh he looked so *fly!*"

The long and short of it, back then, had been: one, that Hank Hotalin had given up on Daisy re Bill Sr. and had joined the Army (to the rage of Aunt Henny, who said that only *bums* joined the Army and that he had disgraced the family); and, two, that he was now out of the Army. And wasting no time. In fact—

Two days later, Daisy announced that she and Hank were getting married. And, "Hank doesn't want to stay here, he wants to grow oranges in Florida. *You* don't want to grow oranges in Florida," she informed Bill. "You want to go to college. Well. What we are going to do, we are going to sell this house. And divide the money. Fifty-fifty, half for you and half for me. And that will take you all the way through college. To study journeyism. How does that suit you?"

He instantly said, "Suits *me*."

And in fact it had taken him half way through college, he hadn't been given his half in one chunk, he was a minor, it had been sent him in instalments. Looking back, Bill realized that he had been lucky, damned lucky, that it had taken him that far. From wanting to grow oranges in Florida Hank had switched to wanting to grow oranges in California. But it had been a bad year for that. Suddenly, there they were, Hank and Daisy, not an orange between them, wholesaling undertakers' cosmetics in St. Louis, Missouri. But it had evidently been a bad year for wholesale undertakers' cosmetics in St. Louis, Missouri, too. Hank, it gradually became evident to his stepson, seldom had a good year. News of him grew wilder as it grew infrequent. When last heard of he had been setting up an ostrich ranch in Sonora, Mexico. By that time Daisy had had it with Hank. With the last two of the last of the hundred-dollar bills, she went into business in Reno. (No, the divorce actually came later.) She opened a small store which sold bakery goods, candy and fruits, plus milk and ice cream and soda pop.

She said it was more interesting in Reno than in Yokums Glen, New Jersey.

She said that she really had no regrets.

But, backing up a bit—

"Yes *yes!*" said Peter Fogarty, the Summer right after the Spring when Bill had realized that the money well was dry—in fact, not even the early Summer: the later Spring. "Certainly I do remember you. Has your soul built thee more stately chambers yet?"

There were still no openings at the *Press*. But Peter made a phone call, took someone to lunch (a very good lunch, followed by three cocktails at Moriarity's), and had in final fact found Bill a job at the *Gazette*. Right across the street. "One hand washes the other," Peter said. "Although it's really just a sort of summer job."

At the *Gazette*, Barney Watson, the city editor, told him, "Don't get your great white hopes up, College Boy. This is just a sort of a summer job. Who was at the Babtiss Church picnic, and alla that Elmer Gantry kine a shit."

When Con Considine, a classmate and close friend, called to invite him to spend two weeks at the family place in Maine, Bill said, "Gee, Con—wouldn't I love to go. But I've got this sort of summer job. . ."

But that was the last time he thought of it in those terms, until one night, that same year, fitting skid chains to the tires of his tin lizzie, it suddenly came back to him. But he was still working. Some years later, he was *still* working. Which, by that time, was certainly more than many, many people, by no means all of

them bachelors without family to support, could say.
Je-sus Christ.

CHAPTER SIX

And Joe Horvath yelled, "*Pull!*"

The men gave a tremendous tug. The mysterious hose went taut. They secured second grips on the wire-bound surface of the mysterious hose. "And—a*gain*." Joe Horvath chanted. "Pu-*ulll!*"

The work crew didn't ho, but they did heave. The hose resisted the second jerk for a prolonged second. Then it gave way, and the men went tumbling and sliding backward. Somewhere off in the darkness they heard a splash—and a sound of something gushing.

"Sunnuvva*biiiitch*," one of them muttered. Then he gave, suddenly, a sniff. And then another. And another. None of them carried a handkerchief, there being a general opinion among the Yokums working classes that fingers had been made first. But the man did not have a cold.

"Jeeze, we broke it for sure," someone said. And then *he* gave a sniff. In much less than a minute, they were all sniffing. A heavy, bittersweet smell met their noses, drowning out the stale smell of the conduit. Joe, who had been moving his head back and forth, and flashing his light here and there, with a puzzled look on his face, now put his head way back, took in a deep breath, let it out.

"That can't *be* what I *think* it is—*can* it?" he asked.

The first answer came in Slovatchko. "Peevah," said one of the crew. His tone was merely definitive; in Europe he had been told that the water-faucets in America flowed milk and honey; he was not now totally astonished to learn that underground hoses flowed with another precious fluid.

"Can it," asked Horvath, once more. His tone this time seemed to indicate it could. "No, but it can't," he said.

But one of the English-speaking D.P.W. men was less skeptical. He took a step forward, his boots squelching. "Maybe it can't—but it is! It's beer!" he yelled. "It's *beer!*"

Like every other city, Yokums had an ordinance against what the ordinance called Hawkers; needless to say, no reference to the ancient art of falconry was here intended. Many of the local merchants had themselves been peddlers once, and, if not they themselves, then their fathers or grandfathers. Having finally, by dint of hard work, long hours, contentment with small profits, diligence, and at least some reputation for honesty and straight dealing, gotten inside the door, then they—or their sons and/or grandsons—finally got around to closing the door behind them. It was no longer possible to buy Yankee notions or piece goods out of a back-pack or a stall on the streets of the city. Some few customer-peddlers still made the rounds to a few loyal patrons, but they carried their wares in suitcases. It was more dignified, and, also, it was unlikely to attract the unwelcome attentions of the police. There were, to be sure, in the warmer weather, a few white-painted trucks which sold "refreshments"—a term understood to mean ice cream, ices, and soda-pop—from a window in the side: but they operated on sufferance. Suffer they were certain to. Did they find some good pitch, did they build up a trade, be sure that sooner or later a police car would draw up and send them packing—

And then! hear the funny foreigners howl!

"Whudda ya wanna from *me*! I juss tryin a make a livin! I gotta kids a support!"

"Don' tull *me* ya problums! I just infawce the Lore! Man owns a staw ann pays renn' ann taxes, yaint got no right come along ann take thuh bread outta his moutt. Come *on*, now, come *on*, gid owda here! Doe lumme hafta tullya *again!*"

Oh, hear the funny foreigners howl!

There were, however, a few exceptions. No one attempted to disturb old "Major" Moorman, whose title had been inherited from his father, a veteran of the Mexican War, when, shaking with senility and fatigue, he offered for sale from a basket set on a small folding chair the wormy produce of his overgrown orchard. And the ordinance was deemed suspended (Yokums's gesture toward a program of National Recovery which antedated the New Deal) in favor of the Unemployed who were offering for sale much larger, much redder, and much less wormy apples (maybe) on certain street corners in The Village, as the old-fashioned still called the downtown section of the city (it had, once, been the Village of Yokums before Village and Town were combined into City). —There were anyway hardly any greengrocers or fruit-stores left in The Village anymore. Ancient old Titus Vanderbeck, whose own father had been a slave, did sometimes sell greens, sometimes fruit, but mostly hot sweet potatoes, from his hole-in-the-wall place in Adams Alley. And I. ("Izzy") Feinbein's Market still held out. Neither offered any objections to the Unemployed selling apples on the street corners. Perhaps Izzy felt that he still had sufficient bread in his mouth. Perhaps Titus was content that he could no longer be sold at auction. *Or* "by private treaty."

And so, and as for perambulating vendors who plied their proscribed trade in the open street, that left two. And as they plied it, slowly, over the whole of the older parts of the city, perhaps it may have been that no store-merchants saw them often enough to feel the white, the rye, the raisin, whole wheat, or pumpernickel being pulled out from between their mercantile teeth. Fred Stevens was one. And Pantaleon Pappadoupolos was another.

Fred operated his business out of a small red wagon, once bright, long dull. It reached up to the bottom button of his vest and its top contained three compartments holding, respectively, hot dogs, hot dog rolls ("buns," if you prefer), and sour crout.

There was mustard in a large jar. There was no relish, and there were no chopped onions. You could have your hot dog with mustard and/or you could have it with sour crout: or you could go look on beauty bare. Or you could go without. The cost, in any case, was 3¢.

The wagon was drawn by a very small pony whose name was generally supposed to be Napoleon.

> Well, I'll be switched!
> The hay ain't pitched!
> Giddee-ap, Napoleon!
> It looks like rain!

ran a semi-popular song of the period. No one, however, had ever heard Fred call the animal Napoleon, no one had ever heard him say Giddee-ap to it. No one, in fact, ever heard him say very much about anything. His conversation was generally confined to, "Mustard? Sour crout? *All* right . . . Three cents, please." His voice was soft, his manner was gentle, he wore gold-rimmed eyeglasses with a gold chain. Once, some lout of a grown-up boy, his friends standing around by and snickering, had grabbed the hot dog (mustard *and* sour crout) and run off with it, an obscenity his sole proffered payment. From some place unknown Fred had picked up a whip, its handle hollowed lengthwise and filled with lead, sped after the bum and laid his scalp open. An attempt was made to prosecute him on a concealed weapon charge.

Fred's defense: "Your Honor, a man who has a horse is entitled to have a whip, isn't he?"

"Absolutely," said old Judge Boodle, who hated louts anyway. "*Absolutely.* Case dismissed."

That was the longest speech anyone had ever heard Fred say.

Presumably the parishioners of the Hellenic-American Greek Orthodox Church of the Holy Wisdom called Pantaleon Pappadoupolos by his Christian and family names. His business vehicle was of a simpler sort than Fred's. It was in fact a baby-carriage, in which a steam apparatus kept roasted peanuts hot and a small steam whistle advised the public of this fact. He pushed the carriage along streets likelier narrow than wide and in between toots of the whistle he sang out, "*Pea*-nuts! *Pea*-nuts!" Presumably the heirs to the heritage of Athens and Byzantium called him Pantaleon Pappadoupolos.

The rest of the world called him "Peanuts."

He sold them for three cents a small bag and for five cents a larger bag. On these enormous profits he supported a wife, five children, a widowed sister and her own two children, and contributed to the support of his paternal uncle, an aged priest no longer able to till the church glebe. All of these lived back in the village of Prodromos on the island of the same name, in the tideless, dolorous, midland Sea: otherwise he could never have supported even one of them. Also, he paid his annual *pentadollarion* to the Archdiocese, smoked one cigarette a day after his one glass of wine after his one-dish dinner. And, more or less once a month, he was admitted to the confidential embraces of a Wallachian widow of very long standing, whom he had courted wordlessly (he had small English and she had smaller) with smiles, goobers, and wild flowers in season from a still unravish'd glade he knew of, behind a railroad embankment. In a way, and all in all, he was a hero. But the world did not call him a hero.

The world called him "Peanuts."

Up on the street level and near an open manhole, another and smaller DPW crew was standing by with a truck on which a sewer-cleaning apparatus was fixed; its mechanical mandibles still gummy with the nasty ichor of previous dips. They talked idly together while they waited on word from Joe Horvath to start dipping up the debris, but their talk didn't deal with the ownership of No Man's Land, a legal nicety of which they were only vaguely aware. The big topics of conversation were, *A*, The Depression, subtopic 1: *Jobs*; and, *B*, Repeal: Would it come or wouldn't it, subtopic 1: If so, *When*?

"Rooz-a-vult," said one of the men. The others nodded. "I,

now, uh, read, uh, someone toll me he read inna *paper*, now, Rooz-a-vult, Guvna Rooz-a-vult, he says, inna *win*ter, they gunna open alla the *Arm'*ries *up*, the uh National *Guard* Arm-ries, so the men who they haven't got no *wuhyk*, n they havn't got no jobs, they uh they kin sleep, they kin have some place ta *sleep*."

"Uh huh," someone else said. "I huhyd that, too. *He's* fa Repeal, Rooz-a-vult."

And a third crew member said, "So is Al *Smitt*."

And the fourth and last member of the above-ground clean-out crew, acting, as one of them had to do, the role of devil's advocate, or killjoy, pointed out that Al Smith had been and Franklin Roosevelt was now, Governor of New York State. And that this was New *Jersey*. Bad news. The men, reminded, shook their heads. Who, in New Jersey, was of comparable stature and status? New Jersey, no one quite knew why or how, had missed its chance on the world scene. (To be sure, in a previous age, the newly installed magnetic telegraph had carried to something less than waiting multitudes the electric message that *Senator Frelinghuysen of New Jersey has declined the Whig nomination.* It was not until the next day that the innovative wire had asked the rhetorical question, *What hath God wrought*? This was much more like a winner for the history books. Too bad, Frelinghuysen. *And* New Jersey.)

Suddenly there was a burst of noise from the manhole.

"Whutsa matta?" one of the D.P.W. men asked. The noise grew nearer, grew louder.

"Somebuddy git huhyt?" his partner inquired.

They had started toward the round opening in the street, and, as they approached, a face appeared. It was excited and disheveled, but it was definitely neither injured nor anxious. "*Beer!*" the face yelled. "*Beer! Beer! Beer!*"

Passersby paused, stopped. Looked, came over to watch what was going on. Why were all the men climbing up from the manhole and why were they whooping as they emerged? Why were they all dancing and capering? True, it was a lovely, crisp early autumn day, but—

"Ah, whudda ya givin me?" scoffed one of the men at the
D.P.W. truck. "*Whut* beer? *Where's* beer?" A sudden thought, perhaps predicated on Occam's razor, and perhaps not, suddenly occurred to him. "Uh, y'mean they found some bottles? some barrels? a *beer*, down there?" He went hastily closer to gaze down.

The sewer cleaners hauled away at something . . . a pipe,
perhaps . . . a newish-looking, copper-glinting pipe . . . or, perhaps, as it seemed rather limber for a pipe, a *hose*? . . . and pulled
it up through the manhole to the surface. A steady gush of *some*
golden-brown liquid came rushing from the loose end, a spiral of
bright wire still dangling where it had been snapped off. One of
the crew bent over and drank. Noisily. *Hap*pily.

Another one exclaimed and explained, equally happily,
"*Naa*, no bottle, no barrels—just like it comes—*beer*!"

"*Hey*!—But, uh, from a *soor*? Ain't that like un*san*iterry?"

The merry drinker paused to protest, his mouth dripping.
"Ah, wuddaya mean, 'unsanitary'? Beer's got alcohol innit,
aynit? So the alcohol inna beer, like, disin*fecks* it!"

"Yur right! Chur right!" cried the skeptic, instantly convinced by this bit of scientific information. His eyes darted
around, looking for a cup or glass; unaccountably finding none,
he took up his metal lunch-box, emptied it into his lap, stuffed
sandwich-boiled egg and (one) piece of fruit—the apple was
smaller than those already being sold on the street corners by
the selected and deserving Unemployed for five cents—into his
pocketses, and, whilst the drinker courteously paused to permit
him—filled the lower section of the box with the, literally, foaming brew. His eyes peered at his fellow-D.P.W. worker over the
brim. They were large and intent. After a moment, convinced of
the reality of it all—it did not after all turn to ashes, it was not
fairy brew—the eyes returned to natural size again. They were
no longer intent.

They were content, though.

The knot of spectators swirled around, calling and hooting
in incredulity. Then the knot flowed in upon the hose. In a moment it had become a group. Then in scarcely any time at all,

it had become a crowd—a crowd which, around the edges, still called out the glad tidings to others, too—for example, to people passing by on the Number 3 trolley car bound for the railroad depot and the end of the line. Some of these passengers ignored the obviously insane information, others peered wildly from the windows, leaped off at the next stop and came racing back to see for themselves. The happy word was passed from person to person, store to store, and house to house. It was carried by men going by in cars—those who did not pause and next, hastily, park —and by people who rushed to the telephone. There had been, in fact, something of a shortage of the substance recently: but *now* —

—there had recently been a shortage of *money*, for that matter—

Thoughtful children informed their parents.

The cry went up all along Main Street, where the discovery first saw the light of day, through *New* Main Street into City Hall Square, the heart of downtown Yokums, up *North* Broadway, down *South* Broadway—"*Beer! Beer! Beer!*"

It might have been bad for business, had business been capable of being much worse. Some of the stores had signs of PRICES SLASHED or EVERYTHING MUST GO or the more specific GOING OUT OF BUSINESS. Some had passed that point, sad little signs which one had to come closer to read, gave addresses where unclaimed items might be picked up: tailors, these, for example, or "French" laundries, or it might be watch-repair places. Some such small signs informed the curious of *key next door*, the effort of a capital letter being often not thought worth it. Some went so far as to say that the place was indeed For Rent. Others made no offer at all, the emptiness merely standing empty in all its dusty drear.

And in so many of the ones which still stayed open, still struggled to maintain business as usual, the casual commerce of former days, with payments in cash or on confident credit, had given way to something which had yet to find a name: the would-be customer, as it might be a woman with children for whom she had come to get shoes, the shoes being gotten, and the purse opened to extract the money, would suddenly find—to her dismay, a dismay equal to that of the merchant himself (though by now half-expected)—that the money had been "left at home."

"Oh my God I musta left it at home. I'll bring it for ya, fuhyst thing inna mawning," here she looks up hopefully—

The merchant sighs. He shakes his head, no genial shake of reproof at such carelessness: a shake the negative of which admits of no doubt. "Ya mean . . . I gotta go all the way back home ann dthen come back wit'th dthe money?" —surely he cannot mean it?

He can only repeat the by now ritual response. "I'm sorry. I'm sorry. If I don't pay my bills they'll close my store." His hand, waved, takes in not only his own place and stock but the now stockless, now empty stores which lie silent and dark in street after street. Silently she gestures the children to take the shoes off, silently they obey, silently they put back on the old ones: dirty, scuffed, heels run down, soles pierced. Silently and with heads down they leave. Perhaps they will try again at another store. Perhaps not.

But . . . now . . . what sounds are these? And what cries from street to street? Merchant and customer look up, listen, look at each other. And some few merchants at least, and more than some few customers, of a sudden make up their minds to hurry off and see for themselves. And some few merchants, who now turn the keys in their door locks, will never even bother to return to open up for business again. Not many, as of this very moment. But some. Some of these shops and stores will never open for business again in the history of the world.

In some cases the gesture is deliberate. In others it is made in a sudden rush, as merchant and customers alike rush out to tap the foaming flow. "Buy at ninety, sell at thirty," the firm foundations on which the structures of the commercial world were set up: and what if when "ninety" comes there is no money to pay for the buy? Well. Put off the answer for another time. For right now—

"Come and get it! Free beer! Come and get it!"

The citizens heard, they came and they got it. They came with cups and glasses, bottles and buckets, jugs, jars, pots, pans, basins; the trays from under the unelectrified iceboxes often not being needed now to catch the drip from the nonexistent because (currently) unaffordable ice—

Ten minutes after the first crows of joy that part of Main Street had ceased to be passable. Automobiles and trolleys no longer went by with passengers curiously craning their necks; instead they simply stopped where they were, and hardly anyone was so deaf to the news as not to disembark and go see. The throng thickened.

—they came with cans, vases, tins, tankards, bowls, nameless vessels of cut glass hastily snatched up from the sideboards where they had stayed in useless splendor for decades—they came, they came, they *came*, they came with just about anything which would hold liquid. Just about *any*thing.

They were very, very happy.

And then, *then*, just as the dancing had barely begun, barely commenced, the steady flow began to slacken, died down to a trickle, stopped dead. A great groan of disappointment went up.

The line of stalled trolley cars reached all the way up to Valleydale Avenue: the first time such a sight had been seen, indeed, since the Great Blizzard of 1888.

The beer, the beer to be sure, had had a faint taste of rubber to it. But after more than ten years of Prohibition, everyone was used to beer tasting of much worse things than rubber. (Ether, for instance: it is hard to realize how large a part of the population must have spent over a decade in a state of partial anesthesia.) Anybody in Yokums who by that time objected to a mild flavor of latex in his brew was liable to stand accused of being a Communist.

Or—what was much worse—an Englishman.

There were anyway two businessmen thereabouts who had not to lock up their premises in order to go see what was going on. Fred Stevens, pony, cart, and all, was slowly heading north. Peanuts was with his steam-powered baby-carriage steadily heading south. They met on the outskirts of the throng. The flow of commerce was for them at least not interrupted by the sudden free flow of suds; it was in fact stimulated. Many purchases of hot dogs and of peanuts were soon being made, with beer to wash them down with. The scene soon rather began to resemble a street fair, and, if there had only been more Italians present, plus the images of Saints Cosmo and Damiano, or the Blessed Virgin of Pompeii trailing ribbons which the faithful were festooning with dollar bills, it would have resembled one absolutely.

For many minutes neither Fred nor Pantaleon had time to even pause and look around and wonder. When they did they did not wonder very much. Business had for long been bad, very very bad. Then, all of a sudden, it was very, very good. Stock was in fact almost exhausted. They looked around at the still swirling (but no longer buying) crowd. Their eyes met. They had never had occasion to speak to each other before. But then, how often does Macy's have a chance to speak to Gimbels? And next, all of a sudden, each made a major decision.

Said Fred Stevens, "A bag of peanuts."

The bag went one way, three cents went the other.

Pantaleon looked at the coins in his palm. He nodded. He thrust them back.

"Hot dog," he said.

All around them the crowd, half-disappointed, half-hopeful, moiled and muttered. Peaceful, prosperous, contented, the two hawkers leaned against their business vehicles and watched and munched.

No one was complaining about the beer's taste, only that there was no more of it. The crowd was for the most part still optimistic until, finally, the police came and began to move them on.

Many opinions were expressed. By now, in the beginnings of the second decade of the 18th, or Prohibition Amendment, that Experiment Noble in Purpose, those who drank beer had been used to obtaining it in a variety of ways both odd and curious. This one, however, was something new to everybody. And the opinion was, that you can't knock Progress.

Whilst the potlatch was still in its beginnings, Joe Horvath, who drank only at wakes and weddings, made his way back to City Hall and into the presence of his most immediate superior, Deputy Commissioner of Public Works Robert "Bob" Bradlaw. Whose eyes gleamed. Whose nose sniffed.

"Hoccome yaint wuhykin?" was his first question.

And, "Whutcha been doin, rollin in a *broowry*?" was his second.

"Hahdja guess?" asked Horvath. And then he told him.

Bradlaw, a man of singularly limited imagination, proved difficult to convince of the simple fact that a pipe, or hose, had been found in the City sanitary sewer system, and when broken open and wrestled to the surface, proceeded to gush forth an apparently unlimited quantity of potable beer into the streets of the aforesaid City.

"Whuddaya givin me," was his refrain.

Alternating with, "Ah, cummon, cumMON."

"*You* come on then, come on, come on, get in the flivver, an' I'll *show* ya," said Horvath. This was the one that did it. Bradlaw was a sucker for free auto rides. And in less than three minutes: *Wow!*

Old timers subsequently shook their heads. "That was where Bradlaw lost *his* head," they reminded one another as they shook their own. "That was when Bradlaw cuttiz own *troat*. In- *stead* of, he shoulda hushed it up righd away: Bradlaw *told*."

It might be said, in at least partial justification, that Bradlaw very seldom after all had very much to tell. And, certainly, nothing like this. But then: who had?

At any rate, after much scurrying and hurrying, Bradlaw once again found himself back at City Hall. Where, seeing the

Mayor's Office in front of him, an office where he had almost never any proper chance to go, he was seized by what suddenly seemed a very laudable intention and performance of duty. He would tell the *Mayor*.

"Emuhygency! Emuhygency!" he panted, hastening past the Sublime Porte. Miss Florence Flaherty looked up, looked down. She knew who Bradlaw was, she knew who everybody was. She did not consider that anything in the nature of an emergency had occurred in the State of New Jersey since the night the Black Tom Munitions Factory blew up. She merely allowed her hand to move a trifle. Then she went back to her work drafting an ethnic "Day" proclamation. The mayor of an adjacent city had once, when asked where he stood on Zionism, replied with enthusiasm, "I have *always* been a friend of the Greek people!" Miss Flaherty did not intend to allow *any*thing like that to happen here.

His Honor listened as the Deputy Commissioner blurted—and, in this instance, the much-misused verb *blurted* was the right one—out the story. He did not bother to turn on the charm, he was not cold, he did not show disbelief or amazement or confusion. He listened. And if the thought of all that good beer running through the gutters of his fair city disturbed him, he did not say so. He waited until Bradlaw finally ran out of breath. Then he asked, "Who else knows?"

Bradlaw said, "Well . . . Iron *Ike* knows. Solid *Ike*?"

Flaherty nodded at this mention of the popular nickname of Isaac N. Hotaling, the Yokums Chief of Police. "He does, heh."

"*Sure*. I *toll* um." The police head had not been any quicker to accept the story than the Deputy Commissioner himself, but his skepticism had been less vocal. He had merely stared for a long, long minute at the informant, as though trying to decide if he should hit him on the right side of the head or on the left. Then he had heaved his big body up from the chair and departed for the scene.

The mayor nodded slowly. Very slowly. Then he, almost absently, placed bottle and two glasses on the blotter, poured, took up one glass, and gave an almost imperceptible gesture—

first, towards Bradlaw, then towards the bottle. *A*lmost imperceptible. "Uhm, *thanks*, Yerahner," said Bradlaw.

They drank.

"Now, Commissioner," the mayor said, in a voice very soft and entirely devoid of anything resembling arrogance, sarcasm, or irony. "Well, now, Commissioner . . . I suppose that you did consider, say, exercising your authority and returning the pipe. Or hose. Whichever. Or whatever—"

Bradlaw, feeling a doubly warm glow, due to the very good Scotch and to being thus addressed, nodded—at mention of his authority (not very much mention was ever made by higher-ups to his authority)—nodded very rapidly. The rapidity of the nods, as the mayor continued speaking, decreased; and finally died away altogether.

"—returning it to the sewer, where nobody could see it. And posting a guard. With instructions to say nothing. *Nothing*. And instructing the D.P.W. men to say nothing. And ordering them away from the site. I suppose that you did consider this. But had reason not to."

There was a long pause. The mayor, looking nowhere in particular, took a long drink.

And Bradlaw, his face first blank, then increasingly uncertain . . . and unhappy . . . said, finally, "Uh, uh . . . *No*. Yer*ah*ner." The pause continued as before. Bradlaw asked, "Uh, you, uh, you, uh, mean I *should*. Of?"

The mayor sighed. The mayor said, "Well it was just a thought. It doesn't matter. Now. Well. *Who else knows*?"

And the by now very unhappy Bradlaw hesitated, then let it all pour out. "Half a the people in Yokums. By now. I guess . . . We'll hafta notify the Feds I guess. Won't we?"

His Honor said, "I guess we *will*."

He did not seem at all happy.

Bill Bomberg and Stelle Wilson were sitting at the same table in Maloney's, talking about their publishers.

"Emery," said Stelle. "Don't talk to me about Emery." Emery was Bill Bomberg's publisher. "If you want to know a real hundred percent vindicative illiterate, make the acquaintance of Herbert H. Ruel."

"Do I have to?" Bill asked. He was content to go on making the acquaintance of Stelle Wilson. That is, he was not really content, he felt that process had gone on long enough and should by now have given way to something much closer. Warmer. In a word, intimate.

"Well, if you don't *have* to, *don't*. It took me weeks to persuade Ed Fleming to let me do a piece on the, what I call, the Do-It-Yourself School of Moonshining, you know? All these restaurant supply stores which sell malt and hop syrups and bottles and cappers and grape juice and grape concentrate—"

Bill, who was looking at her neck and thinking that it really *was* like the snowdrift, said, "Yeah. And crocks and charred kegs."

"—and charred *kegs*," she said, nodding. "What are you *looking* at," she asked, suddenly. "Is the yoke of my dress crooked?" Her hands began to feel and pat.

"I wasn't looking at your *yoke*, I was looking at your *neck*."

"I washed it this morning."

"It really is like the snowdrift."

"Thanks to the manufacturers of Fairy Soap. —*What*?"

She stared at him, he repeated what he had said. Still staring at him, she said, "You're crazy. You mean—*Annie Laurie*? Is that what you do mean? Well, for your information, it's, 'Her *brow* is like the snowdrift, her neck is like the *swan*'—and why any self-respecting woman would want to feel pleased because someone said she had a neck like a *swan*—You really are crazy."

She really did not seem at all pleased, and as he was sure that she would only get more annoyed if he pointed out that *he* hadn't said her neck was like a swan, he said nothing. He didn't even sigh. He said, instead, "And then what? Ruel—"

The absolutely blank look which Stelle used where someone

else would use a scowl vanished. All was as before. "Well, Peter Fogarty liked it, and Peter Fogarty doesn't like just *anything*. The whole *idea* of the piece, you know, was to show that if people want to have beer or wine, people are going to *have* beer or wine: so why not recognize the fact and stop making criminals of people."

Bill said, "Right. Right. And did you mention the directive or directions? 'In order to prevent illegal fermentation from taking place, avoid putting the contents of one can of malt and one pound of hops together with one cake of yeast in four gallons of warm water or keep in a warm place for two weeks together with a pound of dissolved white sugar'?"

She nodded, faintly smiling. "But that's not the right proportions, though. Well. *Anyway*. And Peter Fogarty *liked* it. And do you know what Ruel said? Ruel said, 'Naah. . . ' That was *all*. I spent oh *hours* on it. And Herbert H. Ruel says, 'Naah'. And *that*. Was *that*."

Bill said, "I know. I know. I'm sorry. Yeah. Well. *I* spent an *hour* this morning, listening to old Maw Moomaw give out the same old line of, ah, ma*lar*key—"

Stelle nodded, smiling wryly. "Oh, those hats. Those enormous *hats*. With the still lifes on them. Was she wearing—?"

"Nope. Not today. *Any*way. Same old *stuff*. Nothing *new*. *Noth*ing new. And, no sooner did I get the copy in, then this *beer* —"

She gasped, smiled, started to move as though she were going to lean over and place her hand on top of his, something which she had done once or twice—but this time she stopped, said, "Oh, isn't that the most in*cred*ible—Go on. Go on."

Well, *that* was something *new*. That was something entirely *dif*ferent. Wasn't it? And Bill had rushed over to the scene at once. Witnessed the whole thing, well, almost the whole thing: the people drinking the beer as it poured from the hose, and *e*verything. He'd interviewed the workmen who found the darned thing and asked people their opinions . . . *E*verything. And, as soon as it was obvious that the flow was off, back he rushed and wrote the whole thing up. Would Stelle like to see how the *Press* handled this front page story? This really, well, it was a scoop. A *beat*. "Take a look," he said, handing over a copy of the newspaper.

Stelle rapidly scanned the front page. NO CLUES ON MISSING JUSTICE CRATER, said one headline. KNIFE SLAYER ELECTROCUTED, said another. TEMPERANCE HEAD VOWS "NO SURRENDER", said another. Stelle began a faint look of perplexity. "Well, I don't *see* it," she said, still looking.

"Oh," said Bill, elaborately casual, raising his nicely-defined eyebrows. "You mean it isn't *on* the front page? Hm. DEPRESSION "LICKED," SAYS INDUSTRIAL HEAD—nice to know, but, nope, guess that's not it, either."

Stelle had caught on by now. "Oh you wise guy," she said. "*More* banana oil. Okay. I give up. Where *is* it?"

He took the paper, opened it to page two, folded it so that the right hand columns were uppermost, and, pointing, handed it back to her. Stelle looked at it, grimaced. On the bottom was a tiny paragraph entitled POLICE ARE PROBING SEWER LIQUOR HOSE. "You mean that's *all*? The, the funniest darned story that has ever *hap*pened in this very exceedingly unfunny darned town? And this is *all*?"

"It," he said. "All."

Her face went blank. She said, "Oh. Hell."

"Mr. Publisher Emery said that the *Press* is a paper which families are not ashamed to have on their supper tables, and that, and I quote, 'Families don't want to read about sewers when they're eating supper.'"

Stelle pursed her mouth as though she'd just bitten into a sour plum. "Rather read about Knife Slayer Electrocutions over the pot roast and potatoes. *Sure* they would."

"Lucky if they *have* pot roast and potatoes, way things are going. Lucky to have po*ta*toes, pretty soon."

She gave a quick, grim nod. Then she masked it. "Say, didn't you *read* what Industrial Head said in your very own *news*paper? — Uh oh." She looked at her tiny watch. "We'll both be lucky to afford potato *peels*, if we don't get back to our respective offices."

He said, "Yeah. Yeah."

Bubb Snyder, Maloney's curate, asked, "Whudja have ?"

Bill set a half-dollar on the bar. "The lady had her inevitable cup of tea and I had two Scotch and sodas—"

"Two buddascotch pudding. *Fawdy*-fi cents." Stelle came up and set a nickel on top of the fifty-cent piece.

Bill said. "Oh for crying out loud. Can't I even buy you a cup of *tea*? Oh well."

Outside she said, "Goodbye. Better luck with—"

"I'll walk you back to your—"

She belted her coat, shook her head.

"'I am the cat who walks alone.' So be it," Bill said.

She threw him a quick look. "Say, you're just full of quotations today. First it was Robert Burns, or whoever; now it's Kipling."

"'I am vast,'" he said. "'I contain multitudes.'" He took a half-step forward.

"Well," she said, briskly, "I'm afraid you're going to just have to go right on containing them. Ta ta."

No one called the fall "autumn" in Yokums, no one except an odd schoolteacher or so, from the outlands; the same who called pants *trousers*: and spoke, also, as though eyeglasses were *spectacles*, mirrors were *looking-glasses*, a piece of chalk a *crayon*: and other oddities and unsolved mysteries of the land and sea.

There was no point in all of Yokums where not more than a quarter-mile walk in any direction, except, of course, toward the water, would not bring you to trees. Large trees, old trees. There alas were no more spreading chestnut trees, and alas the spreading elm trees were soon to follow them down the blighted road to oblivion. And there were magnolia trees, the northern magnolia, nothing to do with Roses and Drums, the Fallen Banners and the Lost Cause: but you noticed the magnolia trees and their pink-and-white flowers and their deep sweet smell in the spring and summer. They of course were still there in the fall, but it was not the magnolia trees that you noticed in the fall. There were sumac, too, also called Chinese elm: a vile slander on both China and the elm proper; the sumac was also sometimes called the "tree of life," *God* knows why, and sometimes the ailanthus or acanthus or maybe it was the pithecanthropus: more like some damned evil *weed*, a gross weed, than a decent proper tree: with its vile unnatural growth, faster and ranker than the eucalyptus, its reptilian leaves, and worst of all its stinking smell. It would grow anywhere, and as the great patriarch of the trees died off these cuckoobirds of the tree world too often took their places. Like starlings driving out decent birds, they seemed to drive out decent trees. Let civilization totter, behold the slimy sumac striding like triffids and, all pretence gone, striking mankind down with its poison sting and stink.

But here and there the wild cherry was still seen, its bark a medicament for the old-fashioned and the knowing. Here and there the dogwood and the acacia, or locust tree, also sweetly white-flowered. The acacia lived forever, or so it seemed: in the wide side-yard of the ancient Dutch Reformed Church grew three acacias which had been there when *George Washington* had come to worship: and the classis all there, too, you may be sure, with their cocked hats in their hands—

—but the trees of the fall, *the* Trees. Of the *fall*. They were two in kind, bearing stuff after their kind, the horse-chestnut and the maple. The oak might have been mightier, but its nuts were no comparison to those of the horse-chestnut, nor its leaves so gloriously painted as the maple's. Poets made much of the oak, Vergil and others. But a boy in those months of October and November noticed oaks very little; a boy noticed the horse-chestnut and the maple. A boy learned where to look for the biggest, broadest, reddest and yellowest maple leaves. And a boy learned where to look for the glossiest and biggest horse-chestnuts, some still bursting out of their green husks; but by the time the boy went looking they were for the most part already free of them, lying on the ground amidst the leaves. It was perhaps the sole acknowledgement a boy could give to the abstract principle of simple beauty, for the horse-chestnut had no use at all. None whatsoever. In its bright and shining redbrowness it was merely lovely to look upon.

And by the time the fallen leaves had surrendered their last nuts, by that time the leaves were already being raked into piles and were burning, pyres of the waning, dying year; bittersweet smoke. Signals of coming winter. When all the trees were the same.

CHAPTER SEVEN

The Department of Justice's men had finally arrived at the scene of the almost-carnival. Police Chief Iron Ike Hotaling and his men were already there. During the Spanish-American War, the Boxer Rebellion and Philippine Insurrection, in at least one of which he had earned his nickname, Hotaling had been a fine and chesty figure of a man; there were photographs, occasionally reprinted, to prove it. In the three decades since then, however, the chest had somewhat slipped. And he who had been a fine, big man was now . . . a big man. And also present was Deputy Assistant Commissioner Bradlaw. Not, still. *Again.* Commissioner Quoyte's instructions to him had been brief.

"Giddowda my sight," said Quoyte.

The Federales had arrived, too. There was a certain ceremonious touchiness as the several jurisdictions met. "Captain Farrell," said Iron Ike. "Chief Hotaling," said the Prohi man.

"I didden wanna touch *noth*ing, till you come along," said Ike.

"Preciate that," said Farrell, a tall, thin, oyster-eyed, noncheerful man in an overcoat as grey as his face. He looked like something carved on a totem pole by a gloomy Indian.

There was a pause in these amenities, and, as no one stepped forward to say, "Brave gentlemen of France, fire first," or anything like it, Chief Hotaling said, with a curt gesture, "C'misshner *Brad*law."

Farrell said, "Commissioner." Touched the brim of his hat with one finger, simultaneously bobbing his head about an inch.

Bradlaw said, "Uh—"

This disposed of, the Chief got down to business. "Now, whut *I* would suhdjest," he said, Captain Farrell meanwhile nodding in advance; "*I* would suhdjest we have a cupla men get inna dthis uh *soor*. An, uh, uh, *trace* this, uh, *hose*. To its *sauce*. Huh?"

"Gree with you hundred percent," said the captain.

They both turned to Bradlaw. Who blinked. Then, having said, "*Oh!*" a few times, and, a few times, "*Yeah!*" gave his crew the necessary instructions. To which, with the advice and consent of both Farrell and Hotaling, were added strict injunctions not to sample the merchandise. Just to *trace* it.

It led them—and, so, of course, the combined forces of the law—to an exceedingly dingy garage at the corner of Thompson and Commerce Streets. Thompson was a poor but respectable thoroughfare. Commerce Street was merely poor, the subject of a thousand dirty jokes. This time, however, having sent out scouts and observers, the professional ladies looked from their windows at the constabularies with unworried interest. A large crowd gathered to watch the proceedings. The garage had a door of reinforced steel. It was locked. No one, apparently, was minding the store.

The Department of Justice (in the person of Captain Farrell) turned to the assistance of modern science (in the person of Agent Vincent Hool, plus sundry pieces of equipment). "Open ur up, Hool," said Farrell.

Hool said, confidently, "Ride away, Captain"—and unlimbered his acetylene torch and set to work. He had done this often, of course; very, very often. And he knew that all he had to do, really had to do, of course, was to cut out the lock. But the presence of the press, of the crowd, and of the newspaper photographers, appealed to his sense of the dramatic. And while they all watched admiringly, the Federal agent proceeded to cut an opening large enough for a fat man in a silk hat to pass through. As the panel fell away, Captain Farrell and Chief Hotaling made their way inside.

And at once reappeared, rather purple about the chops.

"Dthere'e another damn daw dthere, wit'th *maw* steel plating!" the chief said.

"Bring that torch in here, Hool: *o*pen it!" the Federal officer ordered his man. The latter hung back, bashfully.

"I can't, Captain," he said, squirming. "I haven't got no more *fuel!*"

So, while the early autumn winds blew early-fallen leaves and always-falling scraps of newspapers up and down the street, the crowd waited patiently until another tank of fuel was brought in, and the second portal breached. Then, moving into the garage as cautiously as if they expected to find the Hunkpapa Sioux barricaded in the grease-pits, the police and Prohibition agents pressed on with revolvers drawn.

A genial odor of malt and hops pervaded the air, and bottle-caps were scattered on the concrete floor; but the place was otherwise empty. In one corner of the concrete floor a trench was gouged out—it led to a hole. Someone idly kicked a bottle-cap into the opening. There was a moment's wait, then a tiny splash.

"What's your opinion of all this, Chief?" asked Captain Farrell. (A rumor, meanwhile, spread through the crowd outside that Judge Crater's body had been found inside. The popular consensus was, that they would rather have beer.)

"I'll tell you what my opinion is, Captain," Hotaling said, portentously, his chest swelling up to its former level, compressing his several chins into (almost) one, "My opinion is, dthat dthis place has been e*quipt*ed and used as a *beer*-bottling plant." Captain Farrell nodded his head slowly at this sage deduction, said that he didn't wonder but what the chief might well be right. "It's my fuhdther opinion," Iron Ike continued, absently allowing the chest and chins to slip back down again, "uh, dthat dthe operator of dthis bottling plant become aware a dthe puhlice surveillance, and removed dthe, uh, e*quip*ment."

Just how the equipment might have been removed without the police surveillance being at all aware of it, was not explained.

"*That* case," Captain Farrell said, reflectively, "the pipe—or hose—may of led here from a brewery. Maybe."

Chief Hotaling canted his huge head to one side, rather like the birdy with a yellow bill, said, "*Maybe. . .*"

After some more of the Sherlock Holmes dialogue, the two savants decided that it might be a good idea to trace the hose the other way, and thus see . . . *may*be . . . where it might lead in the opposite direction. But, as the shades of night were drawing fast, they decided to do this tomorrow. The Department of Justice men went back to Newark, and the local police returned to their headquarters on Bogue Street.

Some of the crowd, disappointed at the lack of action (and, more, of beer) now went home. Some, guided by the peculiar psychology of crowds, stayed on to gape at the empty garage. And some, television being still but a toy in a laboratory, decided to pay social calls at several Commercial Street establishments which were known always to welcome company.

It was, all in all, the best night these ladies had had since the bottom fell out of Wall Street. Causing ripples to spread wide, and far.

Bradlaw, meanwhile, not knowing exactly what to do, but being determined not to be reproached for not doing anything, had told his men that they might as well haul up the hose which lay between the garage-cum-bottling plant and the point where it had been broken. And so they hauled it up. Fathoms and fathoms of it. Looking on, grimly, was the Department of Public Works Commissioner himself, the Honorable John J. Quoyte. He was not in his usual jolly mood. Already too many people had with too little originality asked him why he had not had the beer hose switched around so that it would dispense its liquid largess elsewhere: the "elsewhere" suggested ranging from the Exempt Firemen's Benevolent Association Hall to the Salvation Army Building to his, the Commissioner's own home.

"You ain't a Father Mathew man, are ya, John?" someone, with misplaced joviality had asked, after making the suggestion.

And at this reference to the Founder of the insufficiently renowned Catholic Pioneer Temperence League, Quoyte could think of nothing more sparkling to say than, "Ah, dry up, will ya."

"Dthe *hose* dried up, ann ain't *dthat* a shame, John! Haw haw!"

It was at this unfortunate moment that Bradlaw approached him, diffidently.

"Ah. . . wottle we do wit'th the *hose*, John?" he asked.

Quoyte glared at him. "What in the hell are you asking *me* what to do with it?" he growled. "You went to the mayor before you come to me, didn't cha? Then ask the mayor what to do with it!"

And as poor Bradlaw stood there, his head hanging, Quoyte added a graphic but impractical suggestion of what else the unhappy deputy might do with the hose; then he stomped away. If Bradlaw had by now gotten the idea that his political career had met up with a check, he was absolutely correct.

Still, trying to do the best he could, he had the hose cut into manageable lengths so that it could be stored in the DPW garage. But he was curtly informed that "it didn't belong there." Kindhearted Fat Frank Feeney, applied to with the suggestion that it might be stored in the Police Stable, said, "Suhytinly." There was lots of room *there*, and Fat Frank, who was on the payroll as a hostler, hadn't had much to do with his space or time since the police had gotten rid of their last horses, five years previously. Frank had originally been a patrolman, but had put on weight until his feet could no longer stand the strain of walking the beat. It wasn't that he had been a very gross feeder—it was simply that, since neither State nor Federal governments any longer maintained standards for the quality of the beer dispensed to the general population, kindhearted Officer Feeney had taken it upon himself to sample it at the clandestine dispensaries strategically located around town, in order to make sure constantly of its wholesomeness. As neither this, nor its concomitant effects upon his size and weight, constituted an infringement of the Rules of the Force, and as everyone liked jolly Fat Frank, the Department bought him a motorcycle. Presumably the problem of staying *on* the bike was solvable, since other policeman had managed to solve it; but somehow Frank never could.

"It's dthem gahdamn *cuhyves,*" he would explain, cheerfully.

The solution of making him a hostler was a load off everyone's mind.

The police stable was not invariably empty of horse-flesh, the City Comptroller had been mildly surprised to observe a rather large Indian pony there on one of his rather rare visits.

"Belongs to a *frenn,*" explained Feeney, his red-and-purple face bubbling with good humor. "He pahks it here, now n dthen, pays fuh dthe feed himself, I don' chahdge im nothin fuh rubbin it down and all, and he gives, like, a contri*b*ution. Tuh dthe Ben-*e*volenn Funn."

"Oh, well, that's okay, then," said the Comptroller.

De minimus non curat lex.

In the nice cozy little apartment that she shared with another professional woman (Betty Sills, a bookkeeper at the Steam Laundry), Stelle Wilson—the *E* had been *spurlos versenkt* a while ago, and God help anyone who tried to bring it back up— was awakened by a loud clang. After a second there was another clang, and the sound of a man's voice, cursing softly. She got out of bed and went to the window, where she peered into the street. The gas lamps had only recently given way to electricity on these streets, and—much, much higher up than the old lamps used to be—the harsh white light glared from its unguarded bulb against its white reflector: and showed a man wrestling with a manhole cover. At that moment she heard, or she thought she heard, someone whom she wasn't able to see, calling out something, in a low and urgent tone. Evidently the man down below heard it too, because he lifted his head, and, staying in his half-crouch, said, "*Huh?*"

Then two things happened at once. From somewhere invisibly nearby an auto started, backfired, then, the engine growing louder, then softer, drove off. And she rather thought that the motor must have been on all this time. And, also, that it was a truck and not an auto. The other thing that happened was that a policeman came strolling over, his dark blue overcoat flapping against his legs, and his long night stick swinging.

Stelle quickly slipped into her own longest overcoat, which was *not* as long as she liked, considering the hour—4 a.m.—and so on, but oh well: she grabbed her purse because it had her keys and her pad and pencil, and she darted down the steps and into the street.

"*I* says, Whuddaya *do*in here," the policeman was saying.

The man shrugged. He was wearing a leather jacket with a sheep-skin lining, and either an oilcloth- or leather-covered cap. And was due for another shave shortly. "I come a look for a, now, *pack*age," he said.

"*Whut*, now, package?" the policeman asked, totally skeptical. He saw the other man's eyes go past him, half-turned, saw Stelle, blinked. His lips set for a moment. Then (he was Ed Richardson, a nice-enough young cop) he gave a little sigh, said, "Oh, hi, Stelle, uh, Miss *Wil*son." And, turning back to the man in the street he asked again, "*Whut* package."

The other fellow shrugged again. "I wuhyk fa this guy, drives a truck," he said. "An a *pack*age fall off? So I *get* out, see? An I come a look fritt?"

Officer Richardson gazed around elaborately, "*I* don't see no truck. Whutsya *name*?"

"Louis Lom*bah*di? Where do I *live*? Toity-tree hunnret *Hut*-son Street. In Noo *Yawk*." And he asked, "Whuddaya makin such a fuss abowdit? I just come a look fra missing *pack*age."

Richardson at once said, "Yexpeck ta fine it inna *soor*?"

With what was apparently an invariable shrug, Louis Lombardi said, "I come along an I see the, now, *man*hole cuvva is off. So I put it *back*. See? Any, now, ciddazin, wooda done the same," he added virtuously.

Richardson let his breath out. He did not seem to be convinced.

"Betta come down t' *head*quautas," he said, "tellum all abowd it *dthere*." (Lombardi shrugged.) The policeman turned to Stelle. "You, uh, you comin along? Miss Wilson."

She gave it a brief thought, then shook her head. "No, I guess not. I'm not really dressed for it."

"Nobuddy would *mind*."

She gave him one of her blank stares and he looked away.

"I'll check with the desk about it, the first thing in the morning," she said. "Good night. Officer Richardson."

"Night, Miss Wilson. Cmon, you, Lombahdi."

Lombardi gave them both a quick, sliding look. He did not seem at all disturbed.

Stelle went back to bed, furious. That was how it was, if you were a woman. No matter how long you had worked to prove yourself as just as good a reporter as any man, given the opportunity, always something *suggestive*. Well, Ed Richardson didn't get any change out of *her*. And as for Louis Lombardi, if that was his real name, which she doubted, there was certainly something fishy about *him*. If he had been just exactly what he said he was he would have been pleading and pleading. *Ah cummon, gimme a break* . . . that sort of thing. No. Definitely fishy. Well. Back to sleep. Time enough in the morning.

In the morning—after the one slice of buttered toast, the one slice of unbuttered toast, the one-half grapefruit, the one piece of bacon, and the one cup of black coffee—she called the Police HQ in Bogue Street. The desk sergeant on duty said that she'd hafta talk ta Captain Flynn about that. And Captain Flynn, after asking what he could do for her, Miss Wilson, and being told what, said, "Well, yeah, *we* question him and there didden seem nothing to *hold* him on, so we re*lease* him. What else can I do fr ya, Miss Wilson?"

Stelle Wilson, who really was an experienced reporter, and knew from reason of that experience that the police did not always volunteer every bit of information available, said, "You checked the address he gave? Thirty-three Hundred Hudson Street, New York City?"

Captain Flynn did seem surprised that she asked, but he said, "We *had* it checked, uhuh, and it turn out ta be *false*. Or, anyway, there isn't no such number, Hudson Street, New Yawk *Ciddy*. And, uh, just in case of there might of been some misun-der*stand*ing, we also had a check made in *Newark*. *Lots* of confu-sion, all the *time*, between *them* two places. But no such number, Hudson Street, *there*, either. Not taddit matters, no crime was committed anyway."

In that case (Stelle asked herself, but not Captain Flynn), why did you bother checking his address even once, let alone twice. But all she asked aloud was, "Wonder why he gave a false address?"

Captain Flynn, whose bluff and easy voice had carried a cer-tain small undertone she hadn't quite been able to define, now became good-humored, casual, indulgent. "Ah well, *you* know, Miss Wilson, uh, *some* people, they don't *like* the police ta come arounna their homes. They get em*bar*rassed, if ya know whut I mean."

Stelle thought that she had seldom if ever seen anyone less likely to suffer from embarrassment than "Louis Lombardi."

"I know what you mean, yes," she said, though.

"*Well*. Anything *else* we cn do fr ya, Miss Wilson?"

"Nothing else, Captain Flynn. Now."

After thanking him and hanging up the receiver, Stelle sort of regretted that "Now." But she couldn't resist.

"It will only alert him," she said, aloud. And then, asking herself, "Alert him against *what*?" She found that she had no answer.

Hanging up her coat in the office of the *Press* newspaper, she saw nearby Mr. Peter Fogarty, the senior reporter, and who had in fact been working there since the day he graduated the 8th grade at St. Joseph's School and promptly got himself hired, aged fourteen, as copy boy, office boy, and general factotum: a tall man, with a tendency to stoop, a kindly and homely face and a mouth full of large, long teeth, and many a poem, proverb, say-ing, saw, and totally-respectable jest.

"Oh, Mr. Fogarty, I wanted to ask you," and, her coat slipping, she turned to hang it more firmly.

"*Nihil obstat*." said Mr. Peter Fogarty. "Ask away, my child."

"There. Oh. Oh, are you going to check, when the Police and DPW trace the other part of that *beer* hose? This morning?"

He nodded. In many ways he was *very* unprogressive, and, naturally, with a tendency towards, well . . . almost . . . *big*otry . . . *al*most . . . and Stelle did not understand how he managed to feed seven children (and another on the way, and had you *seen*, *poor* Mrs. Fogarty's *mouth*? At least a tooth gone for every child; the lack of calcium) after two pay-cuts: but he was always a gentleman. "I have already checked, Miss Wilson, my star. And I won't keep you in suspense. You would like to know what they found out. They found out nothing. Nothing at all. Except, of course, that sewers are very *dirty* places, aren't they?"

She stared. "When you say 'nothing'—"

"When I say 'nothing,' I mean nothing at all. They did not find out where the other part of the hose, the miraculous hose, where it went to. Alas."

She stared some more. "But . . . how come? Mr. Fogarty? I mean . . . all they had to *do* was *fol*low the darned thing . . . didn't they?"

He sighed, pursed his lips. "Yes yes. All that they would have had to do would be to follow it. Follow the mysterious cornucopia-hose. Yes. Why didn't they? Well, you see, it wasn't there. You see. The men went down into the catacombs, well, the cloaca, I should say, really, they went down bright and early. I took the early mass at St. Josephs and then I went right down there myself. Not into the sewer, I should say. I am zealous, but there are limits, there are after all limits and Clara has quite enough washing to do as it is and I don't own stock in the Yokums Steam Laundry. *How*ever. The ma*chine*, you know, has much to answer for, but the *wash*ing machine is an unmixed blessing as far as the Peter Michael Fogarty family is concerned. Yes."

"Mr. *Fogarty*—"

He smiled. "Oh yes, forgive me, well. Well, they didn't trace the hose because it wasn't there to be traced. We have the word of many witnesses that there had *been* a hose in the sewer yesterday. It was inadvertently, or perhaps *ad*vertently, broken, wasn't it? Or perhaps it had been weakened by the blows of an axe whilst they were trying to chop out some of the debris there, *Christ*mas trees, would you believe it! And, bless the darling thing, it flowed *beer*, didn't it? And a part of it was traced to its *terminus ad quem*, where the product had recently been being bottled; correct? And although the police force are perhaps not trained in topology or whatever it is, nevertheless they—*and* the Bureau of Prohibition *and* the Department of Public Works—all were able to figure out that *ubi ad quem, ibi a quo:* in other words, now do not be impatient, my dear Stelle, where there is an end there has to be a beginning."

"However," and here he rotated his rather gaunt neck around against the starched white collar, a habit of his, "*where the terminus a quo* might be or may have been must at least for the present remain a mystery, because when the laborers who are worthy of their hire (we must assume) went down into the depths this morning to follow the hose to its origins: surprise! there was no hose."

After a second she said, "And the police—"

He gave a very soft sigh, and, looking her right in the eye, said, "The police profess themselves utterly mystified."

The newspaper buildings faced each other on River Street. The *Gazette* building had been built almost forty years earlier, when the phrase "large, light airy rooms" had been much in vogue among architects of orphanages and schools, and when barges laden with red brick proceeded almost endlessly along the canals and rivers. Some there had been—and still were, though fewer, all men (and women) being mortal—who claimed that the building had been entirely adequate as a school building and that no new school had been needed. There were hints of a "deal," a deal between certain building contractors, certain members of the Board of Education, and a certain publisher. Perhaps no one nowadays could say for certain. A newer school had anyway been built some several blocks away, and the *Gazette*, previously published out of a one-storey wooden structure on Main Street, had purchased the former school at what was said to have been a price much less than what it would have cost the publisher, the late Z.T. Ruel, to put up a new one. And the *Press* building must have looked very bright and clean when it was erected just before the World War, but its light-tan brickwork was now rather dingy.

Stelle often gave silent thanks that so much of the Women's Page was boilerplate and otherwise syndicated. *Dear* Old Dorothy Dix, the advice columnist! Dear dull *Helen and Warren*, the married couple whose magnificently dull life appeared in the form of a daily serial: and all the rest of it—because if so much of the Woman's Page, recipes and all, had not appeared ready-made, undoubtedly she, Stelle Wilson, Girl Reporter, would have had to help make it up: and if she could tell rhubarb from celery that was as much as she cared to. So even though her career had begun, traditionally, as a gopher (Go fer the coffee, go fer the proofsheets, go fer this and go fer that), she was now after all really and truly a journalist. And not a mere extension of the domestic science class. No: she had a desk up in the front like any of the reporters.

From time to time she had noticed that when she was near the immense front windows on the second floor she could see someone—often—waving at her behind the not-so-wide window on the second floor of the *Press* building right across the street. It was no elaborate semaphore, just a casual wave, and, as she was somewhat nearsighted and did not wear glasses, she had not at first known who it was; nor had she at first ever waved back. She did by and by learn who it was, and in this manner:

"Ya boyfriend's wavin atcha," said one of the typists, Mary Stepanski, her face going through the various little twitches and grimaces which sometimes play upon the faces of people who are acting in malice and are anyway without total self-confidence. "Aintcha gunna wave *back* atcha boyfriend?" and she looked away elaborately, while her mouth stretched and wobbled.

"Which one?" Stelle asked, casually, not looking up.

"Billy *Bombuhyg!*" Mary snapped, and then, realizing that Stelle had had the better of it, muttered, "'*Which one!*'" and, her face gone totally out of control and quite ugly, gave an angry sniff and moved quickly away. She never played *that* game again.

"Oh, *that* one," was Stelle's sole comment, and, very casually, she had turned and waved back. A few people had chuckled. But her easy way of handling it had caused it to be forgotten at once. Still. It was sort of a good question, although Mary had presented it as a statement. *Was* Bill Bomberg her boyfriend, in a certain sense, or was he *not*: and if not, why not? Stelle had given the matter considerable thought, and had summed matters up until several headings, entitled (approximately) *Relations Between Mature Single Men and Women.*

First Type: A cool, mutually respectful relationship between (as it might be) professional equals. *Example*: She and Carl Hemling, the *Gazette*'s Sports Editor.

Second Type: A much, naturally, warmer relationship between those expecting to get married, whether formally engaged or not. *Example*: Betty Stills and Bobby Keogh, the Assistant Manager of the Steam Laundry.

Third Type: An *intimate* relationship. *Example*: Peggy Wilson, Stelle's one-and-a-half-year-younger sister, who still lived (officially) with their Aunt Polly in Jersey City, but was actually carrying on an affair with one Robert L. Lacey, an insurance broker: "We're *going* to get married as soon as this damned Depression is over," Peggy said, "so what's the *dif*ference?"

Well, obviously the Bomberg-Wilson, or Wilson-Bomberg, Relation belonged to the First Type. Or it *should*. But did it really? It was easy with Carl. Carl lived with his really horrible old really crippled mother. He *couldn't* get married. And it was no secret that he was a steady customer at Sally Snyder's River Front

Hotel. Which was certainly *one* way for a man to handle sexual matters. You knew where you *were*, with Carl. Carl never waved at you, asked you to lunch or for a drink or quoted poetry at you. "Nice story, today's," was the way Carl expressed a compliment.

As for Type Two, or Second Type, well. What was the *point* of getting too close to Bill Bomberg? He made more than she, but how much more could he be making? He had to be making more because he was a man and men always made more for the same kind of work. Reasons for this ranged from, Men have families to support to Men are available for a wider variety of assignments and work harder and anyway are, well, just *better*, by way of Men don't take any time off because of Cramps: bluntest one.

But—making enough to support a *wife*? Nothing doing. And by now just about every employer in the country was firing women who got married (if they didn't quit anyhow) because it was not fair to pay a woman who didn't need the job when there were so many unemployed men who *did*. —But this was all kind of way ahead of things. Who said either that Bill would want to get married to her even if he could afford it, or that she would want to get married to Bill? Well, as a matter of fact, a number of people did: Sister Peg, for instance.

Sister Peg, however, when asked, delicately . . . about . . . *that* . . . ? *You* know . . . had, first, instantly, wrinkled her face, and, secondly and hastily and of course too late said, "Well, it's all *right* . . . I suppose . . . Well, men *want* it. That's just the way they're *made*, Stelle, might as well get used to that." Maybe *so*. But Stelle didn't see one reason why she had to get used to that right now.

And that, of course, took care of Third Type.

So. Since sex was not such a great big *thing*. And since marriage was not in the cards for the forseeable future *any*way, even if she, Stelle, *was* willing to give up her career. Which right now she *wasn't*. So what would be the use of getting too close with Bill? It would only lead to unhappiness, wouldn't it? To feelings which couldn't be satisfied. To loss of control. And *feelings* and *control* did not refer in this case to *sex*, either.

No.

No.

"Phone. Stelle."

"Thanks. Hello?"

"Hi." Bill. "How about lunch?"

"Where?"

"The Half Moon?"

"Fine. When? Twelve noon? Okay. Thanks."

So, so much for *that*.

Sigh.

The Half Moon, on Main near Valleydale, was all white tile and bustle. There was often a huge red lobster in the window, although, come to think of it, Stelle had never actually seen any-one *eat*ing a lobster. Still, it was definitely not always the same lobster, so someone must. (The only other possible explanation was that there was a sort of Lobster Exchange to which restaur-ants belonged. But it was easier to believe in transmigration or whatever it was that *Cath*olics believed in.)

"And what was your morning like?" she asked.

He shrugged. "Court," he said. "Old Judge Boodle presiding. The usual. The in*va*riable. Bootlegging. Drunk and disorderly. Beerrunning. Sometimes I think that the entire population of Yokums, present company excepted, must consist of those en-gaged in bootlegging and of course those under eighteen years of age."

Stelle snorted. "Hah, that's a hot one," she said, helping her-self to a roll and to some pickles and sour crout. "I must know of at least a dozen bootleggers who are under the age of eighteen."

Bill agreed. "At least." He carefully buttered the small piece of roll he had broken off, which showed that someone had trained him in good manners.

For a moment neither said anything, just nibbled and munched.

Then Stelle said, "You know. I know that every city in the country has beer barons and beerrunners and rumrunners. But does it ever seem to you that Yokums has maybe *more* than its share?"

"Does it ever. Ha. Boy oh boy. Whoopee."

The little frown of concentration settled on the upper part of her face. "Well . . . *Why* . . . do you suppose?"

Bill shrugged, then raised his eyebrows, then smiled a swift smile. "Supply and demand," he said. "Know what I mean? Well, pretend that this table-top, this table-*cloth*, is a map. Here is Yokums, here is Hackamack Bay, here is New *York* Bay, here is the Hudson River. Never mind all the different names, what it is in fact is one large body of very easily navigable water. Very *dirty* water. *And*, over here," he placed a roll on the tablecloth, "is New York *City*. Kay? Okay, back to Yokums. Here, on Charlotte Street, is the National Cereal Company, which, ha ha, does not make Shredded Wheat, it makes near beer. True, near beer has been de-alchoholized, but it is a lot easier to take near beer and *add* alky —and to add, for that matter, *e*ther—than to have to start from scratch. And, ah, here is the Macdonald Pharmaceutical Company plant; never mind the iodine or cod *liver* oil, concentrate on the *e*ther, concentrate on the grain *al*cohol. Got that? And why what is *this*?" *This* was in fact—

"A salt shaker!"

"Ha ha. Joke. *This* is the sugar house. *The. Sug*ar House. And what, pray tell, are the basic ingredients of moonshine whiskey?"

Stelle said, "Sugar and grain and alcohol. Oh. Oh I *see*!"

"Said the blind man. *Well*. Here you have on the one hand all the essential commodities for the manufacture of illegal booze and/or beer. —And *here*. You have, first, the teeming millions, or, al*most*, of the Jersey Shore and hinterland. And *here*," his finger moved again. "You have the literally teeming, or, teeming, literally, millions of the City of New *York*. A great, thirsty, bottomless *gul*let. Of a market. All that is lacking . . . if it *is* lacking . . . is *one mind* capable of tying this all to*geth*er. One master *mind*. So to speak."

"*Now*. Does such a master mind exist? Would you care to try your strength, or *strennth*, as we locals pronounce it if not careful not to, on the mallet, and see if you can ring the gong and *win*. A kewpie doll or a cigar? *Hmmm*?"

Stelle said, hesitantly, "*Well*. . . "

He leaned forward, encouragingly; gestured. "If you look out the back windows of the *Press* building, my dear Miss Wilson, what hills are those you see? What ricks and rills, what woods and templed hills? Those of the Bluffs, right? And, not a million miles away, no, not even in fact *one* mile away, at (as it might be) 439 Upper Bluffs Avenue, *who* is it who is widely and popularly, sometimes *un*popularly, known as 'the King-Pin of New York Bootlegging,' and lives there in domestic felicity like a merchant prince or a giant of industry? Like they *used* to live—only he still *does*? I observe that you hesitate. Why? Are you afraid of getting *in Dutch*?"

"Oh, she said, "Oh! Oh! Oh, of *course*—"

He looked away and looked down. His voice dropped, "Of course. Oh yes," he said. "The Dutchman. The *Big* Dutchman. Albert himself."

"Dutch Stoltz. . ."

CHAPTER EIGHT

P ast a peeling wooden sign, CITY PACKET BOAT WHARF, the rickety wharf itself led a full block in each direction, and in either direction, nowadays, there was never more than one vessel ever to be seen. This was the packet boat *Sadie Howell*, H. (for Horatio) Seymour Clack, Master, Owner, and Captain . . . as he signed himself . . . and the *Sadie Howell* was the last of the fleet of fifty which once—but this has already been said. The paint on the vessel was almost as peeling as that on the sign. In all weathers there was a thin fume of smoke from one of her stacks, and in cold weather there were two. In cold weather there was a fire in the stove in the pilot house, and all year round there was a fire in the *Sadie*'s furnace. The stove was fed with whatever scraps of wood Captain Clack found as he roamed the lower town with a battered baby carriage: it had been new and proud once and once he had wheeled his only child, Howard, in it. The captain was a widower now, and Howard had lived in Florida for the last twenty years, and he seldom wrote home.

The furnace was stoked with lumps of coal which Preacher Babcock fished up with oyster tongs from the State Barge and Canal Boat Wharf, where there was always a certain amount of spillage from the coal scows. Preacher Babcock, who was the color of the coal, was not only the *Sadie*'s Chief Engineer, he was her only engineer. He was in fact the vessel's only remaining crew. The great Depression hit the packet boat a number of years before it hit the rest of the nation, and though the boat had managed, if just barely, to keep on despite the railroads, the trucks had proven too much for it. After four months without pay, Alec Douglas, the last previous employee, had quit, and gone to work as general furnaceman and fix-it for De Vries, who owned ten apartment houses within one two-block area. The pay wasn't much, but it came in regular, and a tiny flat in a basement came with it.

Alec's leaving the boat was not an event which attracted much notice in the world, but it made a difference nonetheless, if only to Alec, Captain Clack, and—the very next day—the short, barrel-shaped Black man who had come along the Wharf with a slow and even somewhat stately tread which shook the shivery timbers. Clack, who was smoking a pipe which contained more dottle than fresh tobacco, regarded him from the deck railing in moody silence.

"Captain, I wawnts to axe you sumpn."

Clack had nodded, said nothing.

"I wawnts a job. I stoke furnace, I tind ingynes, awn the Missipi, awn the Muhzura, awn the Tinnissee—jess about enna river dhey gots boats, I wux awnum."

The captain of the *Sadie Howell* considered this a moment or two. "They got many boats left on them rivers nowadays?" he asked.

A heavy sigh and a slow shake of the head was the answer. "But I *good*," the man said. And added, hopefully, "I kin *cook*, too." Alec could cook, too. He could not cook *much*, it is true, there not being ever much to cook. Nor could he cook well. But Horatio Seymour Clack could not even cook as well as that. He had tried. Lord knows that he had tried. It went into the stove very nicely. And invariably it came out very badly.

"What's yer name, then?"

"Name Eliphalet Babcock . . . but dhey calls me Preacher."

Clack sighed, knocked his pipe. "Well . . . come aboard," he said.

Thus did Preacher Babcock become Chief Engineer of the *Sadie Howell.* Worse appointments have been made.

Now and then the boat took a fishing party out on Saturdays

or Sundays. Now and then, besides the weekend catch, the captain and his one-man crew would catch some few of the fish which still plied the polluted waters. And now and then they would fish up some flotsam and jetsam which was—sometimes —edible, if just barely, and, sometimes, if just barely, saleable.

Sometimes.

Now and then, and in fact, very seldom indeed, she did odds and ends and errands. Never, never, though, nowadays, did she ever have a full hold of real freight cargo. Preacher Babcock was not surprised; he would have been surprised had it been otherwise. The boats he had worked on now sank slowly at the sides of wharfs which were sinking, more often than not, themselves. The *Sadie Howell*, once so proud with fresh paint, was not much of a going concern. But she still functioned. H. Seymour Clack, Master, Owner, and Captain, did not have much in the way of money—in fact, aside from what he was able to put aside against the license fee, he had practically no money at all—but he had Hope.

"You know whut it *costs*, maintain a truck?" he would demand.

"Plenny!" his Chief Engineer would declare, pausing a moment, rag in hand, and standing back to admire the brass-work.

"You *bet*, 'plenny'! Gas? Noil? *Tires*? You know whut them *tires* cost? And . . . and . . ." rapidly he searched his mind, found something else. "*Bridge tolls!*"

"*Oh* yes, Cappin."

"Well. . . " H. Seymour Clack, Master, Owner, and Captain, was a fair man. He stood there now, in his worn, worn, very worn uniform jacket (the trousers had long since passed a point of no return and been replaced by an unmatching but serviceable—and, the crux of the matter—*cheap* pair, boughten from what most of its customers called The Salivation Army), his battered cap set at a still-jaunty angle, he fingered the moustaches which had once, oh so long ago, won him the admiring nickname of "Kitch" for Kitchener Clack: gone grey and ragged and drooping now, and the nickname now sunk as deep as the Lord

K. himself—

"Well. . . . Soons they git that there George Washington *Bridge* built, bridge tolls. Right now, anyway, ferry fares. Yessir, Preach—uh, Engineer—uh, *Chief*"—Captain Clack was a very fair man; if he could not afford to pay his Chief Engineer he could at least give him his full title or its official short-form. "*Sure.* Gas. Noil. Ga*rage* charges. Fares and tolls. And suppose . . . suppose . . . suppose them roads git washed away in some *storm*? Happened be*fore.* And suppose, um, um, suppose there's a *strike*?"

"*Uh*—oh," said the Chief, giving his own grey-polled head a grim shake.

"And maybe the damn *bridge* falls down? Hah *hah.* Oh boy. *Then* you'll see. Coming up to us on their bended *knees*, you bet," Captain Clack wound up, cheerfully, pleased at his beatific vision.

The packet boat *Sadie Howell* would come into her own once more as a prime carrier of prime cargo and freight. All that was needed was a rise in the price of gas and oil and garage care and ferry fares and bridge tolls, plus the roads being washed away in a storm, and the bridge falling down, plus a strike.

This was hope indeed.

But he had it.

And in this the second year of the Great Depression, it was a sight more hope than many people had. Prices could rise to the sky, roads melt like wax, bridges fall as though the House of Usher and strikes proliferate like fever blisters, without giving many people the hopeful vision of the *they* coming to *them*, like so many pilgrims, "*on their bended knees. . .*"

Now restored to a quite good humor, Captain Clack looked around to see what might be done and done presently to make his vessel just that much more ready for the task ahead: and his eye lit upon one of a number of large metal cans located all about the boat and filled three-quarters full of sand: the sand being, in turn, filled with cigar and cigarette butts and spittle. The contents were regularly emptied and sieved and the debris thrown over the side and the sand then poured back in. It now struck the captain's questing eye that the sand could stand renewal, and he said as much.

Preacher Babcock nodded slowly. "I go git some," he said, bestowing his rag in its niche.

"You know *whir*?"

"Thenk so. Beach?"

"Yop. Place the newspapers they call it Sandy Beach, Boys that swim there, *they* call it Bare Ass Beach. You kin take them two *big* cans . . . buckets, almost. . . " The two big cans (buckets, almost) in fact larger than the average bucket, had once contained some food-stuff packed in commercial quantities; C.E. Babcock had fitted them with wire handles to which in turn he had fitted wooden grips made of superannuated broomsticks drilled through to take the wire. Both cans sparkled.

Still under the influence of the beatific vision, Captain Clack decided to splurge. He reached deep into his pocket and came up with an ancient leather change-purse, far too large for its present contents. His cracked and work-dingy forefinger and thumb delved, came up with one, then two nickels; handed them over. "Stop along the way in Bodenheimers," he said, "and gitchew some choon gum and me a bag of Bull Derm." He would have much liked a drink. But—

"Yes Capp'n. Thank you Capp'n."

With the Chief Engineer's measured, heavy, and familiar tread falling away in the distance, the Captain went up into the pilot house and began the immemorial rite of polishing the boat's mahogany wheel. It had been long since the bottle of lemon oil gurgled when tipped, but both it and the rag still smelled correctly. Later, that done, he betook himself to his worn old charts. Suppose, now, just suppose he was to get a freight bound for, say, oh, say, bound for the Gowanus Street Canal in Brooklyn. He would first, of course, swing the *Howell* out into the channel. And *thennn. . .*

In the course of the next hour he had brought the ship to the Gowanus Street Canal, to the South Street piers in lower Manhattan, then back around the Battery and up the North River to

Yonkers (long and long ago he had regularly carried barrels and barrels of soap powder up to Yonkers for the Steam Laundry there) and then . . . then . . . here the captain's imagination had really soared . . . then he had gone south and through the Harlem Ship Canal from Spuyten Duyvil (which he and all other true old-timers called "Spiken" Duyvil) and into the East River and thence into Long Island Sound and all the way to *Bridgeport, Connecticut* for a cargo of lumber down from Maine. . .

All, of course, alas, in his imagination.

He was awakened from these dreams of glory by two immediate sounds. One was the returning tread of his Chief Engineer. It was, however, somehow, a somewhat different tread than it had been when outward bound. Somehow. It was not lighter, certainly. It was just *different*. The other was the sound of a voice raised in song. The voice was that of Eliphalet Babcock, Chief Engineer, and gave great and good support to his being called "Preacher" Babcock, although he was not actually preaching. He was in fact singing. He was singing, in fact, the Hymn called *Jerusalem the Golden*.

Horatio Seymour Clack silently left his charts and went over to look out on and to examine this phenomenon. A faint breeze, only faintly tainted (for a change) with the stale smell of sewage, was on the Bay; and the seagulls flew in from the water and settled, with short squawks of satisfaction, on the pilings of the Packet Boat Wharf. Coming steadily along the Wharf, slower than usual, and carrying both of the very large cans with an almost exaggerated care, came the Chief Engineer. His face bore an expression of grave exaltation.

> *"Dhe sound of dhem dhat triumph"*

he sang.

> *"Dhe sound of dhem dhat feast."*

There was a brief interlude, not of organ music, of silence. Then the Preacher's voice broke into prose, with some air of recapitulating events mentioned previously.

"Comin long *side*walk," he declared, somewhat in the manner of a chant. "Satan he *temp* me. Satan he *temp* me. Satan he say, 'Take dhat money and spenn it awn strong drenk,' Satan say —" Captain Clack heaved a deep sigh. "Satan he cite Scripture faw his puhpose. Oh Satan he temp me and he say, Satan he say, Satan say, 'If dhy soul desire of dhee strong drenk, strong drenk shalt dhou *buy*,' an I say, I say, I say unto Satan, 'Satan, dhou fadher of lies, *git* dhee behind me!' An I stamp muh *feet* at him. I stamp muh *feet* at him. I say, 'O Satan. Satan. Ol serpent and liar from dhe beginnin, serpent shall be trodden under foot. Shall be *stawmp* awn.' An I stawmp muh *foot*. I strike dhe pavement widh muh *foot*. Dhe flinty rock I smite and strike. An dhe rock of dhe pavement open up (Lord, Lord!)! An a golden pipe come issue fawth! Gol', gol', shine like solid gol'! An it flow! Lord, Lord! It flow. Famine great great upon dhe lann, Lord, Lord!" The Preacher was swaying back and forth by now, the Spirit, clearly, being on him. Captain Clack, with circumspection but with determination, had come to stand by the gangplank as the Preacher/Chief Engineer, still swaying rhythmically, came marching up aboard.

"Chief Engineer," said Clack, firmly, "as Master, Owner, and Captain of this vessel, vizz the *Sadie Howell*, licensed as a Packet Boat under the Act of Congress of October the 12th 1875, I demand to know the meaning of this before you go one more step forward."

His Chief Engineer swung one of the bucket-cans down and across and, without spilling one drop, set it at his captain's feet. He then, not looking at the other container at all but looking his captain straight in the eye, swung the other one down at his own feet. And did not spill a drop. He next picked it up with both hands and, raising it to his lips, drank from it deeply, still looking straight into the astonished eyes of Horatio Seymour Clack.

Who next proceeded to do the same thing. Clack, however, merely sipped and tasted. The two men exchanged a long, long, very long look. Then Clack set down his own bucket-can. Then he removed his cap. "For what we are about to receive," he prayed, "Lord make us duly grateful."

"AYmen."

For quite a while there was no further word, only the sounds of sipping, of the smacking of lips, of deep swallowing, gurgling, of (very slight) splashing. Then Captain Clack, with a long sigh, slowly lowered the growler from his lips. "On their *knees!*" he said.

Orpheus T. Brower, Ph.D., was a grain chemist. Most people had never heard of Orpheus T. Brower, but then, most people had never heard of grain chemists, either. Dr. Brower knew, and was indulgently good-natured about this. He did not, in fact, very much care. He had his job as Managing Director of the National Cereals Company, and a very good job it was too: only eight hours a day and a salary of $5,000 a year, plus full and unrestricted use of the laboratory on the top floor of the large brick building on Charlotte Street, in Turkey Island, as that section of Yokums was popularly if unofficially called. He was a thirty-third degree Mason and a Sunday School teacher in the Asbury Methodist Church and a member of the Lions and Rotary Clubs, "Service Above Self," what a *good* motto! He had his nice little house in Gristmill Heights, one of the it is true *old*er houses in that excellent residential suburb ("Restricted"), not one of the newer and larger houses: but it was large enough for Mother and Sister Helen, with whom he made his home.

"No, no," he would say, when the conversation might trend in that direction, "I don't intend to marry. I am quite happy as I am."

"Nor do I," Sister Helen said. "So am I," she would say, nodding cheerfully.

And their mother, darling Mother, would nod slowly and solemnly and say, "Well, *I*. Think that they are *right*. That is what *I* think. My younger son Halcyon married. And they have *children*." Mrs. Brower would say, her face and voice becoming very serious as she mentioned this; "and *oh* the Struggle. *The. Strug-*

gle." Her tone conjured up images of Halcyon Brower, his wife Maude, and their children (Harold, Halcyon III, and Little Helen) wriggling, Laocoön-like, slow-motion, in gumbo mud. But that was their *choice*, she would say, with an unuttered sigh, a faint note of wonder, and a very small shake of the head. What a fine head Mother Brower had, all that fine silvery hair. Bobbed hair was not for *her*, she would say, with a humorous smile. At one time her son, Doctor Orpheus, used to talk of their eventually moving into one of the newer and larger homes in Gristmill Heights: but not recently. For one thing, he had had Losses. In the Market. For another, he had felt obliged to make several loans to Brother Halcyon. And then, too, it was so much easier to keep up a small house. They all felt it was, after all, very *cosy* there with just the three of them. They had their Victrola, and their radio—the old Atwater-Kent, with its batteries dripping acid and its huge horn so often toppling over, had been replaced by a new Zenith, one of their few extravagances: all you had to do was push down a lever and the station turned automatically—and Orpheus and Sister Helen had their books and Mother and Sister Helen had their sewing.

Yes, very cosy.

As for other aspects of Doctor Orpheus's life, he did have other interests besides the day-to-day work as Managing Director with The Company. For one thing, up in his study, when all was calm and quiet and the Victrola and the radio (how they laughed at "Al" Smith and his quaint pronunciation of "raddio"!) were silent for the night, Orpheus wrote. He had been writing a series of stories of the type called Scientifiction, about "space ships" in distant galaxies, adventures of a newer and different sort. Sister Helen alone knew of this, she alone read the stories in manuscript. A few had already been published (pseudonymously, of course). And, for another, in The Company's "lab," Doctor Orpheus Brower was working on a Project.

This one was not a secret.

"What *is* this project, Orpheus?" his mother had asked. And not she alone.

Young Mr. Robert Boykin, the young lawyer who was not only the President of The Company but probably one of its largest stockholders (Orpheus did not pay much attention to these details), Mr. Boykin had asked, "So this is the, uh, *Project*, Doctor?" as he looked around the "lab" with keen interest.

"Yes it is, Mr. Boykin. Yes siree."

Others might say, "Doc," or "Bob" or "Sonny Boy"; but between the two men themselves it was always "Doctor" and "Mr. Boykin." Mutual respect was the keynote of their relationship.

"Well. Well well. Mmm. Mind giving me some sort of rundown on it? Of course I haven't got your scientific type *mind*—"

Dr. Brower shrugged deprecatingly. "Be glad to. I am working on a formula. A new type of formula. For a commercial doughnut mix. You see."

It was not clear that Mr. Boykin did see. He gave his associate a rather curious look. Dr. Brower went on to explain. The usual doughnut mixes of commerce were far from satisfactory. Sometimes the doughnuts took too long to make. Or they took up too much grease. Or they grew stale too quickly. Or were too sweet. Or not sweet enough. Or they *burned*. Or the mix was simply too costly. "I have a several-fold interest, you see, Mr. Boykin. For one thing, there is your pure scientific approach. Can it be *done*? If so, *how*? And, oh, besides the fact that I enjoy the work, the challenge."

Mr. Boykin nodded, his face displaying keen interest, "Yes, Dr. Brower. 'Besides that' —? Mmm?"

Dr. Brower's mild grey-blue eyes gleamed behind his gold-rimmed spectacles. "Besides that, I must confess to you, yes, ha ha. I will admit. There is a com*mer*cial interest—"

Mr. Boykin returned the somewhat rogueish look with which Dr. Brower had made this admission. "Oh. Oh *ho*. There *is*, eh? Ah ha. Weh-hell. Tell me about *that*."

And Dr. Brower *did*. Times changed, yes sirree, times changed, and you had to change along with them. Look at old Bob Hewitt, who had the Stanley Steamer franchise and garage over on Hudson Avenue. Thought the Stanley Steamer was just the best thing, the best automobile that ever came down the boulevard. Which it might *be*. Probably *was* . . . in a lot of ways. But. Old Bob Hewitt refused to face facts, recognize that times had changed. Nobody bought Stanley Steamers anymore. Nobody even *made* Stanley Steamers anymore. True, anybody who did own one, if it needed repairs, this was the only place in North Jersey where they could bring them in for repairs. But how many was that? How often? No—ho.

"Now, it is the same with doughnuts. My dear Mother makes doughnuts, they are simply delicious. But. Takes her all *morning*! Not what your average restaurant can spend time on, now is it? *So.* —And besides, your average young housewife nowadays, *she* isn't going to spend all morning on a batch of doughnuts. Do you see? And then, also." Dr. Brower turned away and fidgeted with a piece of equipment. Someone might have thought him embarrassed.

"Oh don't stop now, Dr. Brower. Go on. You've gotten me very interested." And, indeed, young Attorney Boykin's round, rosy face *did* seem very interested.

"Well. Suppose. Suppose there is a change in the oh the legal situation. Oh just suppose that public taste changes. Suppose that our lovely and natural and healthy product, our malted beverage or near beer, is at some future date not any longer what people *want*? Or maybe perhaps anyway not in such or similar quantity. . ."

Mr. Boykin gave his index finger a sharp shake. "I get your point right away, Doctor. I see the picture immediately. In that case it might be a good idea for The Company to have another iron in the fire? Eh?"

Dr. Brower nodded, slowly, seriously. He started to say something, something more, had even begun a gesture, when the sound of voices below drew their attention. There were two voices, one being drowned out by another, and more profane, one. Dr. Brower frowned, clicked his tongue, hurried to the window, Mr. Boykin following.

Down below was a scene. A man on foot. And another man

on horseback. The man on foot trying to dodge around the horse. The man on the horse heading him off.

"----it!" cried the man on foot. "I gotta right ta pass tru here ta da nexx street, chew ain't got no right ta tell *me* I can't!"

And the man on the horse (more like a rather large Indian pony): "Listen you -----------, donn' chew tell me whut I gotta right ta do ann whut I ain't got no right ta do, juss chew getcher ---- the H--- outta here er I'll blow yer ------ --- *off*, dja hear me?"

And, so saying, the man on horseback brandished a shotgun.

This was instantly persuasive. The man on foot threw up his hands and turned around. "Yer right, cher right, okay, okay, Om goin Om goin, okay okay. . ." His voice fell silent. He went.

Doctor Brower was struggling with the window. His usually mild face was angry. "There is no reason for the use of any such *lang*uage," he exclaimed (the window resisted him). "There are *women* in this plant, and— Even so— There is no *call* for such language. Why—"

Mr. Boykin placed a restraining hand upon his arm. "I'll take care of that, Doctor," he said. "I will speak to the man about that. So don't trouble yourself any further. It won't happen again if I have anything to say about it. And, I assure you, I have!"

The managing director was somewhat appeased, but still he grumbled. "Don't know what we *need* an armed guard for, *any*way," he muttered, slowly moving away from the window, and half-turning back to cast an angry glance. "Do *you*, Mr. Boykin?"

As it happened, Mr. Boykin did. He pursed his rosy lips and nodded. His face was very serious.

"Several factors make it necessary, Dr. Brower. *One* thing, ever since the Depression, people have been trying to sneak in and steal barley. Now *you* know and *I* know, Doctor, that the type barley we use here, it is not the type barley for use in say *soup*. But your poor person doesn't know that. We have had *losses*, Doctor. We have to protect ourselves. Our stockholders: widows and orphans." Dr. Brower's scientific mind had immediately caught the gist of these remarks, and he nodded his agreement. "*Fur*thermore. I am sorry to say. Certain *crim*inal types are *always* trying to steal our malt and hops for the manufacture of so-called home brew. Which, I hardly need tell you, is il*leg*al. After all, we are licensed by the Federal Government for the manufacture of malted beverage or near beer *only*, and we have our legal responsibility, I'm sure that you agree."

Doctor Brower did indeed agree. He was in fact entirely convinced. And young Counsellor-at-Law Boykin assured him once more that there would be no further repetition of such vile language. And on that note they parted.

Several other people and Mr. Boykin had some conversation, too, before he left the plant. One of the Federal Inspectors approached him, asked, "You gotney nooze frus?"

"Why no I haven't," Mr. Boykin said, very quietly, continuing on his way. The man's mouth twisted, and he gave his head a little jerk to the side. But he said nothing more.

"Howya *do*in today, Fritzie?" Mr. Boykin enquired of the braumeister. This man grunted. "How's the *brew* today?"

"Same *pischwasser* like every day," the braumeister said. Mr. Boykin guffawed, slapped him on the back, went out into the yard and thence into Caroline Street, a small thoroughfare which had no sidewalks.

The mounted guard saw him and nodded.

"*You!*" shouted Boykin. "*Come over here!*" The guard's face went slack with surprise. He dug his mount in the flanks with his knees. He came.

"You wanna see *me*, Bobsey?" he asked.

"I don't want to see your *grand*mother. —Listen. I don't care what you say in the night, when you're on *night* duty. But in the *day* time—"

The man was genuinely at a loss. "Whud I say? Whud I *say*?"

Boykin swallowed. His usually pink face was quite red now. "I. Don't want to *hear*. About your opening a dirty *mouth*. Again. Like just *now*. You dumb pa*loo*ka. You under*stand*?"

For a moment incomprehension still kept the guard's face bewildered. Then he gestured towards Lower Bluffs Avenue, whence the would-be-passer-through had very lately entered, and whither he had so soon returned. "Ya mean—"

Giving his head a stiff bob with each syllable, Boykin snapped, "*I. mean.*"

Bewilderment gave way to annoyance. "Say whuddis dthis, some kine of a *kinnergahden?*"

"It's some kind of a *job*, is what it is. You don't *like* the job? You don't *want* to take *orders?*"

"Uh— *No.* I mean—uh—"

"'*No. Uh.*'" Boykin's sarcasm was terrible. "*Lis*-sen. In the day-time. See? Don't use any dirty *language.* See? Do you see? Do you understand what I'm *telling* you? Because, if somebody com-*plains.* And if the *police* maybe come here? Over some goddamn tiny little thing or for *any* thing—You know who isn't going to *like* that? You want a personal interview with *him?*"

The guard's muddy face became slightly grey, slightly green. "Aw, now, Bobsey, ah, now, aw, you wooden tell on me tuh dthuh *big* boy, aw, woodja? Huh? Aw, naw. Aw, not ta dthuh *big* guy? A right, a right, I *will* keep my mout'th shut. I *will*, uh, uh, watch my, now, *lang*widge. Inna *day* time. Like you *say. Okay?* O-kay, Bobsey?"

"Okay, then," said Mr. Boykin. He turned around and walked rapidly towards a waiting car. There were three men in it. One of them got out of the back and made room for him, then got back in beside him. Boykin grunted. Then he said to the driver, "Upper Bluffs. Let's go."

CHAPTER NINE

S telle said, "And what, Mr. Fogarty, is the latest development in the fabulous Beer Hose story?"

Peter Fogarty smiled faintly.

"To my true king I offered, free from stain,
Honor and Faith. Vain faith, and Honor vain."

"Do you know *The Jacobite's Lament*, my star? Lord Macauley? Not? Oh my. What do they teach—Ah well. Well. But do you know the amount of time I put in this morning, writing up my story? Allow me to show you how the art of brevity improves with practice," and he showed her the galleys for the afternoon paper. There, in a lower corner, next to the discreet advertisements of two undertakers, there it was.

LACK OF CLUES IN BEER HOSE CASE

Although the garage is still being watched,
police have not found any clues to the ownership of the beer-bottling plant believed to
have been operating there. The section of hose
is still being held at police headquarters.

"Maybe the police are waiting for someone to come and claim it," Stelle suggested, handing back the proofs. Fogarty chuckled. His smile went fainter yet.

Stelle saw something, asked, "But . . . surely . . . you didn't do all that cutting yourself . . . *did* you?"

"'*Grey-haired from sorrow in my manhood's prime,*' ah, no, the art of brevity, much though I excel in it myself, is one which has been more truly mastered by Oscar T. Emery, our distinguished Editor and Publisher."

Stelle scowled, puzzled. Then her face went blank. "He didn't *like* your story?"

Fogarty's faint smile came and went again. "He said it was sordid. . ."

She opened her mouth but while she sought for a word or words the frosted glass door painted *Editor and Publisher* flew open, and there stood he whom *Gazette* staffers frequently assured each other and all outsiders whom they felt they might either safely trust or safely ignore was the ugliest, stupidest, rottenest, lousiest, crookedest, boobiest, chimp, simp and slob, to wit Old O.E. himself; looking about him with his perpetual Wild Surmise.

"O.E.?"

"Uh Pete! Uh Hackamack and uh Darblay! Uh right away! Uh the uh *street* caved in!" His protuberant eyes lit upon Stelle Wilson. He gestured. "Uh go *with* him, uh!"

In the car, Stelle repeated, "The *street* caved in?"

"Past due," murmured Peter M. Fogarty. There were few or no merry mingled tints of Autumn about the streets here, they merely looked dingy. And poor. The only grace notes were the occasional wreaths of flowers on a door to indicate that someone had recently died within.

"What do you mean, Mr. Fo—"

He turned his large grey-green eyes briefly towards her. "My dear star. Tell you what. I am after all old enough, I believe, to be your father. So why don't you merely call me 'Peter'? What do I mean? Well, my mind having suddenly due cause to dwell upon the matter, reminds me that Hackamack Avenue near Darblay Street has not been torn up in recent years for repairs. Which must make it unique, my dear and cherished compeer, *unique*. He's a nice boy, isn't he?"

Having often enough snorted her contempt on reading fictions in which the heroine "felt her face grow warm," Stelle was both annoyed and astonished at herself to feel that her own face right now *was* growing warm. Nor could she pretend that she didn't know whom Peter Fogarty was talking about. Because she *did* know. So she answered another, if unasked, question, by asking yet another.

"Oh, you aren't referring to the fact that State Committeeman of a Certain Political Party Arthur T. Owens, local resident, is also President and Treasurer of the Hackamack Asphalt Paving Company . . . are *you*?"

He laughed a very little, then he sighed. "Perish the thought . . . Here we be. —Why certainly *not. Post hoc, ergo propter hoc*? Exposed as a fallacy by Emmanuel Kant. Pure coincidence— My *word*!"

For the street had indeed caved in.

A DPW crew was hastily erecting barricades at both ends of the block—the connotation of the populace perhaps rising in revolt was also being strengthened by a brace of policemen who were indeed swinging their clubs. However, they did not hit anyone, were probably not trying to, and anyway the men they were aiming at were dodging nimbly.

Not, though, silently.

"Hoccome ya let dthe *Colo*red Man walk away wit'th his buckets full? Huh, Kelly? Hoccome ya won't let dthe *White* Men get none of it ta drink?"

"Oh *no*!" Stelle murmured.

The well-known genial aroma of hops and malt filled the air around the middle of the street, which had sunken in like an old man's mouth.

Patrolman Kelly, nettled, sang out, "*I* didn't see no Colored Man! 'n I don't see none *now*! I'm wawnin ya, Michael Patrick Aloysius Higgins, gid *owda* dthere!"

M.P.A. Higgins got out of there: but his own mouth opened wide upon words which must remain conjectural, as it shut suddenly upon seeing, first Stelle Wilson, and, second, Peter Fogarty, who said, simply, "Now tell us all about it, Michael."

Michael did. He was sitting up at his window, he said, with an illustrative gesture, when suddenly he heard this big noise.

Big noise, he emphasized. "WhrAWWWWWWMMMmmm!" he mimicked it, throwing wide his arms. And the whole, uh, darned, *street* cave in. He run down, he said, he *run* down, in order to see was anybody hurt. And he saw someone whom he described, with simple particularity, as "This Colored Man"— here M.P.A. Higgins looked all around. But no one of that description was in sight. "He was yellin and hawlerrin, 'Help me!' he was yellin, 'Lord! Lord!' he was yellin. Ann he was tryin ta climb *out*. Ann I see yum grabbin a *hole* a sumpfin, like a, a *pipe*, er sumpfin, ya know, Pete?"

"Go on, go on."

"It was *shin*in. Ann, so help me *God* ann the Blessed Mother —"

"Now, now. Just go on and tell us, never mind the Holy Names."

"Ah, yer right. Well, ah, so help me, he grabs a hole a the *pipe*, ann I could see it *break*—ya know? Ann, nexx t'thing I know, a whole bunch a *beer* is comin outta it! Juss like I hear it happen *yest*aday! Ann this *Col*ored Man he grabs a hole a these two great big *pails*—"

"Everybody onna dthe sidewalks! Everybody onna dthe sidewalks!"

The voice of patrolman Kelly momentarily broke the thread of Higgin's discourse. He and Fogarty and Stelle Wilson left the road, and seeing, as they did so, an official City of Yokums car parked on the other side, were not entirely astonished also to see the burly and frequently genial figure of no one else but the Hon. John J. Quoyte, Commissioner of Public Works.

Who did not look genial now.

He looked, in fact, *moody*.

"Good afternoon, Commissioner," said Fogarty. Quoyte grunted. "What about it, Commissioner? Has the good goddess Grania struck again?"

The Commissioner's heavy face turned almost savage. "I dunno what the—Ahh, *I* dunno what you referring to, Fogarty. Not a word a trut'th innit." He strode forward and shouted down into the collapsed and partially exposed sewer, "You gunna be down dthere fore*v*er? Hahmuch time is it gunna *take* yez—?"

A face peered over the sunken rim. A voice belonging to another face asked, "Who is openin his great big *yap* up there?" The first face murmured something which was perhaps a name. The voice said, "*Him*?" Another voice laughed. Voice and laugh were perhaps nearer to the derisive than the respectable.

Quoyte's face went purple. "Out!" he shouted. "Out! Git on up *owd*da dthere! I wantchez owdda the *soor*! *Now*, djuh *hear* me—?"

The subterranean Voice (or, perhaps, another subterranean Voice) attempted to recapitulate the order, but in a falsetto. The effort was too much for him, and his voice died away into gurgles, and was muffled by the loud, coarse and happy laughter of whoever else was down there along with him; perhaps including the Face, which had by now vanished. And then yet another voice, bass, this one, or at any rate a very deep baritone, began a song. The words were delivered in a measured cadence, and, at each pause, were accompanied with—it may have been—orchestral noises made by striking, say, a monkey-wrench against a shovel and a very large and presumably unbroken pipe. Other voices joined in the chorus; those who did not know the words joining in with *dum dum*, *la la*, and so on.

Had Joe Horvath been there (he wasn't) he could have easily translated: it was the famous folk-song of the Slovatchko or Glagolitski, *Happy Is He Who Hath Slain A Thousand Turks, But E'en Happier He Who Hath Had Carnal Knowledge Of The Beautiful Elisaphetta Daughter Of The Horse-Thief Pishto Varna.*

Slovatchko drinking songs are famous for their lengthy titles. *And* for their many, many verses.

Long, long before the last one was reached, the Honorable J.J. Quoyte had demanded of the police, "Arright, go *down* there and haul lum *up*!"

Patrolman Kelly, however, had belonged to the municipal civil service for many years, and not for nothing, either. "Sorry, Commissioner," he said, gravely, "but d*that's not ahh depahtement.*"

The voices, now grown fainter and lugubrious, next embarked upon the moving and mournful Seven Hundred Fathoms Beneath The Snowy Surface Of The Glagolitic Alps The Sons Of The Widow Feopompushka Delve In The Demi-Darkness For Sundry Cuprous Ores, Alas And Woe . . . All the spectators who found themselves as audience agreed that the effect was very moving.

All but *one*, anyway.

Down (again) came Solid Ike (a.k.a. Iron Ike) Hotaling, the Chief of Police, who was quoted in next day's papers as saying, "I am determined to plumb this to the depths." Down came (again) the Department of Justice's Captain Farrell (Bureau of Prohibition), well-primed with enough fuel this time to cut his way into the Sub-treasury Building vaults.

The hose, which was bound in rather new-looking copper wire which had, it would seem, not had time enough to tarnish, and which did indeed (almost) glitter like gold— the hose was traced from Hackamack Avenue and Darblay Streets, down Darblay to Lower Bluffs to Island Place (a low-rent neighborhood inhabited chiefly by citizens of Nigerian extraction) and through to Hawk Street. It stopped just short of a Hawk Street garage which bore a large VACANCY—FOR RENT sign. But the peace officers, their suspicions unaccountably aroused, forced their way into the vacant building, and found an elaborate bottling plant, plus a vast vat containing enough beer to drown the whole police force,—assuming, that is, them to be reckless enough to go diving for pennies in it without keeping their gullets closed whilst doing so.

"This keeps up," said Farrell, "going to run out of *grodges* . . . Where do you keep the *cars* in this town, anyway, Hotaling?"

"Arrest dthese men!" directed the C. of P., choosing to ignore the witticism. There were nine of the malefactors, and all of them—together with a sampling of the beer—were removed to the Federal Court in Newark. The nine men seemed oddly un-worried by it all.

"And what," asked Peter Fogarty, afterwards, "did the Feder-alists say?" He and Stelle had split up, she going on to Newark, he remaining behind.

Stelle shrugged. "Their laboratory analysts report that the stuff wasn't even strong enough to be rated as near beer. The men were all released. In Fact, they were all gone by the time that I *got* there."

While Stelle was in Newark, he had been back in Yokums, seeing Dr. Orpheus Brower, to whom he had confided a sample, taken by himself, of the liquid in the vats.

The scientist was rather upset. "Why, not only is this liquid not even any sort of malted beverage, properly speaking," he confided, "but it is absolutely a menace to the health, you know."

"How do you mean, Professor?"

"Why—crawling with coli baccili," the chemist said. "And other unhealthy microorganisms."

Fogarty pursed his lips and let out a low whistle. "What do you suppose it *means*, Doctor Brower?"

Brower gazed at him grimly over his eyeglasses. "In *my* opin-ion," he said, "it means that someone has certainly been very careless."

Fogarty considered this, then he nodded. "Do you know, sir," he said, softly, "I believe that you may be right."

Later, back at the ranch, Stelle asked, "And what do *you* think it means?"

Her senior shrugged. "Why, I think that there isn't any much doubt that someone warned them there at the garage in time for them to run several thousand gallons of the Hackamack *Creek* into the vats along with the beer. Fortunately, I suppose there isn't much chance of any of that equipment being used again . . . My old Dutch grandmother, God rest her soul, did I ever tell you, when she made sour crout, she had my father, God rest his soul, trample it down with his own bare feet. Like *wine*. But she always washed his feet and legs first and in seven changes of water, and *then*. She dried them with oatmeal. But of course times have changed, my star. And he *is* a nice boy, now, *isn't* he?"

The best she could come up with also had an echo of the fictions in it. "I haven't the faintest idea what you are talking about," she said.

He gazed at her with what seemed to be a measure of affection, and, also, a measure of faint sadness.

> *"For my true king I gave both lands and wealth away,*
> *And one dear hope which was more worth than they,"*

he quoted. And then he sighed, and gave his head a slight shake. "Ah, yes, times have changed. But surely they can't have changed *that* much? So, now, why don't you invite him over for a nice, home-cooked meal?"

For one thing (Stelle could have said, but didn't), she certainly could not have done so without the knowledge and involvement of her room-mate. And Betty would at once have entered into the matter with a warmhearted, an enthusiastic involvement of herself, Betty, and Betty's boyfriend Bobby ("Oh *good*! I'll *help* you! Oh *say*! Why don't we ask Bobby over, *too*?" And they would then of course have to ask Bobby over, too, a deeply-dull fellow whom Bill deeply disenjoyed), and trot out to admire and be confident about the *whole idea* of engagements which were even if not *official*, well, and oh well, and oh Hell, and oh-the-*Hell*-with-it! Bill would certainly be immensely put off by the whole thing. And she, Stelle, would certainly not blame him. But all that she said now was, "Lots of reasons, Peter. So just don't say anything more about it, please. For now."

He gave one deep nod. "Well. I won't then," he said. "For now."

Bill, meanwhile, for lack of any better thought, had been measuring the various lengths of hose. The total came to more than six thousand feet, or more than a mile of hose which had been pulled up from underneath the Yokums' streets. And, for all the good his questionings had done him, he was himself many miles from any answer or explanation from any of them who had the charge of it.

Captain Farrell: (calmly) *No* idea.

Chief Hotaling: (irritably) Whut dthe Hell yaskin *me* faw?

"More than a mile of copper-colored wire-re-enforced hose-pipe, and neither Federal nor Municipal authority could figure out where in the *Hell* it had been carrying *beer* from," said Bill, over a bowl of soup at Ma Bixby's.

Stelle crushed little round oysterette crackers into hers. "Well, *I* asked *too*," she began, and paused to sip and taste, then continued sipping and tasting.

"And whom did you ask?" he queried.

"Ohhh . . . the usual lot of usually unreliable local sources. And all of them kept shrugging, and saying, 'Probly comes from some now *broory. . .*'"

Bill grunted. "Yeah . . . Probably one in the State of Texas . . . after all, it's the first mile that counts. —Oh. What was the School Board's decision in the Frankie Pollack case, do you happen to know?"

She looked up from the soup with some surprise. Frankie Pollack was a local six-year-old with an odd physical condition as the result of which he had a baritone voice, the strength of a sixteen-year-old boy, smoked cigars, and shaved regularly: such were the facts as known; folklore had already attributed other things. "Yes," she said. "As a matter of fact. He doesn't have to go to school after all . . . they said. They said, because of his 'unusual development'. . . is how they put it. But what—Oh. It has nothing to do with the beer business. You were just curious."

"Kid drinks beer too, I hear. Well. Too bad. And here he had a chance to chase some girls he could probably catch up with, too, to—"

She gave him her blank look. Said, "Well, *I* don't think it's funny! You must have some kind of a *mind*, to—"

"—to give them some chaste schoolboy kisses, I was going to

say. Who's got *what kind* of a mind?"

Well, maybe she'd . . . partly . . . earned that. Better let it drop.

"Which do you suppose is the worst publisher and editor?" she asked. "Emery or Ruel?"

"Ha. Six of one, half a dozen of another," he said. "Ask me another," he said.

She considered this, glancing at the pages of the two newspapers, *Press* and *Gazette,* each had by their soup bowls—newspapers, His and Hers, so to speak. ATTEMPT TO TREAT IN-FANTILE PARALYSIS AT WESLEYAN U. WITH SERUM, she read. CHINESE REDS AGAIN FIRE ON U.S. CRAFT, she read. BLIND HYMN-WRITER IS HAPPY AT NINETY. And MADAME CURIE NEAR NEW RADIUM CANCER CURE. And PRESIDENT SEES QUICK END TO BREAD-LINES. She sighed, shrugged, "Okay . . . I'll ask you . . ." *I'll ask you . . . about you and about me, where is it going and when will we get there, and where and what 'there' is . . .* "I'll ask you, oh! yes! Why is it called Turkey Island?"

He laughed. "Because Colonel Corbett's grandfather used to raise turkeys there."

"*Okay.* That takes care of the 'Turkey.' But why 'Island'?"

He drew lines on the tablecloth with his pencil. "Say! I'm get-ting pretty good at this! A table-top cartographer! Always knew I had *some* hidden talent . . . Uh, 'why "Island"?' Because it really *is* an island. See? Here comes Hackamack Creek. See? And it div-ides. See? And then it comes together again. See? Result—up here —an island. *Turkey Island . . . see?*"

Stelle said, "Well, I see it on your tabletop *map*, Mr. Mercator McNally. But with my very own eyes when I go *by* there, no I do *not* see it, any time. What happened, did it dry up?"

Unlike the Half Moon, which was all white tiles and white paint, Ma Bixby's was all brown: brown paint, brown wood pan-eling, and a ceiling of pressed tin designs, also brown: although whether by reason of paint or some process of aging was as near beyond conjecture as made no matter. Ma herself (widow of a cousin of the late X.X. Bixby), and her daughter Myrtle (some-times addressed as "Ma" by the inexperienced, a form she received without bothering to correct it) took turns between the stoves and the cash register, were both stout and bobbed-haired and wore Keds: they were both of the White (or, as G.B. Shaw has called it, the "Pinko-Grey") race: but, in some indefinable way, spiritually they were brown.

The backs of their necks were neatly shaved.

"No, it didn't dry up!" said Bill Bomburg. "It was *covered* up! After the last water-powered mill either quit or converted to some other kind of, oh, *power*, steam or electricity, why, then, the Creek, right there, I mean both branches of it, were covered up, and—"

"Yes! I read about it in *Les Miserables*! Jean Valjean carrying Marius in his arms through the—"

Bill laughed. Ma and Myrtle looked up, briefly, surprised. People didn't laugh much these days. Then they returned, re-spectively, to the pot roast and the bills. "—Yeah, well, uh, the only thing in common, of course, is that they're all—" His voice stopped abruptly. Their eyes met.

In a small, tense voice, Stelle said, "*sewers*—"

Mrs. Mary Mabel Moomaw seldom raised her voice. It was seldom necessary. "Why, Birdie, he had the temerity to say to me, do you know what he had the temerity to say to me?"

Her assistant put her tiny head to one side. "What, dear?"

"*He*," said Mrs. Moomaw, famous hat on her famous head tremulous with well-controlled indignation, "had the temerity. To say to *me*. 'The Grand Jury moves in its own good time, Mrs. Moomaw, and I can't hurry it, and neither, if you'll excuse me, can *you!*'"

"And *you* said?"

"*Well*. I just gave him *one, look*." Mrs. Moomaw indicated by the expression on her face (lower lip tucked in) the One Look which she had given the unfortunate man. "And I just as it hap-pened I *al*so gave one look at the *clock*." Birdie snickered. "And I said to him, oh just as politely as you please, I said to him, '*Well*, Mr. Morrison, perhaps neither you nor *I* can hurry the Grand Jury. *But. I* happen to *know*. Someone who *can*.'"

Birdie wriggled in delight. "*What* time did Bishop Snooker ask you should be there?"

"He *said*"—not for Mary Mabel Moomaw the curt *yes*, the brief *no*, in answering a question of such involvement—"'Well, we've had just about enough of this nonsense, dear Mrs. Moomaw, and if a telephone call from the Methodist Episcopal *Church.* Will have some effect. So you just make it your business to be there at a quarter to three this afternoon,' he said. 'Because I want you to *be* there in that office at that *time*,' he said. And so I *was*."

"And then this Morrison—?"

Mary Mabel tossed her head scornfully. "Oh, he was still just as brazen as ever, although *out*wardly of course he was still being po*lite*. He said, 'And who might *that* be?' he asked. And *I* said, 'Well, just you wait and *see*, Mr. Morrison. Because unless I am *very* much mistaken, you won't have very long to *wait*.'"

Birdie clapped her little hands together and laughed out loud.

"And *then*?"

Mary Mabel smiled her no-nonsense smile. The fixtures on her hat bobbled with the vigor of that smile. "And *then*, of course, the *tele*phone rang. And he raised his eyebrows and he said, 'Will you excuse me one moment please' and I said, 'Why of *course!*'"

There was a delighted giggle from Birdie. Mary Mabel continued, "Well! You should have seen his *face*. It turned *all colors*! And it was 'Yes Bishop' and 'No Bishop' and 'Well Bishop' and it was 'Well of course Bishop' and 'Oh I wouldn't want *that*, Bishop!' and then after that it was nothing else but 'Yes Bishop, Yes Bishop' and 'Yes Bishop, certainly Bishop!'"

Then Birdie got right down to the nub of it all. "And so," she said, "they, the Grand Jury I mean, they will issue the subpoenas?"

Mrs. Moomaw nodded portentously. "They certainly *will*. The Com*mis*sioner of Public Works and the *Deputy* Commissioner of Public Works. The Chief of Police and the Police Captain of the precinct where the hoses were found. The Fire Chief and the As*sist*ant Fire Chief. The *Water* Superintendent. And, oh various other peoples in the public employ as well, I am given to understand." She nodded her immense satisfaction.

Birdie simply hunched up her boney shoulders and laughed into her hands. Then something seemed to puzzle her. "The *Fire* Chief?"

"Well, of course. That is, well, of course we don't *know*. But who mostly *uses* hoses? And, even if *that* is all clear—and we must certainly assume them innocent until proven guilty— well, we would like to inquire how it was they noticed *noth*ing unusual? While they were making their regular *build*ing inspections?"

The two women nodded this point out between them. And then little Birdie Shallot asked, "Mary. Mary Mabel. I want to ask you. Because *I* have simply been racking my *brains* out. Mary, we all *know* that beer is the original source of liquor poisoning, we all *know* that nobody begins with drinking moonshine because, they say, it is so terribly strong and tastes so absolutely *awful*, and we all know nobody begins with wine either for the same *reas*ons: no, they all begin with drinking *beer* and that is why this is all so important, if you cut off the supply of beer why people will simply not go *on* to drink wine when beer no longer satisfies them, and then if the *poor souls* are not addicted by mind-rotting *wine* they will not go *on* to that vile moonshine whiskey, or, or, or —"

"—or brandy, gin, and rum: yes, dear. We all know. It *begins with beer*. Yes. And so—?"

Birdie looked around the office almost wildly, she gave a despairing gesture and pressed her palms to her temples. "Well. Mary Mabel, am I in*sane*? Am I going out of my *mind*? It doesn't fall from the clouds like *rain*, does it? It doesn't spring up from the ground like, like *oil* does it?"

"No, dear. No, dear, of course it doesn't. *Nature* makes only *benign* substances. It is *Man* that makes *poisons*. But—"

But Birdie would but her no buts. Her voice going higher and higher and shriller and shriller, she demanded, over and over again: where was it coming *from*? Where was it *coming* from?

Wise Mrs. Moomaw, who had after all previous experience with these outbursts of grief on the part of her Assistant, began to feel just a trifle anxious: Birdie was holding her head in both hands and crouching over and making a sound rather like a prolongation of the word, *Grue. . .*

"Well, dear," said Mrs. Moomaw, in her most soothing of tones, "perhaps our asking these questions have hithertofore been too much in the realms of politics. And so perhaps we should now address ourselves to the realms of geography. And *see*. What we can *see*." She looked around the room as though searching for something. Something very tangible. "A map," she said. "A map. A map—"

Birdie let her hands slip from her temples just a trifle. In an expressionless voice and with a vacant look she repeated, "A map. A map. . . "

"A map!" said Bill.

"A map!" cried Stelle. "Where's the nearest place that's got a map?"

"The library?"

"Of course! Of course! The Pulitzer—I mean—the Public Library—"

Simultaneously they jumped to their feet.

Ma (or perhaps it was Myrtle) looked up and wrapped her hands in her apron. Then she unwrapped them. "Two soups," she said. "Twenny sense."

Elmer walked down the street, examining every place with care.

Barbarelli the Barber. That was a funny combination. Sounded kind of nice, though. The red-and-white striped barber pole, turning and turning, turned by some kind of electrical connection, inside its glassed-in case. They *used* to get Elmer's hair cut at Barbarelli's, but Barbarelli charged twenty cents. And Old Man Mohl, who cut hair in an ordinary kitchen chair in his own kitchen, on the Q.T. because he didn't have a license and in his own kitchen he couldn't get one, *he* only charged them fifteen cents. Mr. Barbarelli smelled real nice, he smelled of bay rum and hair lotion and other nice things which he used and sold. Whereas Old Man Mohl didn't have any of those things. And he smelled, well, he smelled *stale*.

But. He only charged fifteen cents.

Back when they used to go to Barbarelli, Elmer always felt himself attracted towards the polished cuspidors, and always, but always, his mother noticed this at once. "Get away from that spit*toon*! Do you wanna get conSUMPtion? —Notchew, Mr. Barbarelli: but who knows who spits in there."

And, also, although in a lower tone of voice, "Get away from there! Put down that *mag*azine!"

"That magazine," that was the *Police Gazette*.

To one side, a sort of shelf, divided into pigeon-holes, and in each one a shaving mug with a name and (*u*sually) a picture painted on it: A horse and wagon and on the green wagon in white paint, *Feinbein*. A big house, with, in curlicued gold letters, *Rafftery* the building contractor. And so on. And so on. And so on. A carpenter's square, for Mr. *Peters*. And always, always, always, whether in English or in Italian: Barbarelli and the other barbers: talking about bets on the horse races.

Always.

◆ ◆ ◆

The Honorable John J. Quoyte looked at the Honorable Francis Flaherty. "Subpoenas?" he repeated.

"Subpoenas," the Mayor said. He was, after all, a Republican. And, it is said, a Republican measures. While a Democrat just pours. Nevertheless the Mayor did not measure either the flow from the bottle or the height of the Scotch in the glass. He just poured. "So much for *my* political future," he said. Then he hefted the glass and drank. After a moment he put it down. "*I* don't know, Johnny. I have a wife, five kids, two automobiles, one house on Laurel Street and one cottage at Lake Prince. Plus four mortgages, figure it out. *I* haven't been collecting that kind of graft. I know it every time I polish my *shoes* and I wonder how long I can get away with not buying a *new* pair—"

Commissioner Quoyte shifted his bulky body in the chair, said, "Well, uh, yeah, uh, sure, Francey. And, uh, well, *you* figure it out. If *I* was collecting, if I was *tak*ing: would I have sent a DPW crew to go down and poke around ezzackly where dthat goddamn hose *was*, if Ida *known* where it was?"

George Washington looked grimly down upon them both from within the frame of his portrait by Gilbert Stuart. Perhaps the General-President was thinking of his famous and famously ill-fitting teeth. Or perhaps he was thinking of the Whiskey Rebellion.

His Honor the Mayor waved Quoyte's comment aside as too obvious to deserve thought. "*What* was it that I wanted? Oh yeah. Vic Vanderdam had a— Yeah." He lifted the telephone receiver off its hook and carefully put it to his ear whilst equally carefully holding the mouthpiece to his lips. "Miss Flaherty, please. Miss Flaherty. Would you be kind enough to find the best one of the downtown area and bring it to me, bring it *in*to me, if you please? —What? Oh. I'm. Sorry. The best *map*. Of the Village? Down*town*? Right. Thank—"

Commissioner Quoyte had listened rather blankly. Now he asked, "You thinkin a goin inna the *real* estate business, Francey?" —and wondered, had he perhaps gone too far.

But the Mayor, who was having another drink, did not seem to take this question amiss. He peered at the Commissioner over the rim of the glass. Then he lowered the glass. Then he gestured with it.

"Listen, John," he said: "before *this* damned mess is over, we may each of us think ourselves damned lucky to have some other business to *go* into. *Come* in—"

Miss Flaherty entered with a long cylinder, which she placed on the Mayor's desk. For an instant he stared at it, as though having no idea in the world what it might contain. The Letter From Prester John, perhaps. Then he said, "Oh, why yes. Thank you, Miss Flaherty." But she had already gone.

"The map," said her nephew the mayor. "The, I asked her for it, the map."

Chief of Police Isaac N. Hotaling and Police Captain (1st Precinct) Casper Clay looked at each other. "*I* never had no goddam soupini suhyved on me buh*faw!*" said the Chief. He was very angry.

"Well, me neither, Ike, uh, *Chief*."

The Chief breathed noisily. "Soupini. That's all I *need*. Juh know whut *dthat* means? Ya know whut dthat *means*?" he suddenly shouted. His voice rang out in the grimy room, with its scarred desk, battered cuspidors, dirty old calendars. "That means *graft*! That means this gahdamn *beer* hose! Any gahdamn-fool *kid* could figure it out nobuddy would dast run no gahdamn hose unner the streets ta run *beer* t'through it, widthout payin *some*buddy off—and payin oh buhlieve-*me plenny*! Who they payin *off*? *You?*"

Captain Clay, stiff in the best gold-braided uniform put on for the purpose of the interview, said, softly, "If they was, Chief, *I* wooden a hafta file fa *bank*rupsey lass munt'th."

Solid Ike glared at him. Then he threw up his hands. "*I*da know!" he exclaimed wearily. "I wuhyk hahd alla my life, homminy years I out inna *dthis* rotten job, *ann* whud've I got ta show faw it? My *salary*! Soupinis! Ya know who call me up this *smawn-*

ing? Chahley *Shuhyt* call me up dthis smawning. 'Dat's nod nice, Ike,' he says ta me. *Oh* yeah. 'Dat's nod nice—'"

Ordinarily Captain Clay would have smiled. Hotaling's imitation of Sheriff Shurt's voice, high-pitched and with a faint undertone of the dying, the almost-dead, Hudson Valley Dutch accent, was famous. The Captain did not smile this time, however; he nodded, very soberly.

"—He says he t'thought we was *friends.* I ask him Whut dthe Hell he's *taw*kin about, well, the long n shawt of it, the long n shawt of it, he says Here *I* am, colleck'n *two t'thousand dollas* a *week*! And hoccome I ain't cuttin *him* in fa nuthin: *huh*? And I ass him: Chahley, whut in dthe *Hell* you tawkin about? *Whut* two t'thousand dollas a week? An, he says he hears I'm colleck'n two t'thousand dollas a week *graft.* F' the gahdamn *beer* hose! *I* talk till I'm blue inn a face: *he* says, 'At's whad *I hear*, Ike, and dat's nod very *nice*,' blah blah *blah.* Fuhyst, soupinis. Dthen the *Sher*-iff is mad at me, fa Crise sake! An fa *What*? Fa two t'thousand dollas a week at *I* nevva even *seen*, Caspa! I nevva even gedda *smell* of it, Caspa! And if *I* ain't gettin nuthin and if *you* ain't gettin nuthin, then fa Crise *sake*, Caspa!—whut the Hell is goin *on* in this Ciddy, Caspa? *Huh*?"

Still stiff-mannered, still soft-voiced, Captain Clay said, "Well, now, Chief. . . I don't *know* nothing fr sure, y'know. But, uh, *may*be, Chief? Maybe the two of us, Chief? Maybe we oughda take a good close look at, uh, now, *map*, Chief. Hmm. Chief? Hmm?"

CHAPTER TEN

Madoc Owens was sometimes called the Wild Welshman, but he didn't look so wild. "A Saint David's Day parade," it has been said, "is five miles long and five feet tall." Earlier the same year, the fashionable Presbyterian Church in Beverly Hills had held its annual St. David's Day Dinner, buffet style; there had been no parade . . . out in the streets, that is: there *had* been quite a parade to the buffet, though. Harold Lloyd was there, David (no relation) Wark Griffiths was there, Myrna Loy was there, lots and *lots* of ham and turkey was there, and many people, it was observed (though not then there out loud) who were perhaps not quite so nattily-dressed as in previous years, and all of whom made several trips to re-stock on the ham and turkey, were there. The Reverend John Caradoc Jones was there, and made one of his justly-famous orations, full of quotations from the Bible, the Mabinogion, and the poems of Taliesin; full of praise for the Protestant Reformation, the Disestablishment of the (Anglican) Church in Wales, and the steadfast loyalty shown by all present in preserving the Cymric Heritage and singing the Lord's song in a strange land . . . and in the Welsh language.

Madoc Owens was not there.

Madoc Owens, in fine and in fact, had never been in Wales. At all. He was born in Liverpool, whither his father had, so to speak, drifted on a coal barge; and whence he himself had departed in some haste, having managed to attract the entirely unfavorable attention of both the Irish Catholic *and* Irish Protestant population of England's second city: plus that of its constabulary. His accents, then, were not the musical tones of Wales, but the less famous, more prosaic ones of the Merseyside. These distinctions did not much matter in the New World.

"Hoccome he *talks* like dthat?"

"He's a *Wel'tchmun*."

Rhymed references to "Taffy" and the crime of larceny as regards sides of beef had, in the early days, been tried on him, but were tried no longer; as several of the de facto bards could have testified if they had not become very suddenly dead. Nor had the name of Madoc been widely recognized, so it had been shortened, first to Maddy, then—this being sometimes taken for a local imprecision of (U.S.) speech—to Matty; and sometimes *this* in turn had been revised and extended into Mathew.

There had been much wealth in Liverpool but little opportunity had there been for Madoc Owens to attain any of it for himself. He had begun small, swiping tiny bottles of tea-milk from doorways, and running very fast; had gone on to swiping scuttles of coal from coal-holes, and running very fast. Next he had ventured to snatching purses, and running very fast; and it was at this point in his career that he found it expedient to keep on running, one day, until he found a Yankee cattle boat which was returning in ballast.

Many years later, one of his friends, hearing the story, had thought it very funny. "Haw haw! Howdja *like* it, Maddy? Howdja like dthe *trip*?"

"*Aw* the stink! I'd've got ahf, Albert, and gone back to given meself awp, but I didn't know how to wahk awn the wahter—"

"Haw haw haw!"

By then Maddy Owens did not resent laughter, provided it was the laughter of equals. It had taken him a while to find himself in the New World. There had been almost an embarrassment of riches. No one in Liverpool, for instance, rich enough to own a large motor car, would have left it quite alone with the motor running; at least one servant would have been on hand. Maddy Owens at once availed himself of the opportunity to drive off the first motor car he thus came upon. The only trouble was, he had not yet had an opportunity to learn to drive: nor did he find one in Sing Sing. What he did find in Sing Sing were a lot of contacts which proved very useful when he got out, and these, in turn, provided him with contacts which proved also useful when he went back in.

He also learned that, although it made good sense to strike out at those who were big and stupid and menacing (strike, and slink swiftly away) and—above all—without important connections—it was equally good sense never to strike out at guards. So, in the land of opportunity, his first real appointment was as a trusty.

It was not at all bad. The State gave you food and housing and a chance to make good and save money; true, the State did not willingly give you *all* these things, but Maddy had already learned an important principle: "Don't bother The Government with bookkeeping." If there were people in the tiers at Sing Sing who wanted to stick quills up their noses, why, Maddy (who had his contacts, let it be remembered) would for a price supply the quills. And, for a price, he would also supply the funny powders that went, first, into the quills, and, next, up the noses.

And so on. And so on.

"Do ye gnaw what I think?" he asked a cellmate.

"Whaddaya t'think, Maddy?"

Owen revealed the thought. "I might maybe open a poob when I get out."

"A what?"

"A pooblic house. A *sloon*, ye cahl it."

The cellmate looked at him. The year was 1919. "Aintcha nevva hoyda Prohi*bition*?"

Maddy had heard of it. He had merely not clearly understood what it meant, nor had he—until then—bothered to try to understand. The cellmate explained it to him. Something about stricter licensing laws, it seemed. Details. Not very important. He shrugged. "Ah, well, then I might maybe open a shebeen. A blind *pig*." Antrim Annie, the fattest tart in Liverpool, whose lover he had briefly been, *she* had kept one. Instead of people coming in the front door during regular hours for beer at regular prices, they simply came in the back door at irregular hours for beer at irregular prices. In a way it was six of one and half-a-dozen of the other. Clearly he had not clearly understood the full implications of the 18th Amendment, but, then, in 1919 . . . and even in 1920, when it had come into effect . . . very few people had.

Maddy understood some few things, though. He knew that you needed a place with more than one way in and out. He knew that you needed a supply of beer. He knew that you had to know whom you could expect to pay you on pay day when they said they would pay you on pay day, and whom you had to tap smartly on the chin . . . or in the stomach . . . or at the temple . . . if they protested your lack of trust or otherwise acted boisterously. He knew that you had to have your own pay day for the police.

And he also knew that although baseball was not a champion game the way cricket was, a cricket bat behind the bar was only a curiosity and a conversation piece, whereas a baseball bat was a very useful implement indeed.

Later, "Where we gunna *get* beer?" one prospective partner asked.

"Where we gunna get *beer*?"

Maddy told him not to be such a croaker. Didn't every farmer have his own malt-house for making his own beer? Eventually, of course, he learned that, whatever might once have been the case in England's sometimes green and pleasant land, *no*: every farmer in the States of New York, New Jersey, and Connecticut did not have his own malt-house and make his own beer; in fact, precious damned few did. But observe the virtue of the valor of ignorance. Long before he fully found this out Maddy had found some farms which were among the precious few. And by the time he learned what good luck had been his, it no longer mattered, the money had come in fast enough to make the farm-house supplies obsolete.

It had also made his status as keeper of a blind pig, soonly known as a speakeasy, obsolete. Why bother supplying the cus-

tomer with pints when you could supply his suppliers with gallons? Maddy's ideas were often fearfully imprecise, one would
say, but he had them so often ahead of time that by the time
imprecisions might have come rising up to bother someone else,
it no longer mattered. Anyway, it no longer mattered to Maddy.
Was there a shortage of, say, rum? Well, go buy *some*! Buy some
where? Where they made it, of course. Uh—*Jamaica*! Just go to
Jamaica, buy rum, bring it *back*. In Jamaica, sure enough! They
had it and they would sell it! The great wave of buying was yet
to begin, business was still as usual. And, "Bring it back," ah yes.
But, ah, *where*? Details, Maddy Owens said. Details. The Coast
Guard was already beginning to stir, to be, if not *semper*, at least
somewhat, *paratus*. It alerted its patrols off the coast of Florida, a logical bringing-in place. Maddy Owens, however, didn't
know anything about Florida. He thought the Connecticut shore
of Long Island Sound seemed like a logical place to Bring It In.
And the Coast Guard had not blockaded the Connecticut shore of
Long Island Sound.

Not yet.

And so it went.

And *went* and went.

And went, and went, and went.

There was, for instance, the Ziggetty Gang.

There had once been, it was said, in New Brunswick, New
Jersey, a Hungarian . . . a*n* Hungarian? . . . surely it would matter
not even to another Hungarian . . . named Szigeti, give or take a *g*
or a *t* . . . but he had vanished, quite vanished; drowned in a vat of
goulash, perhaps. (There were *lots* of Hungarians in New Brunswick. To spare.) The Ziggetty Gang, a one-hundred percent New
Jersey outfit, had done some careful calculating. They had figured out, with Finno-Ugrian craft and cunning, that supplies of
good whiskey, either for cutting and flavoring, or even—though
ruinously expensive—for drinking straight, were gradually running out in the U. States. And, and what was perhaps much
more to the point, the price of such supplies as remained was
rising rapidly. Adam Smith may have told them that this would

continue to happen. Only maybe not. Anyway the Ziggetty Gang had also figured it out that, not a million miles north of New Jersey, in fact probably straight up via New York *State*, was another, neighboring nation, where there was all the real whiskey you could want. And where you could buy all you could pay for. The Ziggetty Gang had figured it out that you could buy blankets in Canada and then stash most of the blankets someplace for the time being and just keep enough blankets to camouflage the whiskey and then, with the documents for the blankets, you could bring the whiskey into the United States. At about half-a-dozen different border points at once. So no one would catch wise. And then the trucks carrying the blanket-covered whiskey would all meet in a very large stable, which had once housed mules for the late Erie Canal's feeder lines, in the dead, dead canal port of Herculaneum, New York. Where *no*body went, anymore. Where the cargo would be unladen, the Canadian trucks and their drivers sent back to Canada, and the Ziggetty Gang would take over *in toto*.

Everything worked out just fine . . . up to a point. *Who* told the Feds, who? Because, scarcely had the last of the Canucks been paid off and sent on their way back to the North Pole when a squad of U.S. Department of Justice men appeared out of the woods, or the woodwork, and arrested the entire Gang and hauled them way in several large touring cars (complete with leather flaps and isenglass windows). Well, the possibility of this happening, though not entirely unexpected, had not been entirely dismissed; so on route to pokey a deal was made. The Feds were paid off. *Plenty.* The money was collected by their captain, a rather short and spare man with a funny accent.

(Well . . . funny, if you didn't happen to hail from New Brunswick, New Jersey.) The Zigs went back to the barn (and the whiskey) bucketty-bucketty.

The whiskey, alas, was no longer there.

Neither was anything else, except some old mule turds. Neither was any*one* else there.

The Zigs brooded about this for a while. Then they started

asking questions.

Conceive the astonishment of Mr. Mathew Owens, who had lately gone into the business of importing blankets from Canada, where they make such good blankets, when a group of men, all heavily-armed, burst into his warehouse near Canal Street, and (he said) began shooting. Naturally, Mr. Owens and his assistants moved to protect their property, and started shooting back. Home team won: the police were agreed that a merchant is entitled to defend himself against attempted armed robbery— and if the police were at all surprised that the merchant's weapons consisted in large part of new-fangled arms called "blooey-guns," the police did not say so to the press—and the courts were not bothered with calls to prosecute. (The blooey-gun was a sawed-off shotgun which fired shells whose shot-content had been first, removed; second, melted down and reformed into one solid shell; and third, replaced in the shell, which was re-sealed. The blooey-gun, excellent as it was for close—very close—firing, was subsequently declared to be illegal; but at the time no one bothered with such technicalities. No one, that is, with good connections.)

And that was the end of the Ziggetty Gang.

However well, though, Maddy Owens may have planned, still, still, sometimes demand *would* outstrip supply; there would simply not be time to bring supplies up from the warm south or down from the frozen north. Sometimes you had to buy supplies from your competitors. Sometimes your competitors got shirty, or greedy, and either asked too much or simply wouldn't sell at all. Sometimes their previous conduct had been such as to make offers of payment contraindicated. In which case—

A man is driving a well-laden truck along a lonely road at night. (At that time all roads tended to be lonely at night.) A car drives alongside and signals the driver to stop. The driver does not stop. The car falls back . . .back . . . back almost to the tail of the truck. Someone, not the driver of the car, gets out of the car, which is still in motion, climbs onto the back of the truck, unrolls a blanket (Re*member*? *Blank*ets?), climbs forward on top of the truck and drapes the blanket in front of the windshield. The truck's driver, not being gifted with x-ray eyes, perforce stops the truck, is persuaded to turn the wheel over to others—

—the truck then proceeds to make deliveries for Mr. Maddy Owens. And Associates.

This fairly simple system of getting supplies came to be known as "high-jacking." (Origin obscure.)

Now, as for Associates. One of Maddy Owens's greatest gifts was that he willingly realized that he couldn't own it all. Many an otherwise well-gifted man failed to realize this sort of thing. And attempted it. Stanford White, for example, thought that he could seduce all the pretty young girls in New York. Joseph Elwell, author of *Elwell on Bridge*, thought that he could commit adultery with the wives of all his bridge partners. Dion O'Bannion believed that he could insult all the Sicilians in Chicago. It was the sincere impression of the Honorable Francis F. Flaherty that he could (if he only tried hard enough) drink up all the liquor in Hackamack County, all by himself. And many and many a man, here and there throughout the Land of the Free, assumed that if he only had vision, gumption, a gang, and enough git-up-and-go, he could control all the bootlegging in his own part of the country. Maddy Owens had never entertained such delusions, whether of glandeur or grandeur. He had never in so many words said that Cooperation is the Soul of Commerce. But he had demonstrated that such was indeed his faith.

When so many of our State Legislatures devised and outlawed a crime which was called Criminal Syndicalism, they did not at any time move to include such businessmen as, say, Alphonse Capone. Or Madoc Owens. Which just goes to show.

"Boy, nevva saw no spread like dthis onna table when *I* was a kid," one of his co-partners, host for the evening, observed one night.

"Nor I. Nor I, Albert, me lod," said Maddy Owens. "Lucky if we had bread-and-drippings, we were. Or booble-and-squeak."

"Bubble-and-squeak!" exclaimed his host. "Whut's *dthat*?"

Maddy waved his hand to help thought. He was not used to being asked for recipes. "Oh . . . Mostly moshed potatoes and cobbage," he said, after a moment. "You put it in a frying-pon. And, as it gets hot, it boobles. And it squeaks."

Everybody laughed. "Say, that's a good one!" exclaimed another guest, one Robert Boykin, attorney-at-law. "'Bubble-and-squeak'!"

Maddy smiled, tucked his linen napkin into his shirt collar. "*Oh* yes. And if we could ever get fish-and-chips, or baked beans on tawst, oh my. Thot was *re*ally a treat! Thot meant the old Dod was *re*ally in the mooney."

Everybody laughed again. "'Baked beans on toast,' fr crying out loud! Didja get dthat, Flossy?"

"Well, Albert. And everybody. I hope you'll like evrything *here* tonight. Mary is a *very* good cook. But I made the *pies* my*self*. So I particularly hope that you like *them*," the hostess said. She turned to the chief guest. "And I made a point, Mr. Owens, of adding some cloves to the *ap*ple pie, because I know that's how they *make* them in England."

Mr. Owens was pleased to the point of being touched. "Well, thank ye very *mooch*, Mrs.," he said.

The host was himself surprised. "Say, howdja know *dthat*, Flah?"

His wife, flushed with pleasure, said, "Why . . . *Al*bert . . . don't you re*mem*ber? My *grand*father was born in England—well, *one* of them was. The other came right off the pickle-boat from Dutch-land, same as yours. He was from—the *Eng*lish one, I mean—he was from *York*-shyre."

Eyes swung to Mr. Owens. Who responded by saying, "*Oh* yes. Good old Yorkshur. Right."

The host smirked, pleased, now, in every possible way: the big spread on the table, the nice wife who had thought of everything, and now: having Yorkshire confirmed as being indeed in England. He looked around and said, "Ha bout summa dthis *wine*, now? Befaw we *staht*? Dthis is nunna dthis red ink the Guineas make, ya know; dthis is from *France*. Huh? Some wine, Maddy? Sonny Boy?"

Madoc Owens nodded, held up his glass. But Robert Boykin asked, "Well, now, but aren't *you* going to take a seat, Mrs. Stoltz?"

Mrs. Stoltz smoothed her hands on the organdy apron which partly covered her black silk dress, and she shook her head. "*Oh* no. Thank you very *much* for thinking of me, Mr. Boykin. But I am going to eat supper with the *chil*dren. I know *some* families, well, there is the mother having herself a good time with her *guests*, and well where are the *chil*dren? Why, eating all by themselves. Alone! Or with the *governess*! Or the *maid*! Well, I just don't believe in that. And of course we can't really have them down *here*, disturbing the conversation with their little-childish *babb*ling. So. If you will kindly ex*cuse* me? And—Albert?—if you *need* me for anything? You can always ring the bell."

"Uhright," said her lord, indulgently. "Here! Take summa dthe *wine*?"

"Well . . . just a taste now . . . *Al*-bert! Do you want to get me *drunk*?"

But not quite yet was she allowed to take her departure. Maddy reached into his pocket and came out with things which clinked and shined. "Here, now, Mrs., give these to the children," he said; "tell them it's from Ooncle Owens. To poot in kiddy-bonk."

And, ever so swiftly, Boykin did the same. Mrs. Florence Stoltz glanced at her husband. He smiled a small smile and nodded a small nod. "Why— Thank you both so *much*! Twenty-dollar *gold*-pieces! Oh, they'll both be *thrill*ed!"

"Teach um ta be t'thrifty," said the old Dad. And so, in another moment, gold in one hand, wine in the other, she was gone. Albert cast another appreciative look around at sideboard and hot-trays. Then he said to Mary's niece, name known only to Mary, who was despite (or perhaps because of) minimal knowledge of English waiting on table tonight. "Okay," he said, with a nod, "staht dishin it out, goylie!"

The ballet, the novels of Sinclair Lewis or Thornton Wilder, the theater, the philosophies of Émile Coué and Bertrand Russell, the economic theories of John Maynard Keynes or for that matter Roger Babson, not one of these were even mentioned.

None of the three had been bred up as a delicate feeder, so the chief sounds for quite a while were those of mastication and gobbling. Eructation and flatulence would come later. The stuffed olives, plain green olives and wrinkled black "Greek" olives came first, followed by celery sticks inlaid with cream cheese and olives, or, for those who had perhaps had enough of olives, plain old cream cheese, plus cream cheese with chives. There were pickled tomatoes, too. Cole slaw. Then there was soup; good solid chicken soup, made with entire chickens, with onions and fresh dill. And dumplings. (Chicken *feet*, too, had been employed, to "strengthen" the broth, the feet well cleaned and then dipped in scalding water to loosen the skin, which, with a few deft digs of her small knife, Mary had peeled off like so much glove. She had soon learned that in America, unlike her native Banat, the chicken feet themselves were removed before the soup went to the high table, so she ate them herself, with only, at first, a shrug, and always, with many a slobber and a smack.)

There were also a few marrow-bones. Boykin alone spread the marrow on bits of bread; the others simply sucked the succulent stuff out.

It was after his second helping of soup and dumplings that Dutch Stoltz asked, "Okay. Repeal. What's the *stawry*?"

Maddy Owens sucked thoughtfully for a second at two of his few contiguous teeth. Then he said, "Let's hear from our legal authority."

"Whuddaya say, Sonny Boy?"

"*Well.*" Their legal authority cleared his throat. "Last week we picked up a report that some bishop, *no*, Albert, *listen*," his host having made a sound of deep disgust, "this is a *Cath*olic bishop. Bishop O'Reilly, somewhere in *Maine*, he was addressing the K. of C., and it so happens he said he hoped that Repeal was on its way—"

"Why dozen he mine his own business? And stick ta re*li*gion?"

Boykin raised his eyebrows in mild incomprehension of the episcopal dereliction, poured himself another glass of the real French wine. "Well, the story probably would've been buried in the local newspaper. *But.* A certain newspaper reporter there. Having been informed that we were *int*erested in such stories. Calls us *up*. And *we* pulled certain strings." His thumb and forefinger met, rubbed. "And the AP and the UP *both* pick the story up. And spread it all over the *South*. With a little *help*. From *us*. And *then* —" Here he held the wineglass up and looked through, and smiled. "*We* found out about a certain *oth*er Catholic bishop. Way out in Ne*bras*ka. With a good German Dutch name. What was it, now? Ah, Steinmetz? Schtrelsinger? *Some*thing like that. And had the AP stringer out *there* interview him. And, of course, *he* said: he agreed with Bishop O'*Reil*ly. A hundred per*cent*. And we saw that *that* got plenty of publicity, with front page attention. All *over* the South." And he smiled into his wine glass once more.

The host scowled. "Whut dthe funk izza point a *dthat*?" he demanded. "Whut good does alla *dthat* do?"

His lawyer's round, rosy lips opened, first, upon a silent, if small, reproach. Then he said, "Why, Albert, don't you have *faith* in the fundamental bigotry of the American people? *I* have faith in the fundamental bigotry of the American people. They *hate* the Catholics in the South. They hate the *Ger*mans in the South. And not *only* in the South. The Protestant churches, why, the, uh, Methodist and Baptist and Presby*ter*ian Protestant churches, not the Lutherans of course, they are scared to *death* of people with 'foreign' names, as they think of it. Outfits, oh, like the National Family Temperance Union, the Anti-Saloon League, why half of their stock in trade has *al*ways consisted of telling the reubens that beer and booze are *foreign* things, Albert. So *I* figure: Hammer the point *home*. Albert. Hammer the point *home*."

But Albert wasn't entirely prepared to allow the point to be hammered home. Quite yet. "My great-*grann*mudtha?" he said, "*she* was an Old-Time American. Huh name was Van *Tass*el, fuh Crise sake. Ya know whutchee tell me? When *I* was a kid? She *tell me* that huh fahdtha tell *huh*, dthat dthuh Revulutiona Erry Waw? ya know? The Revolution Erry Waw? The American Revolution Erry *sold*juhs? Dthey fought the goddam Waw on *rum*! fuh Crise sake. Not beer, okay, I grantcha dthat. But *rum* . . ." His voice died away into a growl, then revived. "Alla dthem *Patriots*? A buntcha *rum*dums!"

This long-echoing testimony to the inflammatory powers of The Demon Rum was interrupted as Maddy Owens sucked on another tooth, or, perhaps, the same one. He said, reflectively, "Well, ye gnaw, Albert, the boy is right. What was it beat Al Smith? Nought the Tariff issue: The *Wet* issue. And the Catholic, the Religious, issue. In peoples' minds: the same thing. Foony thing, ye gnaw. I remember, in Liverpool? The Orangemen, they would have the great parade, ye gnaw, on Boyne Day. Big banners. *Big* banners." He gestured. Then he quoted. "'Gnaw Pawpery.' And 'Temperance'. And more o' the same. 'Gnaw Pawpery' and 'Temperance' and 'Temperance,' till ye'd have it cooming out o' ye're ahss-hawl, 'Temperance.' And *then*, ye gnaw, and then they'd all turn out to the Protestant poobs and *drink*? My word! Till they were rawling in gooter." He shook his head, fondly reminiscent.

His host and partner had listened in silence, if without enthusiasm. He next said: "Yeah, well. Still. I dun*no*. Ya know whut I *do* know, though?" he asked, in a burst of emphatic speech. His guests shook their heads. *What* did he know?

But there was an interruption. Mary's niece, glossy with sweat and incomprehension, had felt that the next step of the dinner had waited long enough: who knew but that was what the big boss-American was now, so obviously, angry about? She took a heavy step forward. "You, meat—now?" she asked.

Albert Stoltz, suddenly awakened to his duties as host, said,

"Uh—*yeah*. Yuh cn bring in dthe meat now. Good goyl," he added, as one who praises the dog who drops the slippers at one's feet. And as she proceeded to deliver up a giant turkey . . . an enormous ham . . . and a vast standing rib-roast of beef . . . he said, "I'll tellya whut I *do* know. Whut I *hear*. I hear that some *banker*? Up in *Bawston*? Uh, his name, his name, his name is, uh, *Kennedy*? Joe *Kennedy*? I hear he's, all of a sudden, now, he's buyin up stock inna *bottle* cumpnies? Whuddaya *want*, Maddy? Summa everyt'thing?" He stood up and posed with the carving tools.

Madoc Owens considered. Then he nodded. "Soom of everything," he agreed. "Ah, ye did right not to have mooton, Albert. Ye can't *get* good mooton in America. Dawn't *gnaw* why," he said, gently shaking his head.

"One of life's little mysteries," Sonny Boy Boykin said, lightly, looking on.

"The hom is fine," Madoc observed, as slices of it piled up on his plate. "The chicken is fine. The beef is fine. Even the lomb is not bod. The toorkey is chompion. But not the mooton. Domn foony thing." Abruptly, he somewhat changed the subject. "Ah, but there is nothing like a good home-cooked dinner at home. The best restaurant meal is not equal to it. Eh, Bobsey, boy?"

"Mm-*hm*!"

For a long while the sounds of grazing were all that was heard—except that, from the kitchen, besides the occasional clatter of plates and pots and pans, the quaint exotic strains of the Tastie Yeast Jesters oozed forth from the radio for the amusement of Mary. Then Dutch Stoltz said, his mouth only partly full of prime beef, "Well, dthat's whut *I* t'think. A big money man in *Bawston* stahts buyin up *bottle* cumpnies, whut *faw*? Alluvva sudden? *I* t'think he's gotta *know* sumpthin. I mean, fuh *whut*? Orange *Crush*? *Nephi*? *Moxie*? *Sasparella*? Naah. . . "

He gave his head a scornful shake. He swallowed. Maddy Owens reached over and helped himself to an especially fine, crisp, brown piece of turkey skin. Then Stoltz said, "So, whut *I* t'think. *I* t'think: *Re*peal. Is in dthe, like, wind. Be*cause*. If it evva *does* come. Everybody in dthe *country* is gunna go out and staht *buy*in stuff. *Ann.* If y' only make one. *Penny.* On each *bottle.* — Wow."

Mary's niece brought, in relays, the cakes, the custards, the junkets, the jello, and, finally, the famous pies.

Sonny Boy Boykin said, "Well, we are continuing the regular quarterly contributions, via one of our fronts, the Citizens' Law Enforcement Foundation, to the Dry organizations. And, of course, the usual retainers are still being paid out. Don't tell *me*, Albert, that with this Depression still going on, that anybody trying to make both ends meet on a government salary, is going to give our retainers up."

Albert was evidently not going to try to tell him that. Instead he told something to the waitress. "Uhrright, goylie, yuh cn go eatcha own dinna now," he directed. "Fwee *want*cha, we'll *call*ya." He watched her go. He said nothing for a long moment. Then he gave an enormous burp. Then he asked, "An, uh, so, uh, whuttabout dthe broory inspectors? Dthe, uh, *beer*checkers? Hm?"

Sonny Boy shrugged. "Same demands. Dollar a case. For every case of non-de-alcoholised beer they allow to leave the brewery, they want a dollar. Instead of the usual four bits. Harrison won't budge, and neither will any of the others budge. Well, the hell with *them*, Right?"

Stoltz nodded his agreement that this was right. Then, a sudden thought occurring to him, he asked, "An, uh, *hom*much we payin off the Chief a Puhlice?"

Sonny Boy considered a moment. "Two thousand, five hundred dollars per week."

"Dthat's a lodda money, Bobsey."

Bobsey looked up from his pale pink junket, surprised.

"What, 'lot of money'? *That*? Twenty-five hundred dollars a *week*? Why, listen, Albert, that goddamn suds shop brings in a clear profit of *ten thousand dollars a day*! A. Day. *Albert*. Now, just figure that out. Over the course of a *year*. Why, even allowing for unforeseen incidents and holidays, say . . . say, only fifty weeks a year . . . uh, uh, well, say . . . approximately . . . well, that's over three million dollars a *year*, Albert! Why, twenty-five hundred dollars a week is nothing. And twenty-five *thousand* dollars for re-enforcing, for hose re-enforced with copper wire, to get the beer out of the brewery secretly, without having to pass the Fed inspectors and pay them off, is nothing. And—"

Albert sat and listened and from time to time he raised the index finger of his right hand and fingered his broken nose. Then he said, "'*Nothin*' is too much if ya don't get nothin *faw* rit. We pay it fuh pro*tec*tion, don't we? So whut kine a pro*tec*tion y'call it 'f dthey keep bussin open dthe *soors* an bussin up the *hoses*: huh?"

The young lawyer sighed. "Well, you see, we paid the police. We didn't pay the Department of Public Works. We didn't *think* of that. We—" Suddenly, all so very suddenly, Albert Stoltz was not in his seat at the head of the table. He was next to Bobsey Boykin and he was holding him so that he also held the man's left hand whilst crushing the man's right arm and hand against his own body. He was holding the man's left wrist with his own left hand and with his own right hand he was holding a revolver and he was pressing this into the other man's face. It did not look at all well there.

"Well, ya conk sucka!" Dutch shouted, his face scarlet. "Ya liddle *prick*! Why *did*den cha t'think a dthat? I'll kill ya, ya doidy lousy son of a bitch! I'll *kill* ya I'll *kill* ya I'll—" His voice ran down. He stopped short. Bobsey was speaking, whose tones, astonishingly, were perfectly calm. Maddy Owens ate ham, with mustard. *Lots* of mustard.

"Albert," said Bobsey, speaking very softly, "that brewery was registered in the name of our front, old Lawyer Bremen, you know. But then, you know, he took sick, and we had him sign it over to me, because if he died, you know, then the brewery would belong to his *family*. I don't have any *life* insurance, you know, Albert, I couldn't *get* any life insurance because I'm in the rackets—but if I were to die suddenly, Albert, you know, my family *would* in a way collect life insurance because if I were to die suddenly, Albert, the brewery would belong to *my* family,

Albert. . . "

The Dutchman had already calmed down. He smiled. The revolver suddenly disappeared. He threw his arms around Boykin's shoulders. "Why, Bobsey," he said, affectionately; "why, Sonny Boy," he said, "ya know dthat I wouldn't hoyt a hair on ya head," he said.

Maddy Owens looked up and smiled at both of them. "This is great cahfee," he commented. "The cahfee in America is chompion. But not the tea, now. Cahn't *get* good tea in America. Dawn't gnaw why."

Bobsey Boykin wiped his forehead with his heavy linen napkin. "Anyway," he said, calmly, "*one* of the hoses is still pumping."

Dutch Stoltz cleared his throat. Obviously he was going to speak. The others looked and listened. "Let's alla vus eata lotta dthe *pie*, now," he said. "Udda wise Flossie's *feel*ins would be hoyt. . . "

CHAPTER ELEVEN

The Judge Boodle family was one of the older families of Yokums and the Judge's father, "Old Ben" Boodle, was still remembered, although it would perhaps be an exaggeration to say that he was still remembered fondly. The local press of course referred to him, on those occasions when reference was necessary, as "the late Magistrate Benjamin Boodle," and indeed a portrait of him in judicial robes was in existence: it hung, in fact, in the living room (Grandma Boodle still called it the parlor) of the family home on Jersey Street: but, not only was it said by some scornful (possibly jealous) few, that the portrait had been painted very posthumously and from a tintype, they also denied that "Magistrate Boodle" had ever worn robes in either an official or an unofficial capacity. Had he even been a J.P.? Some said Yes. Some said No.

"What he was," the No-sayers said, and sometimes they said it with a grim sneer or snort, "he was the *Hog* Warden, that's what he was. Sure!"

This antique and obsolete office entitled, if indeed it did not require, its holder to patrol the then-unpaved streets of the (then) Village of Yokums with a stout robe as, so to speak, badge, or, certainly, equipment, of office: did he see "any Pig, Hog, Sow, Boar, Shoat, Gilt, or other Swine running at large in violation of the aforesaid Ordinance," he was "then and there or at such other time as might be convenient to captivate the same and retain it in such Pound or other safe place as he shall provide" and to charge a mulct or fine, ranging from five to twenty-five cents (depending on size) and moreover to obtain a fee of five cents per day for the animal's upkeep. If these sums accumulated to the amount of one dollar, the hog was sold at auction and the proceeds divided equally between the warden and the village.

It was even said (by the same croakers, of course) that when business was slow, "Old Ben" (or "Boar-Pig Ben") was not above opening a gate or removing a fence-rail in order to let the hog(s) *out*.

And sometimes the libel was even embroidered to say that if Warden Boodle was seen prowling the streets and alleys, "the wild Irish kids" would "whistle their hogs home"—and that sometimes they would even pelt him with clods of dirt, or even nastier substances.

Ben Franklin Boodle may not have been, exactly, a magistrate: but his son was certainly a judge, and *his* name was— or had been—Winfield Scott Hancock Boodle. Who remembers General Hancock? A brilliant record in the Civil War he did have and the Democrats did nominate him for the national Presidency and the newspaper reporters did ask him how he stood on the tariff and he did say . . .didn't he? and if he did not, everybody believed that he did: "The *tariff*? *That's a local issue.*" Garfield won. The general's namesake was always careful with reporters (not that any of them ever asked him how *he* stood on the tariff), he was always careful to point out that, as his full name was too long, it should be set down merely as Winfield Scott Boodle, "—or just plain Judge Winfield S. Boodle." And if any new reporter was dumb enough to ask, "Why not Winfield S. H. Boodle, Judge?" His Honor would explain, "Some very low-type minds find the letters 'S.H.' suggestive, young man."

"Oh, uh."

"*That's* why."

The Judge had a grey face and a long nose and, owing to a nervous condition of long standing, suffered from a severe convulsive facial tic. Experienced lawyers had to caution inexperienced clients not to stare at him.

"Court will take a brief recess. Five minutes, huh*hunk*," as Court cleared its throat. As the door closed on the robes:

Lawyer: Say, didn't I *warn* you not to *stare* attum?

Client: Hey, I didn't *stare* attum. I ws just lookin um in the eye. Show that I got nothin ta *hide*.

Lawyer: Well, *don't* look him in the eye! Or he's liable t' throw the *book* atcha. Whether you got nothing to hide or *not*.

Client: Well, whut *makes* him like that?

Lawyer: I *told* you. He's *nervous*.

Client: *He's* nervous? *He's* nervous? Say what does he got ta be nervous about?

Clerk: Awe rise, Onnable Caught.

The Honorable Court had told Bill Bomberg, when Bill Bomberg was still a cub reporter, "Any time you have any questions, young man, Mr. Om Bomberg, just come right into my chambers and ask me. Ask me personally. Always glad to be of help to The Press. *Glad* to." Which was more or less true. His Honor may not have been a *very* nice man, but as long as no suggestion was made by The Press that his salary be reduced, he *was* glad to be of help.

Police Officer O'Donavan: And inside the suitcase I find six bottles a whiskey.

The Court: Witness has no doubt as to its being whiskey?

Witness: The labbatory says it was whiskey. Judge.

Prosecuting Attorney: Ask leavetenter laboratory report as evidence. YrHonor.

Defense Attorney: (Nothing)

The Court: ... ordered ...

The Court: Well . . . Novack. Seen you here before. Haven't I. Seen you here before. Several times. *Many* times. Seen *you* here before. Novack. Given you more than one break. Fine way you reward The Court's kindness. Rotgut whiskey. *Rotgut* whiskey. Novack. The law of the land, means nothing to you. *Awful stuff.* Don't know how you think you can get away with it, time after time. Impoverishing the poor, can't buy *milk* for their children. Breaking up *homes. Awful* thing. Patience of The Court exhausted. *So—*

The Court reached to pick up a document. The Court's hand

seemed to give a slight leap, to close convulsively upon the empty air. The face went into a flurry. Eyes blinked, mouth quivered, nose twitched, cheeks danced—

Everybody carefully looked everywhere else.

"Court will take a brief recess. Five minutes, huh*hunk*."

The Judge made sounds of vague assent as Bill came into his chambers after him. There was a newspaper and a Zane Grey novel on the desk. Neither one looked very new, or very looked-at. Inside the desk was something else. The neck of the bottle clinked against the glass. The Judge's teeth clinked against the judge's teeth, then against the glass. The Judge gave a loud sigh. Then he asked, "You got a medical problem, Mr. Um Bomberg?"

Bill had been there before.

"Well, a very *slight* one, Your Honor." He gave a stage cough.

"Then let me leave to give you a very slight prescription of *spiritus frumenti*. Oh, yeah. *This* is no rotgut. This is good, sound rye whiskey. Pre-War. Legal, of course, perfectly *leg*al. Medical script. My doctor. Nervous condition, *on*-ly thing that helps. In the long run. Bromides: no help at all. People don't know. Only nother jurist could know. Strain a the Bench. Day in Day out . . ." The Judge's voice ran down. He gave another long sigh. He made another few several clinks, but this time his teeth were silent.

"What I wanted to ask, Your Honor. Not asking as a reporter. Case of Renzo Washington."

Judge Boodle frowned slightly. Then he nodded rapidly. His face was almost composed. "*Not* as a reporter. No no. Course not. Couldn't print it. Family newspaper. Huh*hunk*. Well. Whatabout it?"

Bill explained that the very respectable Colored woman who did his shirts happened to be the common-law *Mrs.* Renzo Washington. The Prosecutrix. And, also, had happened to have second thoughts.

"And asked you to Use your Influence on Old Judge Boodle, eh?"

Bill faintly smiled his recognition of the judicial good will. "Something like that. She said that she took it to the Lord in

Prayer—"

"Too bad her *hus*band, so-called, too bad *he* didn't take it to the Lord in prayer. Instead of taking it where he *did* take it. Well. Don't mean to sound in any way shape or form sacrah *lige*ous. Um. Uh. Oh yeah. And how old is the *girl*?"

Bill said that he thought that Cleo's daughter was either twelve or thirteen. He said he could look it up. The Judge shook both head and hand. "Thirteen. Maybe *four*teen. *They* don't know how old they are. Half the time. Fourteen. Same as eighteen with us. *And*. Half the time they think, they get a woman, woman has a girl, a daughter, think the girl comes *with* the woman. Do as they *please*, they think. Mind you, though. Poor *Whites*? Just as bad. *Worse*. Fact. Well. Mother a good respectable church-going Colored woman? Kay. She is willing to drop it, *Court* is willing to drop it. Favor to *you*, Mr. Awm Bomberg."

"Thank you, Judge."

The Judge shook his hand. "Getting back now. Time and tide and the court calendar, *ho*yeah." Suddenly the judicial face crumpled. "Oh Christ. Oh God. Sixty-eight years old, Bomberg. Two more years: retirement. Don't have a penny. Not a button. Hoped to my God *rest,* on the beach. *Flor*ida. Put it all in *reel* a state. Oh lost my *shirt*. The rest went in The Market. Every goddamn cent, Bomberg. Xept for my salary, don't have *shit*!" Without another word he turned and shambled rapidly out of the room.

Clerk: Awe rise, Onnable Caught.

Court: . . . right. Novack. Stand up. October. Soon be Christmas. Court's present to you, Novack: temper justice with mercy. Know you have wife and family. Turn over new leaf. Get honest, uh, honest work. Get—

The Judge's weary small face went vacant. Then it began to twitch. Then it turned to the clock. The clock ticked. Otherwise the stuffy courtroom was quite silent. The face (Bomberg stole a swift glance) was in agony. But it was too soon for another "brief recess." Much too soon. And how soon was retirement on the tiny pension? Not soon enough. And yet, also: much too soon.

CHAPTER TWELVE

Elmer was out on the streets again. He had hoped to avoid coming home from school altogether that afternoon, but nature had caught up with him and frustrated those plans: and whom did he find at home, much to his surprise, for relatives from The Other Side of the Family were seldom seen there, but his father's sister Aunt Neddie's husband Uncle Bob.

"Ah here he is *now*," said Uncle Bob. "Cuhmere Elmer, we're *talkin* abowtcha."

"I gotta go t' dthe bat'throom," said Elmer, invoking sanctuary. Though not, of course, for long. Almost enviously he regarded the peeling brown paint on the narrow walls; much as he would have liked to have remained there, his presence unknown and unsuspected, his person unmolested, to try out at leisure some new fantasy, some new technique, once the mere necessity of urinating was out of the way. But it was not to be. With a sigh he placed his peter back in his pants, pulled the chain, went out.

"Uhright," said Uncle Bob, giving his head a prefatory jerk. Elmer's mother repeated the gesture. "Uhright. Yuh mudder's ulweeze comin over ann bellyachin," he said to Elmer, just as though his mother was not there and listening and glaring, furiously, at them. "Gettin dthe Ole *Lady* all wuhyked up, ann dthen dthe resta vus haft a suffa. She wantsta know, hoccome we don't *do* sumpin faw yuz. Uhright. So we *ah* gunna do sumpin faw yuz."

His mother said, looking at the wall with rage, "Bob is the only one a the whole *bunch* who's got *any* human feelings."

"I speak ta dthe *lannl*awd," Uncle Bob went on, waving aside the compliment and the interruption. "I *speak* ta ya lannlawd. I tellum, 'Lucano, whut dthe hell izza sense a tawkin about e*vict*in um. Whut dthe hell ya gunna gain by dthat. Either dthe place is gunn a stay empty,' I tellum, 'aw even if ya *do* rent it, ya gunna hafta pain it fuhyst, nen ya gunna hafta give a munce concession onna *rent*, aintcha. Ann nen ya gunna hafta fix *dthis* an ya gunna hafta fix *dthat*, becuz dthe way t' things *ahh*, nowadays, anybody who's *got* some money ta pay rent, uh, dthey cn pick ann, uh, *choose*. So, all in *all*, Lucano,' I tellum, 'it's gunna cawss ya *maw* dthen two munce rent. Ya gunna hafta pay dthe *Mah*shall fa su-hyvin dthe papers, even, ya wanna evictum. So be sensible. Ann just don't col*leck* dthe rent fa two munce, becuz dthey ainn *got* it,' I tullum. So he say, 'Okay.' Dthe Guinea bastid," Uncle Bob wound up, dismissing the mercy of Mr. Lucano, who had chosen to pay his savings earned by standing on his feet twelve hours a day cutting hair, to the mortgage department of the bank instead of to bootleggers or bookmakers; a lesson to *him*, no doubt.

"Thank you, Bob," Elmer's mother said, with a deep sniffle. "You're the only decent *one* a thum."

Uncle Bob's benevolence, however, was not yet finished. He gathered up their total attention with his small grey eyes, and drew forth from one pocket two one-dollar bills and some small change. "Ann dthis is faw dthe gas ann the yelectricidy," he said. "Yeah, yeah, yeah. I know yowe um maw. But dthissl keepum from tuhynin it *awf*, fa while. *Now*," he said, suddenly, turning to Elmer. Who went stiff, and calculated the distance to the door, *Now* being his own father's signal that he was about to take his belt off and give Elmer the strap. However, such was not the case at the moment, with Uncle Bob.

"Whut dthey say, whut dthe resta dthe Famly say, dthey say ya gotta quit school ann getta job, Elmer."

And at this Elmer's mother raised her head and gave a great scream of "Nooooo!"

And Uncle Bob half-turned, and in a rather gentle voice (for Uncle Bob, gentle), said the words, "Valley *Brook*?" And Elmer's

mother stopped in mid-breath for another scream and fell absolutely silent.

Valley Brook was the ancient County Alms House and Poor
Farm.

Elmer, his heart cold with shock at hearing the dreaded
name, as well as observing his mother reduced from scream to
silence, felt a sudden surge, nonetheless, of excitement and of
joy. *Leave school and get a job*! why, who was it who did *leave
school and get a job*? Why, The Tough Guys, that was who! And
you saw them, later on, lounging importantly on the street
corners, nodding indulgently as you went by, and they didn't
wear knickers anymore, they wore *long pants*! And they openly
smoked cigarettes! And they spit in the gutter, like grown-ups!
And they spoke, openly and confidently, about Doing *It* to girls—

But a sudden thought spoiled these beatific visions.

"Yeah, Uncle Bob, but gee Uncle Bob, uh, uh—"

Uncle Bob suddenly seemed very tired of it all. "Drop dthe
udda shoe, Elmer," he said.

"But, uh, Uncle *Bob*? I'm not fourteen yet! I couldn't get
working papers. And, uh, the Truant Officer—"

This seemed to revive Uncle Bob. "Wuhykin papers! Dthe
Trune Awfissa! Who's gunna ask ya f' wuhykin papers? Ciddy
Hall? Ann, uh, dthe Trune Awfissa! *He* ain't gunna bahda yuz! Ya
lucky enough ta *get* a job. Dthese days. —Leave *me* worry about
him!"

There was a silence. Broken by Elmer's asking, deferentialy,
confidently, "Where am I gunna get a job, Uncle Bob?"

But this was clearly the wrong question. The mixture of
scorn, command, benevolence, vanished abruptly from Uncle
Bob's face. He opened his mouth. Then he closed it. Then he grew
annoyed. "Hoddoo *I* know where ya gunna get a job? *Look* fuh
one!"

Elmer did not know where he was going to look for one. But
he did know one thing. He knew that he was under no circum-
stances going to remain alone with his mother after Uncle Bob
left. He got up from the kitchen chair as though goosed. And he

said. "I will, I will! I'll start right away. Right now!" And, with nods of farewell which did not involve his looking directly at anyone, he walked quickly out of the house.

Behind him, after the sound of the closing door, he heard Uncle Bob say, in a tone of weary but compulsory approbation, "—lotta moxie. Kid's gotta lotta sand."

And on the thrill of this compliment, Elmer walked out to seek his fortune in the world.

CHAPTER THIRTEEN

Miss Murkle, the Librarian at the front desk, looked up at the sudden clatter of feet. She frowned. All *sorts* of people were taking to coming into the Library these days, many of whom did not seem at all interested in reading the books. Most of them did find their way into the Reference Room, though. (*Not* her department.) True, the Library was warm in the cold weather and cool in the hot weather. But. After all. After *all*. And yet. Still. Even after two pay-cuts, and another one threatened: it *was* A Position. And where could one go look for another? So she merely lifted her eyebrows at these two young people, a young man and a young woman, and touched her index finger to her pursed lips.

"Can we see a map?" the young woman demanded. Yes, really de*man*ded!

"A map! A map!" the young man exclaimed.

"*Shhh . . .*" said Miss Murkle, urgently. She gestured towards the Reference Room.

"A map! Where are the maps? We want to—Oh. In there, Stelle," said the young man. And off they galloped. Miss Murkle shook her head. She gave a long sweeping look around the rotunda. But everything else was in order. There was no one to hiss at, no one to snap fingers at. Miss Murkle sighed, returned to her perusal of the new Edgar Wallace. A*nother* thing about The Position: you could get to read the newest books before they were either catalogued or shelved. The Depression sank out of sight, noisy young people and slouching old ones were forgotten. Miss Murkle, in a police motorcar, drove slowly through the dark streets of Manchester (England). Would they find the Gang Leader? They would. They would. The Inspector was so clever. They would find him.

But, please, Lord: not yet.

If Miss Murkle found The Position more taxing than in the years before, conceive of the problems faced by Miss Showalter, who had been in charge of the Reference Room for *years*. Ever since the Hudson-Fulton Celebration. Sometimes hours used to pass without anybody bothering her at all, leaving her quite free to bring her scrapbooks up to date. Mr. Constantine Leo Maria Fitzhughes was certainly no trouble. Mr. C.L.M. Fitzhughes had vowed to read through the Catholic Encyclopedia entirely, and arrived early every morning to embark on this learned and pious task: it was true that he was a *slow* reader. But he was also a very *silent* one. Another favorite patron of the Reference Room was Miss Eldridge the Elder: so interested in Genealogy! But required no help whatsoever. Only, well, sometimes, well, sometimes to be sure, sometimes Miss Eldridge the Younger would slip in to consult her sister about something; they always did speak in whispers but truth was: their dentures clacked. Clack-clack. Hsis. Hissle. Clack-clack. Shwissshwiss. And after school sometimes the brighter sort of schoolchildren would come in to do research for an assigned project. Miss Showalter always had her scrapbooks put away by then. That hour or two hours: tiring. True.

However, all that was nothing to what she had to put up with nowadays! *Look* at all those *Men*! Sprawling over newspapers! Muttering and mumbling, often *talking* right out *loud*! And she was under more or less *orders* from Mr. Wunck, the Chief Librarian, to let them *be*! "There is a lot of Communist activity going on," Mr. Wunck explained. "These are the times that try men's souls. It is well known that Leneen wrote most of his propaganda in the famous British Library. And I want you to keep an eye out for that sort of thing. Do not provoke any of them. Ah, merely inform me at once." Said Mr. Wunck.

And . . . *well*! What was *this*? People simply *gal*loping in? *Two* of them!

"A map! We want to see—"

"Hsssshhh . . . Please lower your voice," Miss Showalter requested, in her lowest tones. "This is a Library!"

Then! Wouldn't you know it! One of the dozers woke up, asked—loudly—"Say, Miss. Where's Libetty Magazine? Huh?"

And so poor Miss Showalter had to do everything at once. Fortunately the newcomers knew exactly *which* map they wanted: the large-scale City one. So *that* was out of the way. The current *Liberty* was In Use. But the man was just as satisfied with one of the bound volumes. And so, finally, she was able to get back to her scrapbooks.

Oh my.

"See," said Bill, into Stelle's ear, "the first hose came right along here, down here. See?"

"*Yes*," said Stelle. Forgetfully not turning her mouth to Bill's ear.

"Hsssshhh!"

Stelle threw the old dragon an apologetic smile. And, into Bill's ear, she said, low-voiced, "And here's where they found the second one." It was odd the way his hair grew, there, on the back of his neck. Nice, though. Somehow. And he smelled faintly of bay rum. And, faintly, of himself. Also, somehow, *nice*. Stelle had never really noticed any of these things before.

"Oh I wish it were a more modern map," Mrs. Mary Mabel Moomaw moaned, in the N.F.T.U. office. "Still, still, we must do the best we can. Now. Let us *think*. Where was the first hose *found*? What do *you* think, Birdie?"

Birdie's little face screwed up into a tight ball of unhappiness. "Oh I don't even like to *think* of hoses!" she said. "—anymore."

Mary Mabel sympathized. Still. Duty was duty. "Well, dear, but we *must*, you know. We owe it to the Women and Children of the Community. As well, of course," she added, very slightly distastefully, "*the men.*" Birdie shook her head, gave a little gasp. Anxiously, her friend looked up. "Is it very hot? It *is* very hot. More like September than October, today. Do you feel faint? Should we send Herman the Janitor for some nice, cold root beer?"

Birdie's eyes, pressed tight, sprang open. She looked at Mrs. Moomaw somewhat reproachfully. "*Beer!*" she said.

"Hm. Well. Oh yes! The map! *Well!*" She turned her head to it again, spread out on the desk, its sides curling, its Tuscan letters faded with age. "Let, us, *see*. Where shall we be*gin!* What have we here? The Packet Boat Wharf. Well, *no—*"

Memory of a recent slight—to be sure, merely the recent-most—occurred to Captain Clack. "I seen this big fella," he said, "steppin outa this big limma-*zeen.* Ann I sez ta myself, 'Faint heart never won fair business, Raysh.' So I steps up ta him—*big* fella, with a kind a broken nose, clothes onnum that you cd sure bet didn't come from no Sears ann Roebuck—ann I takes off my cap politely ann I says, 'Say you look like a businessman or mannafackcherer,' I says, 'in which case lemme inner duce my-self, because I am the Master, Owner, and Captain a the Packet Boat *Sadie Howell* ann maybe we cn move some freight er cargo fr ya at a good low price.' Ann he give me a kine of a *look* ann then he says, he says ta me, '*Yeah*? Ann whut woodja move fr me? *Whale* oil?' Ann everybuddy busts out laughin, fit ta kill, juss *laughin . . . Thuh* son of a bitch. . . ."

His Chief Engineer, who had perhaps himself experienced a few several slights in his own right in the course of days, gave two grunts, gave his head two emphatic shakes. "*Nem*mine, Captain. Day come, dhey goen sing *dif*runt tune. See plenny in mah Bible, bout boats an ships. Ainn nevva seen nuthin bout trucks. . . "

Captain Clack gazed over the wide waters as he nodded his

agreement. "Be comin ta me on their hands and *knees*," he muttered. "*On their hands and knees!*"

"*Well*," Mrs. Moomaw said, "the first hose was traced between the point *here* and the point *here*. And the *second* one, the one which was found when the *street* caved in, *it* was traced up to, ah," her finger moved, at first slowly, then with growing confidence and speed, "up to *here*." She pursed her lips. Here, very well, then, there. But . . . What of it? What then? And— "What, dear? Hm? What did you say?" For Birdie had smiled, murmured something.

"It says," Birdie pointed, "'Turkey Island.' I never saw it actually on a *map* before. Written *down*. I only heard the people speak of it. 'Tuhykey *Eye*-lin,'" she mimicked the common accent of the region's uneducated; she smiled.

Mary Mabel was encouraged by her assistant's sudden, if mild, good humor. "*Yes*, dear. Evidently it was originally a genuine place-name, not merely a, well, not exactly *slang*, but— Turkey Island. We can almost *see* it from our window, over there. Well . . . see where it *was*. It is of course all dry land now. In-*dus*trialized." Already her mind had half-forgotten about it, her eyes returning to the map, her finger still pressing down where it had been after tracing. Some vague, evanescent thought flitted through her mind, was gone in far less than a second. "The National Cereal Factory is there. About all that *is* there, nowadays, I suppose."

"Yes," said Birdie, equally abstracted. "That malted beverage factory. . ." Her own finger came tracing up the streets, paused. "A garage . . . here. And . . . a garage . . . *here*." A tiny frown-line furrowed the skin above the bridge of her nose. "Oh!" she exclaimed.

"What, dear? *Yes*. *Both* garages . . . they *are* near, they are rather near to Turkey Island. The garages where those shameful people had the illicit bottling plants. Oh!"

Birdie looked up. "What did you—?"

Mary Mabel cleared her throat. "Well. Oh, why. I was just *think*ing. That *some* people. Who did not *know* what kind of *good* people they are, there at the factory. Might be tempted to *think*. Out of *ig*norance. That perhaps the illegal *beer*. Came from *there*. Merely because it is the only brewery one *knows* of. And also because it is so *near*. Not *real*izing, you know, that it is *not that kind of beer*. For *one* thing. To say nothing of, of, how *poor* Mr. *Har*rison and *poor* Dr. *Brow*er, oh what they would *think*. To think that *they* should be suspected!"

Birdie sighed, shaking her head. "Well, *we* won't think of it."

"No, dear. Oh *no*, dear. We will just put it out of our heads."

The map, released, curled itself up in a rush. Mrs. Moomaw reached out to straighten it, but Birdie stopped her. "Mary Mabel, it *is* hot," she said. "And even if Herman the Janitor *did* go to bring us a cold drink it would be warm by the time it got here: well: Almost. So—"

But she did not need to finish her sentence. Mary Mabel nodded. "Yes, it would, Birdie. Well." She looked at the clock. The clock looked at her. "*Well*. Why don't we just put on our hats and go down to Blakewell's? It is always *so* nice and cool inside there. And have a nice, cool soda? Say . . . sarsaparilla? And some of Blakewell's nice French vanilla ice cream? That they make *them*selves? *Mmmm*?" she suggested, temptingly.

Birdie nodded her head rapidly, her little face filled with almost child-like pleasure. "Oh yes! *Could* we?"

They could. And, "*Why*?" asked Mrs. Mary Mabel Moomaw, rhetorically, "*Why* will people put that loathsome *poi*son into their system, when there are so *many*, *whole*some things to drink which are *so* refreshing to the taste?"

But to this of course, there was no answer; Birdie just sighed and shook her head. Artificial cherries bobbing on their straw hats, the two ladies walked out into the corridor together.

"Uh, uh, *no* thanks, I had enough, enough, Francey," said the

Honorable Commissioner of Public Works of Yokums, New Jersey, putting his hand politely over the top of his glass.

His Honor the Mayor of Yokums, N.J., looked at him in amazement. "'Enough'? How, John, how can any one man have enough? Dolly says to me, *too, she* has this absurd concept of there being an 'enough,' and she says to me, the dear good woman, mother of my children, 'Francis, oh, Francis, haven't you had enough?' And my *aunt*, out there, that wonderful woman, my *aunt*, the Sister Superior of City Hall, she no longer even *asks*, you know, John. No. But her disapprobation shows in every move she *makes*. What is 'enough'?"

He lifted the bottle and poised it over his glass. "Is there enough in this," he poured, "to relieve the pressure of people coming, coming, *com*ing, saying, 'Lower my taxes for the sake of Christ Crucified or I won't have a roof over my head in my old age!'? *Is* there? Or is there enough in this," he poured, "to clear my ear of the pressure of people beseeching me every time I walk down the street, 'Ah, Francis, get my man a job or the furniture will be on the sidewalk because there's nothing for the *rent*: and I'll *pray* for you, Francis'? And is there enough in this to pay even *last* month's payment on the house on Laurel Street, where my wife and I and our five children and my white-haired old mother live?" He poured. "*And* the meat *and* the bread *and* the milk *and* the potatoes *and* the clothes *and* the shoes *and* the school fees *and* the school *books* over there at Sacred Heart for those same five children?" He poured. "And as for putting anything aside for their future, and as for the non-amortizing mortgage, may God bless *its* heart, on the summer cottage," he poured, "is *this* enough?" And the payments on the two *cars*—"

He paused a moment in thought. "What else, now? Is it enough for my so-called career? What happened to *that*, would you like to know?—And if you would, John, well, so would *I*, John: so would this be enough for *that*, now?" And he poured. And he drank. And he drank. He drank.

Then he sat a moment, silent. Then he looked around, vaguely. "*Ah* yes. The subpoenas. From the Latin, well, ah, the

Hell with *that*. Let us look upon this map before us, John. And see if we can wonder what the brewer buys one half so precious as the stuff he pipes. And whence. And perhaps whither. And certainly by *whom*. *To* whom. Allow me," he said, with slow, grave courtesy. And did nothing.

The Commissioner of Public Works, by now just a bit uneasy, "Ahm, *Francey*—"

The Mayor's head jerked up. "Yes, Of course. Well, here it is. Here is the city. *Not*. The City of God. The City of Yokums, New Jersey, a town every bit as ugly as its name. Here are its streets. And, underneath the streets, the what? The *sewers*. And in the sewers, what? Why, sir, the *rats*. The *rats*. John. Fat on grain and graft and mash, John, and on the body and blood of the *people*, John. Of this great re *pub* lic. Which is *bound*. Hand and *foot*. By a barbarous and a bloody *law*. John. Which hath cor*rupt*ed them. And shifted the *power*. John. Into the hands of *brig*ands. John. And power tends to corrupt. John. And absolute power? Corrupts absolutely—

"A great historian said that. John. A great *Catholic* historian. John. *Sir* John. His name was. I forget the last name. Ner. Ner mine. John. So, ahm, y'm, lettus look at the *map*. John. Of our fair city. Which hath become a, a, a *laughing*stock. All who see her pass by and jeer. Jibber. Hiss. Throng tumultuously. And ah hoisten the ah hems of their *gar*ments. Looka the ma, ma, uh, thum. Map. John. . ."

John J. Quoyte said, "Yeah, well, yeah, uh, I *know* alla that. Uh. Nothing *new*. I mean, if *this* one doesn't 'take,' then *that* one does. And, uh, as for the map. What is the map gunna tell ya thatcha don't already, uh, *know*, Francey? Where the beer is coming from? Where else *could* it be coming from? If it's *beer*, ya know, well, somebody *brewed* it. And if it was *brewed*. Then it musta been brewed in a, now, brew-ry. And, come on now, Frances, pull ya self tagetha now, *will* ya? After rawl. There *is* only one gahdamn brew-ry inna whole gahdamn *Ciddy*. So, I mean, whuddaya need a *map*— Ah, now, Francey. Ah, fr Crise sake!"

The Mayor sat hunched over the map. His elbow was resting on it. His hand was pressed against his forehead. His eyes wept many tears.

CHAPTER FOURTEEN

Bob Blaine, the Rewrite man, was down on marriage. "Wham, bam, thank you mam," is the only way to do it, he said. "Put on your shoes and go home to your own peace and quiet."

Bill Bomberg eyed him sardonically. "At least you do take your shoes *off*, then. I hadn't suspected you of such a degree of delicacy."

Blaine shrugged, gave a one-sided smirk. "As some wise man once said, 'What is marriage after all but bad words in the daytime and bad smells at night?'"

Off on their shelf, the teletypers clattered away their dole of doom and woe, their tale of optimism and (any day now) Recovery. (Both Depression and Recovery had already gained the status of capital letters.) Some mad, vile old man had confessed to the murder of a dozen children. Some Eastern financier had denounced Federal insurance of savings banks as a Jacobin plot. Mothers who lacked the bribe of food to keep their kids at home now feared to let them go out and play.

"Trouble with you, Blaine," Bill said, "is that your work as Rewrite man has affected your brain. And your body, too."

"It's a pretty good body," said Blaine, aggrieved. "I haven't had any complaints about my body. Before."

Bill gestured this away. "You know what I mean. You are so used to cutting things down to what you think of as basics. But, you know. Marriage isn't *just* sex. Sex isn't just a quick *bang*, pull it out, wipe it off, 'put on your shoes and go home.' There's lots of other nice stuff connected with sex, you know."

Bob Blaine said, "*Ahhh.*" He said, "You've been reading Louisa May Stopes again." Gave a fart and a scornful chuckle and went back to cutting to ribbons the newest reporter's newest story.

Dick Riley, from Sports, had come in and listened silently. He handed Blaine the papers in his hand. "Red Hot Extra," he said. "*Hice*-cool football. Central vs. Heights."

"Bull-y. Just puddit down somewheres."

Riley turned to Bomberg, said, "Ah, I envy *you*, Billy. You roving repawtas, *you*'re the boys that get alla the nookey!"

"Ah, come *on*, now—!"

Riley, lighting a Between the Acts Little Cigar, his mouth occupied, lifted his eyebrows to show that he stood by his statement. Then said, "Never mind, 'Ah, come on now!' Who is it that the buhrieved widows, they grab ahold of their hands and leadum off inta thuh bed-droom, to, uh, like *com*futt them?"

"*Aw*—"

Riley waved his finger horizontally, dismissing the "Aw" as well as other disclaimers. "Some red-hot mamma, she and her boy-friend they have a *fight*? And the *cops* come? *And* the roving repawta? And the cops grab ahold a the boy-friend and take um away ta cool *off*? till *maw*ning? And the lady-friend, she figures, Well, why waste thuh shank a the evening? Ur any *other*, uh, shank, fa that matter?" He clutched an imaginary bathrobe around his skinny midriff, performed a pirouette. "'Come ahn *in*, Mr. Repawta! And I'll, uh, reveal alla the *de*tails. Faw yuh.' *Huh*?"

Blaine said, "Haw Haw!"

"Aw, now, Dick, that hardly ever happens," Bill protested.

Riley pounced. "But it *does, happe*n! In thuh cawse a yuh *wuhyk*. Whereas, in *thuh* cawse a *my* wuhyk. Whuttum *I* gunna do, if *I* get hawny? Hump one a thee athaletes?"

Blaine gestured one of the Little Cigars for himself. "Been known t' happen. Not *you*, Riley, I hastily hasten to say. But, uh, look at that son of a bitch, Lord Alfred Douglas—"

"*You* look attum," said Riley, venomously. "*All* a thum lawds: Limey bastids."

"Yes," said Blaine. "And look what he did to Oscar O'Flahertie

Wilde, a nice Irish boy, for you."

Riley, his interest quickened, asked, exactly what *did* Lord Alfred Douglas do to Oscar Wilde? Blaine instantly replied, "Stabbed him in the back, as you might say."

After a moment, Bill, his face red with laughter, said, "Oh, yeah, but, uh, Bob, I never heard that the noble lord was an athlete—"

Blaine said, "Sure he was! He was a boxer! His father made up the Marquess of Queensbury Rules. Alfred used to wear boxing gloves every time he and Oscar, you-know-what! He was not only athletic, he was an athletic supporter. . . "

But this was by no means as good as the previous quip, and Bill, with a noise of disdain, got up and left. The conversation had gone not quite in circles, but he was left with some thoughts on the semi-initial subject, viz. Sex. Well . . . viz. Marriage. *Marr*iage and Sex. Sex without Marriage he was familiar enough with; Marriage sans Sex he hoped never to encounter at all. "Marriage *and* Sex," he said to himself, in a low, thoughtful voice. "Now and forever, one and inseparable." Which, finally, brought him to something which he now resolved to face: often enough had it popped up in his thoughts: always—before—he had drawn a veil over the thought . . . though perhaps not always immediately over it—What *were* his essential thoughts about Stelle Wilson? To deny that he was attracted to her was to deny that he was attracted to fresh air. Well, sure, you had to breathe: and if you couldn't breathe fresh air you would have to breathe stale. Would this attraction someday grow stale? It didn't, now, seem that it ever could. But common sense told him that it might. He had known passion, love, to turn stale, to turn to lassitude. Even, alas, to disgust. Sometimes in the course of a single evening. Sometimes it had taken longer. Sometimes it had not gone to that extreme. Sometimes he—sometimes she— had folded their tents like the Arabs, and as silently stolen away. And sometimes the break had been noisy indeed. Once—his sole venture into inter-racial romance—a West Indian named Celia, had, first, accused him (unjustly) of attempting to start up again a previous liaison with another woman; had, next, driven him out of the traditional cottage with traditional blows and imprecations; had, lastly, while he was gone, smashed all his glassware and crockery, slashed all of his clothes not then out to wash, and had deposited his pillow in the middle of the bed and had deposited under the pillow a fork with the tines down: an obeah sign one of the most dire.

And had vanished.

As it happened, the damn sign, or curse, had worked, too. For the next co-occupant of the cottage, a part-time waitress named Gladys, who had the most remarkable breasts he had ever seen (they not only turned up at the ends, they turned away from each other as well), took advantage of Bill's absence one afternoon to entertain a gentleman friend. Presumably she had made him free, too, of the remarkable breasts; certainly she had made him free of her other intimate equipment: Bill, coming back earlier than usual, saw them from the far end of the block as they left the cottage for the opposite direction.

Again, the pillow lay in the middle of the bed; this time, however, as he picked it up, he saw no fork. The caller had simply left his signature upon the bed sheet. And the ink was still wet.

Bill had, first, cursed. Then he stripped the sheet off. Then he took all of Gladys's belongings (plus one of his towels, which she had evidently used at the termination of the recent interview), tied and rolled them up in the sheet, tied its corners with knots, and set it on the porch. With her hat on top of it. And while he was still standing on the porch wondering what the Hell to do next, his landlady suddenly appeared. She had, it seemed, received news. Although she had received it late.

"I heard you were keeping a negro woman here," she said.

"I was."

"You'll have to go."

He stared at her. Then he spoke to her more bluntly than he was used to speaking to her. "Why the Hell should *you* care, Mrs. Snyder?" he demanded. "Your River Front Hotel is the biggest goddamn whorehouse in town, and for Christ's sake don't tell me it isn't, because I have patronized it, as well you know."

Her heavily-powdered face was as expressionless as ever. "That's right," she said. "And you may have noticed that all the girls were *White* girls, too."

So, with a shrug, he packed up his things and stowed them in his car and drove to engage a room at the Y while he searched for some other place to live.

But that was a while ago. There wasn't a lot of money available to him nowadays for large-scale dalliance . . . or, for that matter, anything else. He had once established a savings program, but, since then, two pay-cuts had effectively disestablished it. And as for his venture into the Market—Well. He was still working, he was "working every day," he wasn't going hungry, maybe he could af*ford* to get married. *She* was working, too — *Oh* oh. There it came again. And there *It* came again. The picture (mental) of *Stella desnudata*. Was that it, mainly? Was that at the bottom of it? Well, and if it was, so what? Well, and plenty "what" . . . *Dope*, he called himself. And so the same old thoughts about it all, over and over and over again: in whirling circles. Until, finally, he came out where he went in. Which was at Bob Blaine's maxim.

"If you can think of one single reason not to get married," Blaine said (and said and said), "then don't get married."

By this time Bill was home again. He breathed through his mouth as he went up the stairs, trying to ignore the marital cabbage of The People Downstairs—a certain deathblow to romantic notions. He would not think of Stelle. He took off his coat, unbuttoned his vest, sat down in the Morris chair, picked up the copy of *The Bridge of San Luis Rey*, read one line with deep attention, and immediately began to think of Stelle again.

CHAPTER FIFTEEN

Captain Clay and Chief Hotaling had their heads together over their own map. "I stood up all lass night," said Clay, "tryinn a figgya dthis out. Fuhyst awf, natchrally, I figgya: dthe *broory*. Right? Ain't dthat logical? *Buh-*ut. 'En I say, 'Naaa. *Cum*-mon, Caspa; dthat broory is le*git*.' So, dthuh suds musta come from somewhere *else*. *How* it coulda come from somewhere else in the Fuhyst Preet-sinct widthout *my* knowin abowd it, wull, dthis I godda figgya *out*. If it's comin from somewhere else in dthe Fuhyst Preet-sinct . . . it ain't comin from Washinnton, D.C. . . Huhybut *Hoova* ainn sennin it . . . but cha cann' pipe beer only so *fah* . . . Ann I go ova dthe funkin map twenny, fawdy times, Chief. Where could dthey be anutha place where maybe someone was, now, makin beer? *Awe:* Maybe bringin it in from somewhere *else*, ann pipin it out from dthere? . . . if *dthat* makes any sense . . ."

Chief Hotaling grunted. His red, freckled hands, thick-fingered, like a pair of huge spiders, crouched upon the map. Then they began to move about it. "Here's the fuhyst place dthey fine anythin. Ann dthen dthey trace it upta *here*. *Commuhyce* St. Dthuh goddamn guh-*rodge*. And. Layta dthat *night*. Dthey fine some palooka foolin width dthuh *man*hole cuvva. Right . . . *here*. And so if he ann his pals, if dthey wasn't pullin up sa *maw* a dthuh hose— So it musta gone on at leas' as fah as where dthuh *man*hole was . . ." His fingers inched along, along.

He asked, "Alla dthum ole buildings? Been empty since dthuh Wuhyld's *Waw*?"

Captain Clay shook his head. "Naaa," he said. "Naaa. I check um out *good*. Ann Bobby *Morrisey, Fire* Chief Morrisey? *He* check um out good, too. *No*, Chief. Uh. *Uh*. I *tell*ya, Chief. I tellya. Eidtha it comes owda dthe t'thin air, Chief. Ur else it comes owda dthat *broory*, Chief. Legit. Ur *not* legit."

The Chief flung up his hands, looked at the ceiling, veins swelling in his great, thick neck. Then once again he was glaring at Captain Clay. "What? Tcha trying a tell me that dthis ole sissy, Professor Brower? *He*'s inna dthuh rackets?"

"*He* donn' own dthe place, Chief. He's juss like, dthe, now, managin di*rec*ta. *I* donn' t'think he knows his ass from his *el*bow, Chief. *Who* owns dthe place? Well, I haddit lookt up. Of*fi*cially, Chief, dthe, like, owna of record, Chief, is old Lawyer Bremen—"

Chief Hotaling made a face, as though he were at that moment tasting old Christian Jacobus Bremen, Attorney-at-Law, and found him—with his hairless and liver-spotted head, tremulous lower lip, and old-fashioned (and rather dirty) clothes—not at all to his taste, at all, at all.

"Yeah, well, Chief, ya know. Sometimes dthese businesses, dthey, now, change *hands*. Ann ya don't awe ways *know* about it. At the *time*. So I *ast* a rown, Chief, *I* ast a rown. Ann ya might not like whut I got ta tell ya Chief. But *who* is it who awe ways come a rown dthere ann he acts like *he* is dthe boss? A*nudth*a lawyer. Ole Lawyer Bremen, he's, dthey say he's a priddy sick *man*. But dthis *uttha* guy, Chief, he's *young*. Who'd I mean? I mean Mr. Rahbit Boykin. Father is still a nawdinerry duhyt fahma, up in Buhygen County. But the *son*. Well. *You* huhyda *him*, Chief. Been in dthe papers maw dthen *once*, Chief. Sonny Boy Boykin? *You* huhyda *him*, Chief. *You* know whose mout'thpiece *he* is, Chief."

Chief Hotaling's face went, first, grim. Then slack. Then he said, "Son of a *bitch*. . ."

Very, very softly, Captain Casper Clay said, "Well, dthat might *be*, Chief. Dthat might well *be*. Beside dthe point, Chief. *My* guess, Chief: dthat dthis, now, *broory*, Chief? Dthat it, now, in effeck, it belongs to our fellow-townsman, as ya might say. And as ya might callum. Mister, ah, Albert Stoltz? *Dutch*?"

"Son of a *bitch*. . ."

Captain Clay nodded slowly. Perhaps, even, a trifle sadly. "So I dunno whut we do about *dthat*, Chief. Yump. Uh-huh. In *fack*. If he sits inniz own *house* ann if he leans owda his own *window*, Chief, ann, uhm, if dthe wind's in dthe right direction, Chief: he could just about *spit* right onta dthe *roof* of it. Just a*bout*. . ."

In the silence that followed, the voice of a belligerent drunk, becoming less belligerent by the moment, was heard from a few rooms away, protesting that he had his rights.

Chief Hotaling then said, perhaps repetitiously, in a low voice, filled with trouble and with perplexity, "If *I* ain't gettin nuthin, Caspa, ann if *you* ain't gettin nothin, Caspa: Then who in dthuh *Hell*, *is* gettin sumpthin, Caspa?"

Captain Clay lifted a hand and smoothed his silvery hair. He said, "Two t'thousand dolla's a *week*? the sheriff tellya? Fifty-two weeks a *yea'h*? Ann, me, last mont'th I file fa *bank*rupcey? Why, f' two t'thousand dolla's a *yea'h*— Well. That's *my* problum. Well. Who. Yeah. I dun*no* who, Chief. But I do know *one* t'thing, Chief. Whoevva he *is*. He's gotta be *some*body priddy *big*...Chief. . ."

CHAPTER SIXTEEN

The Grand Jury met in the old Federal Building, still popularly called "Federal Hall." After this was later torn down to make room for a much-needed empty lot, many voices were raised declaring it to have been an architectural treasure; it had taken two years to build and two weeks to destroy. But this all lay in the future. The chambers in which the Grand Jury met still held a rather full flavor of what is often called "a more gracious era," but no one in those middle-early days of the Great Depression gave a thought to that. Mouldings? Panelings? Furniture? For all that anybody cared, the Grand Jury might just as well have been meeting in a popcorn warehouse, or a furrier's loft.

In charge of things was Assistant United States Attorney R.C. Spears, a youngish-looking man whose hair was crew-cut: at the time, considered rather daring and dashing.

"I want to make it clear," he said, quasi-apologetically, "that I am not accusing *anyone*. *We* are not accusing anyone. All that I would like to know," he said, a trifle desperately, "is just how more than a mile of four-inch hose could be run—I don't even know if any officials of the City of Yokums had ever *heard* about the hose line before it was publicized. All I'd like to know is this: How is it *poss*ible. That more than a *mile*. Of four-inch *hose*. Could be run under four, city, streets? Without *any* knowledge on the part of city officials? *Or* employees?"

He paused. He gazed around the large, musty, dusty room. But if he was waiting to hear someone pop up and volunteer the information, he was doomed to disappointment.

"More than six thousand *feet* of hose?" he said, pleadingly. "Worth more than 25,000 *dol*lars?" Again, the pause? And, again, the silence. Assistant U.S. Attorney Spears sighed. He said, "Call Isaac Newton Hotaling."

Nothing of what might be supposed to be deeper feelings showed on Iron Ike's great purple face. Nor did any hints of any difficulty in enunciating appear, later, in any public source (such, as it might be, in newspapers): the public utterances of public officials, like those of members of Congress as finally appearing in the *Congressional Record*, being subjected to a process of copy-editorial sand-blasting or steam-cleaning, in which dialects disappear, participles are never left perilously to dangle, *ums* and *ahs* and repetitions are neatly removed like so many warts. So:

"I am informed by the Deputy Assistant Commissioner of Public Works (Hotaling was described in print as having said) that all the sewers in which the hoses were laid were wide enough in diameter so that it would be possible for men to remove a single manhole cover and thread the hose for as great a distance as they wanted to. Suppose the policeman on beat was somewhere else on his post at the time? In such a case, detection would have been impossible."

U.S. Attorney Spears gazed at him with stupefied astonishment. "In other words," he asked, after a moment, "if a policeman saw six thousand feet of hose slithering into a manhole, he would suspect *noth*ing?—unless there was a man attached to it in plain sight?"

This was perhaps unfair, as the six thousand feet represented the total length of all the hoses. Perhaps Iron Ike felt the unfairness of it; at any rate, iron-hard, he said nothing in reply; and Spears did not press for an answer. Instead, he dismissed the Chief, and summoned the Commissioner of Public Works.

"What is your opinion of this hose, Commissioner?"

"It ran downhill," the Commissioner said, promptly. (Actually, what he said promptly was, "it run downhill," but his grammar was also subject to plastic surgery through the medium of print: a free press is a strange and wondrous thing.) "It ran downhill, and it is my further opinion that it was *floated* down-hill, too." And he pressed his lips together and gave an emphatic nod.

After waiting a moment for the other shoe to drop, Spears asked, "Floated downhill to *what*?"

"To whatever it was floated down*hill to*," said Quoyte, gazing on Spears with well-controlled astonishment. Spears stared at him a moment, but nothing happened.

"Now, Commissioner," Spears said. He paused, cleared his throat. "Now, Commissioner. The hose, you know. The hose couldn't go floating around *cor*ners, you know, making angles from one street to another, without someone opening manholes and going down to guide it. How is it *pos*sible," he burst out, querulously, "for all this to be done without being seen?"

But the Honorable John J. Quoyte had no idea how.

The Honorable Francis F. Flaherty had no idea, either. "Well, then, Your Honor," asked Attorney Spears, "have you any idea who owns the garages that these pipelines have been traced to?"

The Mayor's face, impassive for far longer than usual, lapsed into a very slight smile, which in turn dissolved into a sort of spasm: in a moment he was as before. "We are engaged in trying to trace the owners, sir," he said. "But the properties are owned by corporations which in turn are owned by corporations, and so we have not been actually . . . *able* . . . to determine with any degree of legally requisite exactitude, you know . . ." His sentence and voice ran down together. He stared with glassy eyes upon a dust-obscured canvas on the farthest wall, of a gentleman in an-tique costume engaged in parley with a remarkably oleaginous Indian. And, after a rather long moment, the Mayor was excused from further questioning.

Fire Chief Robert E. Morrissey assured the United States At-torney that the garages in question had, on the occasion of their last being inspected, either been quite empty, or had contained nothing but the usual collections of flivvers and tin lizzies and Mack or White trucks. Certainly nothing in the way of bottling plants had been observed.—And as for the hose itself? A specimen of it was handed up to him, it not having been thought essential to introduce all six thousand feet.

"Well, for *one* thing," the Fire Chief said, thoughtfully, and he gave his head a little bob or two—either in affirmation of testimony or as the result of a habit induced by having fought many preliminary boxing matches long ago and before entering the greater security if lesser glamour of the Yokums Fire Department: "for *one* thing: the hose is especially heavy. Especially heavy. Yes *sir*."

"Why is that, do you suppose, Chief Morrissey?"

Chief Morrissey said that he could only guess. But that his *guess* would be that the hose was especially heavy in order to prevent seepage from the sewers. Heads nodded all around at this. This at least was no mystery. The users of the illicit hose had certainly practised a commendable solicitude for the health of their customers.—But what was the purpose of the *copper wire*?

Chief Morrissey said that he could only guess. And that his guess was that this may have been done, the wrapping of the especially heavy hose with copper wire, so as to help assist the hose to withstand pressure (and his head went bobbetty-bob).

"*Pressure?*"

Morrissey looked at the U.S. Attorney as though the latter had just emerged from a neutral corner. "Well, yes. Sir. *Pressure.* Liquids, confined to a narrow space—the interior of a pipe or a *hose,* for example—through which they were being pumped, the liquids were subject to pressure. Considerable pressure. Liquids floating downhill inside a confined space, even without being pumped, would exert a considerable pressure. Hence the heavy copper wire carefully wound around the especially heavy hose. Uddawise," he said, lapsing into his native Doric, "it could, now, like, buhyst open."

The Fire Chief was succeeded on the stand by the Honorable Lawrence O'T. O'Brien, Commissioner of Water Supply to the City of Yokums. The Mayor's face had twitched, but the face of the Water Commissioner remained as free from grimaces as his head from bobbing. Yet the face commanded attention. The face, and in particular the nose, had in fact been subjected to mysterious influences which had tinted it, perhaps for patriotic purposes, in a rich variety of reds, whites, and blues. There was perhaps a general impression that this Commissioner had refrained from oftimes samplings of his own chief product: but if because he considered it unwholesome or because of a commendable fear that it might render his official judgement the less impartial, was not known.

Had the Water Commissioner known of any unusually large uses or users of water supply such as might for example hint that a beverage industry was going on at any place not licensed for the purpose?

The Water Commissioner had not.

Did the Water Commissioner, then, know anything—anything at *all*?! (Spears was getting rather tired)—about beer-*running*?

The Water Commissioner declared with great fervor that he had never heard of such a thing. So far as he knew, no one in the City of Yokums drank anything stronger than Orange Crush.

And, finally, and after some prolonged discussion with his own assistant, Assistant U.S. Attorney Spears called to the witness stand Mary Mabel Moomaw, Director of the Northern New Jersey Region of the National Family Temperance Union. Had Mrs. Moomaw any ideas about the illegal beer hose situation? Mrs. Moomaw had.

"Our respect for law and order," she said, and she said it both slowly and clearly and in a voice which if not unduly loud was certainly in no way subdued, "has been under attack in the name of Repeal. Many people seem to have the idea that the 18th Amendment is going to be re*peale*d. Well, they are *wrong*! It is *not* going to *be* repealed. Sewers are the right place for beer! Let us put an end to this Repeal talk! Stiffen the anti-liquor laws *and stiffen their enforcement*! No home can be happy and safe where the sting of the liquor serpent is felt, and while the bootlegger is abroad in the land!"

Attorney Spears thanked her, politely, but Mrs. Moomaw had

a lot more to say and he had to thank her twice more before she had quite finished saying it.

Bill Bomberg and Stelle Wilson turned in long stories to their respective papers. And their respective publishers said, respectively, that People did not want to read long Grand Jury reports, that People did not want to read about sewers at their supper tables. The *Gazette* ran a piece on the history of the lute (a Spanish lute group was then touring the U.S.): evidently just what their readers *did* want to read about: their readers were enabled to trace it to the Arabic "al-ud," and to discover its connection with the medieval theorbo and cittern, the Biblical psaltery and the modern zither. And the *Press* went to press with GRAND JURY TO DEFER LOCAL CASE TO CONSIDER OTHERS (one paragraph), and CHIANG KAI-SHEK BAPTIZED. JOINS METHODIST EPISCOPAL CHURCH (one column).

It was probably not the exact triumph for which Bishop Snooker had hoped, but, to do him justice, he did really rejoice more in the sinner saved far away than the sinner chastized at home.

There being for the moment no *Love Nest Raid* stories, the New York City newspapers were pleased to give maximum coverage to the beer hose. And this, in turn, enabled vaudeville, then in its death-throes, to dust off one of vaudeville's oldest and dustiest.

Stage Englishman: Can you inform me of a good hotel?

Stage American: A good hotel?

Stage Englishman: Yace. A good hotel.

Stage American: Well, how about the Waldorf?

Stage Englishman: The Waldorf? Is that a good hotel?

Stage American: Oh, a very good hotel.

Stage Englishman: And, ah, does it, ah, have a good view?

Stage American: Does it have a good view? Say! You bet it has a good view! Why, on a clear day, you can see Yokums!

Stage Englishman: (long, puzzled pause) Ah, what are Yokums?

It may not have opened at the Palace. But, ultimately, it may have helped close it.

The metropolitan newspapers, which did not share the local press's inhibitions about stories concerned with sewers and such, continued, intermittently, to give the story a fairly big play. The New York City tabloids were particularly popular among the local population for this purpose. See, for example, a man in the cap and leather jacket of those who have no pretensions towards upward social mobility, see such a one slide out a tabloid from a pile on a newsstand and drop down two pennies and start swiftly to leave. See, also, the swift reaction of the vendor.

"*Daily News*, tree cents, ya gotta gimme anudda penny—"

See the astonishment, finely done, of the purchaser, baffled in his plans for quick departure, turn to annoyance. "TREE cents? Suppose ta be TWO cents!"

"Two cents inna Ciddy and tree cents inna subuyhbs."

Grim creases appear alongside the purchaser's mouth. He shakes his head. "*Jeez*-uz. Tryinna BLEED d'people." But, he pays, he pays. The *Mirror* is no cheaper. And, as for the *Sun*, the *Telegram*, the *Herald-Tribune*, or the *World*, one might as well try to read the Encyclopedia Britannica. (As for the *Times*, the vendor does not even carry it.) The *News*, however, has easy prose, big type, lots of pictures, and specializes in crimes of passion and of violence (sometimes but not always the same thing). The *Daily News* has never run an article on the history of the lute.

Elmer Dugan was back home. He had not found a job. He had found a dollar, though, and as he knew his mother would never believe that he had found it, he told her he'd earned it. It had for a while acted as an anesthetic of sorts. For a while.

Then, "Sayy, Momma?" he asked.

Instantly his mother cried, "I doe wanna *hear* abowd it!

Don't tell *me* abowd it! Tell yer rotten *Fa*'dther abowd it! Ah tell yer gahdamn *Grann*modther abowd it ann yer lousy rotten Aunts and *Unc*les abowd it! I wasn't good enough fa dtheir prize packidge ta marry!? So I cn sit here ann *stahve* ta deat'th—Whuddaya *want*, Elmer?"

He said, Reflectively, "Say, Momma. Ya know. About this *beer* hose?"

"Whud abowd it?"

"Well, om. Ya know. Ya remember that *day*? When I come home and I ast ya, Hoccome the Telephone Cumpney was puttin a *hose* inna the *sewer*? And *you* said, *you* said, It was probley a *cable*? For the *tele*phone? Well, om—"

"*No*," said his mother promptly, her *No* cutting into his *Well, om* and cutting off the words which were to follow. "*No*," she repeated, shaking her head till her hair came loose. "NO!" She reached up both hands and started fixing it into place again. "Uh uh. You never toll me nothin. I never said a wuhyd."

"Well, I was just thinkin. Maybe whoever it was, who *put* that beer hose down there—"

"No! No!"

"—maybe they had a *truck,* Momma? Painted ta *look* like the Telephone Cumpney's truck, huh? And so maybe *that*'s why hoccome nobody notice't? I mean, uh, uh, that, uh, plenny a people *notice't. But no buddy *thought* nothin of it? Huh, Momma?"

His mother glared at him. "You shutcher mout'th," she said, venomously. "Don't be such a liddle wise guy! Yer gahdamn *Fa*'dther, he's such a wise guy! And look whut it *got* him! Ya never saw nothin, ya never *saw* nothin, ya never t'thought nothin, ya never *toll* me nothin! Y'unnerstann? DO. YOU. UN. DER. *STAND*?"

Elmer sighed. He nodded. "Yeah, momma. *Okay. Okay.*"

But her security measures had not yet been firmed sufficiently. "Re, mem, ber whut I say! Cross ya haht and hope ta die! If, you, ever, *tell*, anybody, one, *word*. Do you want some gorilla ta shoot chew dead wit'th a *tommy*-gun? Like dthat Vincent Mad Dog *Coll* did? Some *child*? May he buhyn in *Hell*?"

Elmer's mind quickened. A pleasurable thrill passed through

his body. He had gotten an unexpected dime and went one Saturday to see The Chapter at The Itch, the neighborhood cheap movie house. And there he also saw the newsreel showing the funeral of the very child mowed down, perhaps by *accident*? only maybe *not*? by the very gorillas? And the child's mother was a large woman, and a heavy woman, an immense woman, in a cheap print dress which concealed nothing, certainly not her grief. Her vast body heaved and shook, and she tried to throw herself into her child's open grave. Elmer suddenly thought of himself as lying at the bottom of that grave. Buried! Buried alive! Tears came to his eyes. "I promise, Momma," he said. "I promise! I promise!"

And then he left the house very quickly because that his few tears were about to start a more numerous flow on her own part and he did not at all want to be rocked back and forth in his mother's arms while she wept and cursed and ranted. But? As to Where To Go. Valleydale Avenue? Well. No. There were to be sure lots of *stores* there and if he found no job he would at least look in the stores—no. People on Valleydale Avenue in the stores, they were not as nice as they used to be. The Lots? Maybe some of the boys hanging around there had heard of jobs, a job. Well, again no. There were a lot of bigger boys hanging around The Lots these days. *Mean* ones. No school *and* no jobs, for them. Well . . . uh . . . how about The Water?

Memories pale as winter butter came to his mind, of perhaps it was his grandfather Dugan or maybe it was his great-uncle Pauly Dugan, *ann I leff school when I was ten years of age and I went down to The Water and I got meself a job. . .*

Luck was with him. First of all, he found a nice long pole. It was always interesting to go fishing in The Water, either from The Beach (although lately there were also a lot of bigger, meaner boys at The Beach, too), or from The Wharf, where the Hackamack River disembogued out of its covert into the Hackamack Bay; not for fish, for that required tackle, a thing he didn't have; to "fish" for whatever might be floating by—once he had found a lady's purse, with a two-dollar bill in it! Second piece of luck, there were no bigger, meaner boys hanging around The Wharf, looking for trouble. And third of all, there were some men on the deck of The Ship (as Elmer always thought of it) and they were talking to each other. This in turn was a two-fold good, because it meant they probably wouldn't notice him and tell him to Go Home; also they might say something interesting. About ships? Pirates? And, uh, exciting adventures?

So, very quietly, Elmer made his way to the edge of The Wharf and idly plied his pole in the cluttered, clotted waters, and listened to the conversation. There was someone sitting way down at the other end of The Wharf. Looked like a Smokey. As long as he stayed where he was, well. Smoke. That meant some kind of alcohol mixed with water. Only the lowest class bums drank *smoke*. Sometimes they died, drinking it, poisoned or frozen to death without even noticing it; or sometimes they built fires to huddle around while they drank it and sometimes they fell into the fires and burned to death without even noticing it, and sometimes. . .

"Couldn't the Senator help ya git some business, Raysh?"

"Who, him? The Senator? *Oh.* You mean, ah—"

"*That's* the one."

A sigh. Rank pipe smoke drifted down. "Ah, *I* d'know. Oh, sure, we went t'school t'gether. But that was *years* ago. I doubt, oh, I doubt I'd know whut he even *looks* like. *Now*adays."

A grunt. "Whut he looks like? He looks like a chief o' police. Whut he looks like. Yeah. He looks more like a chief o' police than the chief himself looks like a chief o' police. Couldn't *he* gitcha some business, Raysh?"

A sigh. A mutter like a verbal shrug. A shadow fell across the water and Elmer looked up. A man was there, looking down with a funny, crooked grin. The man from the other end of the wharf. The smokey. Who said, "Fishin up the merry widows, huh, kid?"

Elmer said, "*What*? Oh. Those *white* things? What do you callum?"

The man said, "*Fish* skins." He smirked, moved closer closer.

Despite a strong feeling of dislike, Elmer felt curious. "You mean, uh, you mean, the fish shed their skins? Like snakes? Is *that* what they are? *Oh*." Another mystery of the sea, but this one solved.

But the man said, "Naaa," smirking more, moving closer, more. "People drop um in thuh terlets. Ah, you wanna come witt me, Ah'll *show* ya—" He had his hand almost on Elmer's shoulder when someone else spoke.

"You'll show him nothing, you dirty pogue; you'll get the Hell out of here: right *now*!"

It was one of the men on The Ship!

The smokey's face writhed. He showed his filthy teeth. "Ah, why'n'tcha mine jer own business, ya funkin conk-sucka!"

Oh how quickly everything happened! The man jumped off The Ship and onto the dock so quickly that his cap flew off and he smacked the smokey with the flat of his hand so hard that Elmer could hear the sound of the smack echo and a ropey plug of snot flew out of one nostril and a jet of blood flew out of the other and the smokey drew back crouching and turning with his face bright with fright and terror and he ran and he ran stumbling as the man from the ship hopped after him on one leg as the man was swinging a kick with the other—

"Help! *Hellpp*! Moyda!" the smokey howled, just as though he were putting it on: but he *wasn't*; it was for *real*! Oh how the smokey ran away!

One of the men still on the deck said, "Goddamned de*gener*-ate!"

And the other man, a Colored man, said, "You done just right —"

The first man, breathing heavily, stopped, stooped, picked up his cap. And, for a second, everything seemed to stop. Elmer read the word on the badge or plaque fixed to its front.

Instantly, Elmer forgot almost everything. He forgot the ill-fitting shoes, forgot the empty stove at home, forgot all the stores where he was no longer welcome either because his family no longer bought anything or because he had been seen hooking stuff, he forgot all the places where he could no longer play because they were being taken over by older boys who could find no work and were mean about it, forgot the implied threat of the alms-house and the words unspoken in his mother's wrath that she could (if worse came to it) herself return to live with her own parents if Elmer himself did not have to be fed, and he even forgot the trolley-cars he loved to ride and now could not because he had no nickels. He walked up to the man who was brushing off the cap.

"Say, Captain," he said, "do you need a cabin boy? *I'll work for nothing!*"

CHAPTER SEVENTEEN

The Hotalings and the Conklings, all but aboriginal in the Hudson Valley, have been described somewhere or other as "vast tribes." Isaac N. Hotaling was somewhat vast himself, he was six feet tall to the inch and he weighed somewhere over two hundred pounds. He had seen and smelled powder, first, in those black clouds hanging heavily over the Spanish lines near Matamoras during what was once described (sincerely, by more than a few), as "the War for the Liberation of Cuba" . . . and then in more than one domestic shoot-out. Even the sovereign State of New Jersey has had its own equivalents of the Fight at the Okay Corral.

But recently, very, very recently, he had found himself engaged with an enemy whose lines showed no black smoke at all. And he honestly did not know what to do about it. Captain Clay's comments had not altogether taken the heart out of the Chief, his heart was too big and too tumultuous for that. But that they had added to his burdens could not be denied. And he did not attempt to deny it, even to himself. Vexation, indecision, frustration, fury, and, finally, rage, caused that heart to beat more and more rapidly, more and more heavily, as the day went on. And so, finally, although it was not the usual hour of the day nor any of the usual days of the week, he got to his feet, closed and locked his door, changed into his second-best civilian clothes, unlocked his door and said to his clerk, in the gruff, abrupt tone in which he always said it, "You know where ta find me."

"Yes, Chief," the clerk said. He had gotten the job in the first place on the basis of a barely civil examination, consisting of the one question, *"Can ya keep ya mout'th shut?"*

Some men who had two cars had the other car for the convenience of their wives. Not Ike Hotaling. "Isaac, don't you think it would be a good idea for me to learn to drive," Etta had asked him—once.

His answer, in its entirety, had been, "Naa." He hadn't bothered to look up from the funny papers. Etta went back and basted the ham, and didn't even sigh. Isaac was a good provider, and one of his provisions was for his wife's stepmother, an evil-tempered besom whom none of her own sons would tolerate. Etta did not indeed love the old woman, but she perhaps hated her less and yet feared her more than did her stepbrothers and stepsisters. As long as Isaac paid the fifty dollars a month for Ma's board and keep and pin-money at the Dutch Reformed Church House for Widows and Spinsters, the chances of Ma's appearing to rant and rave staid close to zero. There were worse things than not being allowed to drive a car. Etta basted the ham.

Ike drove his other car away from Bogue Street but not in the direction of his home address. He parked the Ford and went in the side door of a very nearby building. Myrtle was perhaps more surprised than she was pleased, but she did not show any displeasure. She never did show it. Hotaling had a certain way, either of selecting compliant females, or of educating them into compliance.

"Newton!" said Myrtle. Nobody else had ever even thought of calling him by his middle name. A good thing, too. "Oh, gee, what a great surprise! I wasn't ex*pec*ting you, honey!"

They embraced.

Women said of her, "Oh she's just a little bit of a thing." They said it indulgently. She looked modest and drab enough on the street, she even scrubbed off her make-up before going down to the corner store. They didn't know, at the corner store, that her toe-nails were painted. Let alone did they know there that it was *Newton* who painted them. There were a few things that they didn't know, there at the corner store. Although, to be sure, they knew quite a lot.

"A cup of tea, let me get you a cup of tea, Newton," she said, he having finally released her, after silently rocking her back and forth for rather a long while. "And some *cookies?*"

He pressed his hand flat against his forehead and slowly dragged it down to his chin, mashing, in the process, his Indian Chief nose. He looked up from the flowered carpet. "Only if dthey're *yours.*" Myrtle had a canny way with cookies—small and delicate and yet crisp and flavored in subtle ways unknown to the kitchen at his legal residence. Etta went in more for soggy crullers and pale, heavy pies. She was great at basting hams, though.

"You can't *baste* a ham too *much!*" she used to say.

He drank, noisily, two cups of tea (tea! what would they have said at the Station if they knew that Solid Ike drank *tea!*), and ate a pile of her cookies with abstraction.

The wallpaper was bright, and there were doilies on the chairs.

After a long moment, Myrtle said, very quietly. "Well. Something is wrong. Want to tell me about it?"

"Oh Jesus Christ Muhyt somebuddy is makin out dthat he's *me* and he's cleckting over two t'thousand dolla's a week pruhtection money fa dthe broory and dthere's notta a gahdamn t'thing I cn *do* about it!" His voice grew thick and heavy towards the last words, and he put his huge hand to his huge face and burst into tears. "Two, t'thousand, dolla's a *week,*" he sobbed. "*Oh my God, two t'thousand dolla's a week—ann I can't get a penny of it!*"

Her bag of tricks was perhaps small, but she had never known them entirely to fail. She leaned on his arm, rather lightly. She waited till he had gotten control and didn't look up as he wiped his face and blew his nose. Then she said, lightly and softly, as she placed her tiny hand on the knot of his necktie, "Hey, I know what. Let's go play Oops-a-daisy. Hm? It'd make you *feel* better, maybe." After barely a second, she said, "I know it would make *me* feel better. . ."

A small pursey smile began on Iron Ike's purple lips. "It *would,* huh?"

She looked away, shyly. Nodded her head. And, after another moment, she began to slip down the knot of the necktie.

◆ ◆ ◆

At no time did she lose her head.

◆ ◆ ◆

Dr. Lloyd McKinney, the Police Surgeon, was a big man himself. And he brought with him two of the biggest men on the Force. (Fat Frank Feeney was probably *the* biggest: but he couldn't have kept a secret in a fire-proof safe.)

"I couldn't *lift* him!" said Myrtle, in the same desperate and breathy whisper in which she had called the Chief's clerk. "I tried to get his *clothes* on. But I couldn't *lift* him . . ." They stood there, gazing at the big, silent body, face-down in the rumpled bed. After a while she said, breaking the silence, "He said he was tired. He said he just wanted to take a nap."

No one believed her for a second, but, in their hearts, they honored her for pretending.

"Died in his sleep," Dr. McKinney said, instantly. "Heart attack. Sudden. I suppose. Autopsy will show for sure. But no doubt in *my* mind. *Well.*" He reflected. Nobody said a word, although one of the policemen, Matt Keogh, slowly crossed himself and, after a second, so did the doctor. The doctor came to a decision, nodded. "We don't want any scandal, now, do we; no," he said. Just as they expected him to say. He turned to Myrtle. "Just wait outside for a few minutes, please," he said. She nodded. It was a doctor's voice. A doctor's orders. "Get his clothes on," he directed the men, as he followed her out.

In the nice, bright living room McKinney looked at the clock, checked it with his pocket-watch. "All right, then, so here is what we better do," he said. "I very much doubt that anyone will *ask*," he said. "Because we are going to hush this up, but absolutely: if anyone *should* ask: He left here over an hour ago. Got that?" It seemed as though he were going to say more, then he suddenly seemed to hear something, and, with an abrupt intake of breath, he turned and went rapidly back into the bedroom. Said, holding out his hand, "Yes, right, I'll *take* that, Harrison, Keogh."

The looks exchanged then—Harrison to Keogh, Keogh to Harrison, Harrison and Keogh to McKinney, McKinney to Harrison and Keogh—were not friendly. But Harrison did release what he had (five double-eagles, as a matter of fact; or, in the common speech, five twenty-dollar gold-pieces). "We just didden wannum ta drop onna flaw, Doc," Harrison said.

"Yes. Right. *Thank* you."

Harrison felt impelled to say something else. He said it softly. "*You* know, Doc, dthe old saying, Y' gotta pick up dthe dead man *some*how. Ann dthe *bess* way, is by dthe *pock*ets . . . Fifty-*fif*ty?"

McKinney's moustache twitched. His lip, under it, lifted. Then it fell again. "I'll make sure that you are both with me when I hand it over to Mrs. Hotaling," he said. He had had a fleeting notion that there was someone nearer to hand who was in the long run going to be needing it more than Mrs. Hotaling, but it was certainly now impossible to do anything about it. "Get his *britches* on right, damn it! And oh make sure the buttons match the button-holes."

The living room had been bright with the last rays of the sun; by the time they were finished, though, it was dark. Nobody saw them get him into the car, the second-best car, the Ford, back in the side-alley. But then there was another problem. Dr. McKinney's plans had depended on a church with open doors. This description would have fit the church of his choice, St. Peter Ad Vincula: but the Deceased had been a Protestant. The Deceased had in fact *left* the faith of his fathers over a semantic difference with the Dutch Reformed minister, Dr. H. Berryman Buren—that is, as Solid Ike had put it, "Alla dthum big wuhyds, who'n dthe Hell cn unna*stan*' 'm?" and had taken himself off, at least provisionally, to the Free Baptists. But a quick investigation proved that this conventicle was, except for stated occasions, locked tighter than a chastity belt.

However, the (so suddenly) late Chief *had* been known to visit, now and then, his equally late mother's church, Saint James Episcopal, a foundation almost as old as the Dutch Reformed; and a perfect maze of gates and doors and seldom-used corridors; Doctor McKinney, who prior to his marriage and conversion had been a communicant there, knew it like the back of his hand. And there—having paused twice en route, just in case, to check the security at Full Gospel and English Lutheran (nothing doing, either one) — there they deposited their charge.

Neatly, in one of the best pews.

DIES AT HIS PRAYERS, said the sub-headline in the *Gazette*.

Hotaling was succeeded in office by Captain Clay, who owing to the rise in salary, was able to compound with his creditors, and thus after all avoid bankruptcy.

Myrtle was not so fortunate. Myrtle was not fortunate at all. Even though Mrs. Snyder gave her back her old room at the River Front Hotel.

CHAPTER EIGHTEEN

Down in the big, big basement of the industrial premises at Numbers Five through Fifty-five Charlotte Street (in fact, the only premises on Charlotte Street since Nightingale Ned Smith, "the Musical Blacksmith," had closed, eight years before), Stan Sawyer was talking to his assistant, Hamilton Swift.

"Put down the shovel fr a minute, now, Ham, and leave me explain couple things to ya," he said.

Ham Swift, an immense young man in a filthy undershirt and blackened dungarees, gave his shovel one more scrape through the coal pile, then let it rest, stuck in at an angle. "Yeah, Mr. Sawyer."

Stan had once been every bit as tall and broad as Ham. He was in fact still as broad, he was in fact now broader, but the effort of holding his increasingly vast belly up had finally defeated him; and he now slouched when not on dress parade, so to speak. "Got a nuff coal fr now, a nuff steam in thuh boiler. See?" He gestured to one of a bank of dials and gages.

Ham nodded. Steam. Boilers. Gages. These were impressive things, in fact, these were the Higher Mysteries. Ham's Uncle Jefferson "Jeff" Swift had for forty years been engineer on the old West-Jersey and Indianville Line, with three trains a day carrying coal from the old canal to the old Foundry. Ham had shoveled coal at the canal barn since he was twelve. Uncle Jeff had always promised that Ham would be fireman on Number Four . . . one day . . . whenever Black Bob died or quit. But, without any warning—without, anyway, any warning observed by the Swift family, who did not read newspapers (or, for that matter, any-thing else)—the Foundry had closed. The canal had not exactly closed, but for all commercial purposes it might as well have. One morning Number Four had been waiting in the roundhouse for the signal as it did six mornings a week; with Number Three and Two rusting on their old rusty rails (Number One had been turned into Minié balls sixty-odd years earlier)—

And the signal did not come. The West-Jersey and Indian-ville Line had, without the Foundry's coal-carrying trade, sim-ply ceased to exist. So had all jobs connected with it. There was not even a watchman any more. Who would steal a locomotive engine and a train of two coal-cars which did not even connect with any other railroad?

Black Bob just vanished. But Uncle Jeff put on his Sunday clothes, filled all the pockets with coal, and walked off the Deer Creek Bridge.

Stan Sawyer had come back for the funeral, had seen Ham, huge and mute, had said—after the funeral—"Young fellow, you come back with me and I am going to give you a job."

Ham's mother, who would have been a widow had she ever actually been married (a formality not usual in those parts and that family) to Ham's father, said, "The Lord must of sent you, Mr. Sawyer. Ham ain't too bright."

"Don't matter."

"Couldn't keep him in school. Can't read."

"Don't matter." Stan Sawyer reached his cup for a final cup of coffee. "Got a foreigner working for me now. I'll fire him." And so he had. The foreigner had said nothing; at least he had said noth-ing in front of Stan Sawyer and Ham Swift; and if he had said something in his own home and in his own language, why who in the Hell cared. Ham was introduced at the plant, where his size and musculature proved all that was necessary in addition to Stan Sawyer's introduction. Ham was also introduced at Mrs. Wilmer's Rooming House, where he and Stan Sawyer innocently shared the same broad bed. They worked together at the boilers, at the furnace. At the furnace they broiled their own bacon and pork chops and ate their half-loaves of bread at a time. As Ham was not good at counting change, Stan made the purchases. Once a week Mrs. Wilmer filled out the money-order Ham sent home. Once a week the two men went together to the River Front Hotel but Ham was the one of the two who went upstairs once a week; Stan only went upstairs once every two weeks: the other time he played cards and drank beer, only. And once a week they went to the movie thee-*ayter*. Tom *Mix*!

"I gotta go march in thuh *prade,* like I told ya, Ham," Stan said, now, in front of the furnace.

"Yeah, Mr. Sawyer," Ham said, lifting up the front of his undershirt and wiping his face with it. He knew that Mr. Sawyer was a veteran and that veterans had to go march in parades. It would be nice if he could go watch the Columbus Day parade as he had gone a couple of times to watch the Fourth of July parade back in Indianville. But they couldn't both go because then there would be nobody to shovel the coal. Ham was very happy shoveling the coal. It was as good as shoveling the coal from the canalside. It was as good as shoveling the coal on Number Four engine would have been. True, Ham did not altogether understand what they were shoveling the coal here *for*, but there were a lot of things which he did not understand. There were a lot of big machines upstairs, probably that had something to do with it.

"Now remember what I told ya about these gages here."

"Yeah, Mr. Sawyer."

"Pressure gits past *ten*, turn this here little wheel here."

"Yeah, Mr. Sawyer."

Mr. Sawyer nodded, gestured that Ham could resume his shoveling. Mr. Sawyer had brought his good suit to work and hung it up on the toilet door. Now, having carefully spread newspapers on the floor, he changed into it. And into his good shoes. He then put on his veteran's hat. Then he looked in the tiny cracked and faded mirror. Then he waved his hand and walked up the stairs, stepping in time as though he had already heard the fife and drum. Ham shoveled coal. From time to time he looked at the gage. It was like a clock and it had numbers all the way around it. Ham had never learned to tell time, either, but he did remember that there were numbers all around a clock. He wasn't sure, now that he thought of it—and he thought of it very, very briefly—that there was a number 100 on a clock.

He scraped his shovel against the floor under some coal. He liked the shivery sound it made. So he did it some more. He laughed, and threw more coal on the fire.

For some reason at that moment the voice of Miss Livermore came into Ham's mind. Miss Livermore had taught the old school at Three Points. She had tried to teach Ham. She had tried hard to teach Ham. Her voice seemed to be speaking to him right now. "One with an O, Hamilton . . . One with two Os, Hamilton . . . One with three Os, Hamilton . . . Hamilton? Hamilton? Oh, my . . ."

Ham laughed. The flames danced. "I'm strong," he said, to no one. "I'm pretty strong."

CHAPTER NINETEEN

"What's up?" asked Jordan Steinmetz, the *Press's* Rewrite man, getting to his feet and looking across the street.

Stelle asked, "What?"

"Looks like everybody from over at the *Gazette* is leaving . . . *What* the...dickens! Fire-drill? No. *No!* They're coming over *here!*"

And—sure enough—they *were*. *All* of them? Stelle certainly did not know everybody at the *Gazette*. But it did look like all of them. She got up to watch as they all walked into the big room there on the second floor of the *Press* Building. Sure enough. In came Bill Bomberg. And came right over to *her*. "To what do we owe the honor of this visit?" she asked, trying to sound as if she weren't rather scared at this unprecedented occurrence.

He looked as though he were a little bit scared, himself. "You can search *me*," he said. "All I know is that we were all told to get on over here. Maybe war's been declared. Maybe Hoover has abdicated and Indian Charley Curtis is President now."

Stelle said, "Haw!" and then looked around to see if anyone had heard this almost-laugh. If anybody had, nobody seemed to care. Very shortly the big room was pretty full of people. Certainly, even if everybody from the *Gazette* was not here, everybody was from the *Press*. And at that moment up spoke H.H. Ruel, the *Gazette*'s Publisher. Who had *never*, so far as she knew, even entered the building before.

"Make this brief," he said. "Have everybody's attention? Economics of the situation. Not room any more for two daily papers in this town. Mr. Emery and I. Same conclusion."

There was not a sound.

"I've sold him the *Gazette,*" said Ruel. "Bless you all."

Oscar Emery cleared his throat. "We'll uh be using this uh building," he said. "It's uh it's uh newer uh equipment. Uh and as for uh jobs it's uh matter of uh seniority. You uh all uh know how long uh you've uh how long uh you've each *worked* here. Over uh five years uh you've uh still got your uh job. Less than uh five years uh sorry uh sorry but uh that's that."

Not a sound.

Ruel had the last word, Emery having turned away and started out. "Show must go on," he said. "Still working, back to work. *Press-Gazette*, now."

Stelle found herself downstairs on the front steps with her hat and her coat on. Someone said to her, "What are you going to do? Do you know?" It was Bill.

Numbly, she shook her head. "I don't, either," he said. She looked at him. Her heart felt swollen and sore. He looked about the same as she felt. Then a little smile came on and went from his face. "Whatever we're going to do," he said, "let's do it together." Still she didn't say anything. She started down the steps. If he had taken her arm at that moment she would have jerked it away. He didn't take her arm. He walked close to her. He walked very close to her. And when, at the bottom of the steps, she slowly turned to go down the street, he turned and went with her. And they didn't say anything to each other but they kept on walking close to each other.

Until they were touching each other. As they walked.

CHAPTER TWENTY

Ham Swift shoveled on another load of coal. Then he took his rake and worked it through the flames. Then he applied himself to the damper and the grate, chuckling at the noise. Then he paused. There was, he felt, something he should do. What was it? A slight pressure in his bladder at once caused all other thoughts to fade, and, opening the snaps of his fly, he urinated into the space beneath the grate. The hissing of the steam also amused him. He could not for the moment think of anything to do next, so next he did nothing. After a while he sat down on the sturdy wooden box placed there for the purpose, and stared in happy vacancy into the glowing coals.

As the good women of the NFTU gathered on the sidewalk in front of their Hall preparatory to walking down to join the Columbus Day parade, Mary Mabel Moomaw took the chance to say a confidential something into the ear of little Birdie. "I am *so* glad," she murmured, "that Attorney Spears didn't say anything about Dr. Brower and the, uh, *factory*."

"Oh *yes*, Mary Mabel! so am *I*!"

"Because. Besides the em*barr*assment. I was *so* afraid, you know. That he would suggest that we all go and *visit* the place. And, oh, Birdie! I just didn't feel that I *could*. *Again*. The *smell*, you know. The *awful, smell*."

Birdie gave a grave nod. "Of . . . *beer*," she said, lowering her voice.

Mrs. Moomaw compressed her mouth. Then she loosened it for final comment on the subject. "Of . . . *beer*," she agreed.

One after one the various units for the Parade fell into place, some on the sidewalks, some in the street. Patriotic parades in Yokums tended to contain all the same elements; however, in some official recognition of this being Columbus Day, the Grand Marshal was His Honor Former Assistant Judge Louis P. Belcampo, who was assisted on this occasion with a list of all the units participating. There were, for example, all of the American Legion and VFW posts. There were all the High School bands and all the fife and drum corps. There was the Bagpipe Band. The Catholic War Veterans. The Jewish War Veterans. The United Spanish-American War Veterans. Boy Scouts and Sea Scouts. The Knights of Columbus and (judiciously apart) the Knights Templars, a Masonic body and, ditto, the Order of De Molay. The National Family Temperance Union. And so on. And so on.

Pride of Place was given, of course, as always, to the Grand Army of the Republic, a veterans' organization composed of the survivors of the U.S. Armed Forces in the Civil War, who were placed just after the NFTU, not because there was assumed to be any particular connection, but because it was hoped that any spectators who might tend to become restive during the passing-by of the NFTU would respectfully cease to be so upon catching sight of the GAR. The GAR units consisted of several sections, in fact. First of all, of course, would be the Gallant Veterans themselves. And after them, the Ladies of the GAR. And then the Loyal Legion. And then the Sons of Union Veterans.

At the last previous parade, for the Fourth of July, there had been five Civil War survivors. Since then, however, Color-Sergeant Lassing (Sixth New Jersey Sharpshooters) had passed on to his reward, to be with his Savior in the Heavens; and Major Levi Fischer (Brooklyn Zouaves) had passed on to San Diego, to be with his grand-daughter and her family. (The newspapers had quoted him as having said that he would of course be sorry to leave the scenes of his childhood; his actual comment had been, "Jesus Christ, another one of them son of a bitch winters would kill me.") And today, and at the very last minute, someone of the family of Corporal Ernest Anhalt (Freylinghuysen Fencibles) had phoned up to say that "Uncle Erny just isn't up to it today, we all feel terrible but he is in *bed*."

"So who does that leave?" Grand Marshall His Honor Former Assistant Judge L. P. Belcampo, wondered out loud, consulting his list.

Well, it left exactly two. Two members of the Grand Army of the Republic for Which it Stands. Two surviving veterans of the Irrepressible Conflict. And they both of them realized this at about the same time and so they both gave each other official nods of recognition, in which was mingled some note of common triumph over Time and Chance.

Private Don Carlos ("Daddy") Wilkerson's uniform tunic was so eroded by years and by usage that one would scarcely have known what it represented. But his GAR campaign hat, now: darkest blue, semi-broad-brimmed, golden cord braiding it about: everybody knew what *that* was. "Twon't rain, now will it?" old Daddy Wilkerson kept asking. "Twouldn't do t' git me hat wet. No, no. Twouldn't do t' git me hat wet. Couldn't git another one, ye know. Not any more. No. Not any more."

Also on hand, and even more obviously on hand, was Commodore John Calvin Clutterbuck, in full fig, including sword and cocked hat with feathers. "I trust we shall have good weather for the occasion," he said, taking a reading. "If these plumes get wet, they're as good as ruined, and you have no idea how difficult it would be to replace them nowadays."

The eyes of the two old warriors met, finally. For a long moment they only looked at each other. Then each nodded. And touched hat in informal salute. Nodded.

Clutterbuck's nod said, "Ah, you were a mere private foot-soldier who never went to the Academy and never felt the salt spray upon the picket-line at sea nor smelt the smoke of the blockade-runners. But, still, you did serve on the right side in the War Between the States; so I do acknowledge you."

Wilkerson's nod said, "Ah, you were a mere middy-boy and you never had to fear the Parrot cannon-guns nor never had to stoop down and drink rainwater from hoofprints left by the Rebel horse. But, still, you did serve the Union in the Great Rebellion: so I do acknowledge you."

Thus, the nods of these two old, old, very old men to each other.

A message-runner came and spoke to the Grand Marshal. Who nodded and sent his own assistant with a message for both old men: "The Mayor is sending the City Limousine for the Gallant Veterans to ride in, because of the heat." The Gallant Veterans swiftly scanned each other. Rank has its privileges. Commodore Clutterbuck spoke first. "My comrade Wilkerson may ride, if he chooses to. I, of course, shall walk." Private Wilkerson gave his head a tiny jerk in which one might have read a tiny measure of scorn. "My comrade Clutterbuck kin ride, if he gits tired," he said. "Course, I'll walk."

And so that, of course, was that.

The Mayor had emerged from the private room of a conveniently-located restaurant, where he had taken aboard a little something for his nerves; and was given the news. He sighed. "Giants in the Earth," he said. "Well, Patsy, we might as well get the show on the road . . . don't you think so?"

"*I* think so," the Grand Marshal agreed. He gave a signal. A whistle sounded. A bugle blew. Drums began to beat. Children jumped up and down and clapped their hands. The first balloon of the day escaped. And the first little girl announced that she had to go to the bathroom.

Real bad.

The parade was on its way.

The new publisher of the *Press-Gazette* was giving last

minute instructions to his oldest reporter.

"Now uh remember Mr. uh Forgarty," he said. "No more uh stories about uh any uh beer pipes or uh beer hoses. That story is uh dead. And uh uh uh," he groped for the *mot juste*.

"And 'buried'?" suggested Peter Fogarty.

The publisher all but leaped to catch the word. "Yeah! Uh. Yeah! And uh *buried!*" he exclaimed.

Fogarty suppressed a sigh, assured his employer that he understood. On the way down the stairs, though, he uttered aloud a sudden thought. "Say, I wonder where he got the *money* to *buy* the other paper?" he exclaimed.

A ghostly chuckle sounded. Willey, the ancient janitor, leaned on his push-broom and showed his tortoise gums. "Say! Dontcha know *that*, Petey?"

"No," said Peter Fogarty. "But I suppose that you do, Willey." He had forgotten that Willey was popularly supposed to know everything. But now he remembered. And he waited.

"Why *sure*," said Willey. "*Sure*. The Senator *loan* it to um."

"Oh *ho*. Oh ho." Fogarty waited another moment. But Willey was again just an old man at work. His puckered lips pursed as though ready for a whistle, he slowly marshalled a tiny heap of dust, in which were several wooden matchsticks, the tag from a sack of Bull Durham, a piece of orange peel, part of a Hershey Bar wrapper, and a soggy part of a soda bottle label which read TA-TION STRAWBER.

His long face longer than ever with thought, Peter Fogarty walked on slowly down the stairs. He sighed. "In a speculum, en-igmatically," he said. And, then, "Seven children, seven children, a wife and seven children." And he sighed once more.

The Mayor and the Grand Marshal had been the first to march, and they were the first to leave off marching. The usual reviewing stand had been set up in front of the City Hall, and there, behind bunting, they took their places, silk hats in hands. Before them, feet—many, many feet—marched and stamped rhythmically upon the street. The patch of asphalt was also there in the street before the reviewing stand. Part of the roadway had sunk a few several inches. Perhaps the asphalt was only there as make-shift. Perhaps it was there as a marker. Or reminder. The Yokums streets were torn up for repairs with frequency, and as to those who argued the *post hoc, ergo propter hoc* which Peter Fogarty had once mentioned in connection with the fact that a leading local politician was also a leading paving contractor, why, probably they were just jealous.

Be all that as it may have been. Minute after minute and quarter-hour after quarter-hour the marching feet went *stamp-stamp-stamp*. On the reviewing stand His Honor the Mayor and His Honor the Grand Marshal moved their silk hats so as to cover their hearts whenas The Flag went by. It went by often.

Ham Swift wanted a drink of water, and, on his way to the faucet, he passed the bank of dials and gages. He slowed, he looked at them, he did not stop. On his way back: there they were again. Again he slowed. Again he looked at them and this time he did stop. He looked at them for rather a long time. And, once again, a voice sounded in his memory.

"Yeah, Mr. Sawyer," he said. There. *There*. The needle. It was there, fluttering away. Sure enough, it was by a number. A one with an *O*? A one with two *O*s? For a long moment he stood there, hesitating. Then he said, "Yeah, Mr. Sawyer." He reached over to the wheel, and he turned it. Mr. Sawyer had told him to.

And indeed Mr. Sawyer had. Mr. Sawyer had not, however, told him which way to turn it. Not that Ham realized this omission. The matter did not occur to him. He gave the wheel a turn. It resisted him. So he gave it another turn. And it came off in his hand. For another long moment he looked at it. Mr. Sawyer hadn't said anything about this. Maybe that was what the wheel was supposed to do. Ham set it down very carefully. Then he went over, and, taking up the iron hook, opened the furnace door. A delightful flicker of blue flames met his large, and largely vacant, blue eyes. All was in order. He sat down on the box. The incident of the wheel did not worry him. It did not *not* worry him. He had already forgotten all about it.

Daddy Wilkerson and Commodore Clutterbuck marched side by side. The whole parade. At the end of the parade was the reviewing stand, upon which both would stand whilst one of them (the Civil War veterans took turns, year by year) would read General Logan's Order #1, commanding the decoration of the graves of the Union dead—no. That was for Decoration Day. This was Columbus Day. It was, for October, hot. But neither one would indicate the least fatigue. Finally—*finally*—there was a pause. A stop. Each one recollected what still lay ahead. To wit: Speeches. Lots and lots and *lots* of speeches. *Too much sugar for a penny*, Don Carlos Wilkerson thought to himself. *Not even a hoofprint to drink from* . . . He swung his head slightly around. His eyes met those of his comrade Clutterbuck. They faced each other.

"Hot day," said John Calvin Clutterbuck, Commodore, USN (ret.).

"Yes sir. Tiz. *Tiz*," said all that was left, locally, of the Army of the Shenandoah. The two old, old, very old men licked their withered lips and looked around. In vain. There was not a sutler's tent in sight.

Then, both together, they said, "*Very* hot day. . ."

There had once upon a time been three hoses. Each one had, so to speak, worked an eight-hour shift. Then there were two. And each one had worked, as it were, a twelve-hour shift.

Then there was one.

And it had been working around the clock.

True, it was a thick hose. True, it was re-enforced with copper wire.

Still...

And then the pressure had started building up. And still the hose held out. If the pressure had been turned off at that point, all might still have been well. But the pressure had not been turned off. And now, in fact, with the wheel broken, there was no way to turn it off. And so, finally—

The National Family Temperance Union filed into place in front of the reviewing stand on the steps of City Hall. Hard behind them came the Sons of Union Veterans of the Civil War. There was one loud stamp of feet. (The Sons had been well-trained.) And the mended patch of asphalt sank, dissolved, vanished.

A spume, a gusher, suddenly appeared. It rose over the heads of the in-comprehending multitude. It flew up in the air. And then, whilst the flow still continued, the head of flow condensed from flow into liquid. It drenched Mrs. Mary Mabel Moomaw from the stuffed bird on her hat to the buckles on her high-buttoned shoes. One slightly tipsy oldster did indeed cry, "*Thar she blows!*" Some there were in the crowd who at first thought that a water-main must have burst. But not Mrs. Moomaw. The full horror of it all burst upon her in one single second. She *knew*!

"Help!" she cried, trying—vainly—to escape. "Help! Oh, help!" The press of the crowd held her fast. "It's *beer*!" she screamed as she struggled. "BEER! HELP! *BEER*!"

Private Don Carlos Wilkerson's eyes flew to the eyes of his comrade Commodore John Calvin Clutterbuck. It had been a *long* march. It was a *very* hot day. With one simultaneous and decisive gesture the two old warriors swept off their hats. With high-kneed steps they flew to the very spot of the miraculous flow.

They were not the very first to be there. But they were the first to be there with anything to drink from.

The rest of the throng was right behind them.

The Federal Inspectors at the near-beer brewery paced list-lessly. This had once been a beaut of a job. Fifty cents a case rake-off on each case of un-de-alcoholised beer they had illicitly let pass. Then, and, after all, this was the Land of Opportunity, was it not? they had struck for a *dollar* a case. And had not gotten it. Very well, then, so only *near*-beer had gone out. But had this after all put any money in *their* pockets? It had not.

The lassitude of the day was suddenly broken by the sound of running feet. The man on pony patrol went out on the gallop, came back at once. Following him was a well-known figure.

"A dollar a case, okay!" it gasped.

One of the beer-checkers had started to nod, wide-eyed. The other one pushed him aside. "*Two* dollars a case!" he declared. Demand's danger is Supply's opportunity.

The newcomer tore off his hat, threw it down, stamped on it. "Gah*damn* it! —Okay. Okay," he capitulated. "They'll just hafta pay *more* for their beer, in New York, then," he said. "Alla the gah-damn *hoses* is boysted!" he yelled. "—Staht *bottling*!"

And then someone else appeared. It was the chief inspector of the beer-check squad, Hubert Harrison. He wagged both hands in front of his face. Everything stopped, once more. "They're watching the Holland Tunnel for beer," he said, sorrow-fully. "The Department of Justice is. *And* the ferries," he added.

There was a long silence, then. And then someone said, slowly, "Dey're gunna die a *toyst*, in Noo Yawk."

This appalling prospect spread before them, all faces fell. All heads were scratched. And then an automobile came rolling into the yard. Almost before it stopped, the chubby figure of Sonny Boy Boykin came tumbling out. "Did you start bottling already? No? *Good*! Where's Old Man Morse and his helper? Huh? The *coopers*? Lemme see the coopers! The barrel-makers! The Big Guy just had a wonderful idea!"

There was steam in the box, there was always steam in the box: the Chief Engineer of the vessel saw to that. It had been his first order and was, regardless of other concerns, always his chief concern. He gave the gleaming brass another loving wipe. Then he looked up. What a commotion on the wharf! What a rattling and echoing of ricketty timbers! But Preacher Babcock never rushed. It never payed to rush. With deliberate pace he went on deck. The Captain was already there. The new cabin boy peered, wide-eyed.

Coming down the Packet Boat Wharf was a truck. Laden with barrels.

All stenciled WHALE OIL.

Behind it was another truck.

Behind *it* was another truck.

Behind—

The first truck stopped. Two men came tumbling out of the cab and went running towards the gangplank. Horatio Seymour Clack took his place. "Hold on, there. *Hold* on," he shouted. "*I'm Captain here*! What's going on?"

The first man had attempted to stop, but the momentum had been too much for him, and he tripped and he fell. He did not wait now until he regained his feet, but, leaning forward on the backs of his knuckles, he shouted, "*Charter! Freight! Cargo! New York City?*"

H. Seymour Clack, Captain, Master, and Owner of the Packet Boat *Sadie Howell* (Licensed according to Act of Congress), drew himself erect. Slowly he surveyed his vessel fore and aft. Then he said, calmly and triumphantly, to his Chief Engineer: "See? What I told you?

"*On their knees . . . On their hands and knees . . .*"

ABOUT THE AUTHOR

Avram Davidson (1923 – 1993)

Avram Davidson was born in Yonkers, New York, in 1923 and was active in SF fandom from his teens. He was a Marine medic during WWII. He is remembered as a writer of fantasy fiction, science fiction and crime fiction, as well as many stories that defy easy categorization. Among his SF and Fantasy awards are two Hugos, two World Fantasy Awards and a World Fantasy Life Achievement award; he also won a Queen's Award and an Edgar Award in the mystery genre. Although best known for his writing, Davidson also edited *The Magazine of Fantasy and Science Fiction* from 1962 to 1964. He died in 1993.

ALSO BY AVRAM DAVIDSON

Vergil Magus

The Phoenix and the Mirror (1969)
Vergil in Averno (1986)
The Scarlet Fig: Or Slowly Through a Land of Stone (2005)

Kar-Chee

Rogue Dragon (1965)
The Kar-Chee Reign (1966)

Peregrine

Peregrine: Primus (1971)
Peregrine: Secundus (1981)
Peregrine Parentus and Other Tales (with Ethan Davidson) (2016)

Other Novels

Joyleg (with Ward Moore) (1962)
Mutiny in Space (1964)
Rork! (1965)
Masters of the Maze (1965)
Clash of the Star-Kings (1966)
The Enemy of My Enemy (1966)
The Island Under the Earth (1969)
Ursus of Ultima Thule (1973)
Marco Polo and the Sleeping Beauty (with Grania Davis) (1987)

The Boss in the Wall: A Treatise on the House Devil (with Grania Davis) (1998)
Beer! Beer! Beer!(2021)
Dragons In The Trees (2022)

Collections

Or All the Seas with Oysters (1962)
Crimes & Chaos (1962)
What Strange Stars and Skies (1965)
Strange Seas and Shores (1971)
The Enquiries of Doctor Eszterhazy (1975)
The Redward Edward Papers (1978)
The Best of Avram Davidson (1979)
Avram Davidson: Collected Fantasies (1982)
The Adventures of Doctor Eszterhazy (1990)
Adventures in Unhistory: Conjectures on the Factual Foundations of Several Ancient Legends (1993)
The Avram Davidson Treasury (1998)
The Investigations of Avram Davidson (1999)
Everybody Has Somebody in Heaven (2000)
The Other Nineteenth Century (2001)
Limekiller! (2003)
Skinny – A short Story (2021)
AD 100 – 100 Years of Avram Davidson (2023)